THE

ST. SIMONS
ISLAND CLUB

John Le Brun novels by Brent Monahan

The Jekyl Island Club (Book 1)

available now

The Sceptred Island Club (Book 2)

The Manhattan Island Clubs (Book 3)

available March 2016

The St. Lucia Island Club (Book 5)

new release for Fall 2016

TURNER
PUBLISHING COMPANY

THE
ST. SIMONS
ISLAND CLUB

A JOHN LE BRUN NOVEL

by

Brent Monahan

Turner Publishing Company
424 Church Street • Suite 2240 • Nashville, Tennessee 37219
445 Park Avenue • 9th Floor • New York, New York 10022

www.turnerpublishing.com

The St. Simons Island Club, A Novel

Cover design: Maddie Cothren
Book design: Glen Edelstein

Library of Congress Cataloging-in-Publication Data

Monahan, Brent, 1948-
The St. Simons Island club : a John Le Brun novel / by Brent Mona-han.
pages ; cm
I. Title.
PS3563.O5158S7 2015
813'.54--dc23
2015024123

Printed in the United States of America
14 15 16 17 18 19 0 9 8 7 6 5 4 3 2 1

for Ian Monahan,
who thinks his dad is as good at
detective fiction as Poe and Conan Doyle

CHAPTER ONE

March 18, 1908

JOHN LE BRUN REGARDED the sun rising over St. Simons Sound. He squinted against its blinding splendor in the cloudless blue sky. A gentle breeze blew from the southwest, creating a second sea from the pickerelweed, arrowhead, bulrushes, arrow arum, and other vegetation bending in lazy waves over the salt marshes of Glynn County. Le Brun carried the final, "deathbed" version of Walt Whitman's *Leaves of Grass* in his left hand. He had purchased the poetry collection in Atlanta the previous year but had only begun reading it during the past week. Now that the Yankee tourist season was coming to a close in Brunswick, he was resigned to absorbing "the precious lifeblood" of master literary spirits in lieu of live companionship.

A shady bluff signified the far point of Le Brun's habitual late-morning strolls. He groaned softly as he eased his nearly sixty-year-old bones onto a mossy mound. He had read only the first poem when he recognized the voice of Sheriff Warfield Tidewell calling his name behind him. He waited patiently without turning, a faint smile elevating his cheeks. He knew the only thing that would cause his successor to interrupt Le Brun's solitude was police work.

As the pebble-covered pathway crunched under Tidewell's shoes, Le Brun angled his face once more toward the sun and said, "The very reason for callin' this region 'The Golden Isles.' It's no wonder the ancient Greeks decided it was Apollo ridin' his golden chariot."

"No wonder," Warfield echoed.

John's smile grew broader. The game had begun, whether Warfield would first state his dilemma or John would betray his continued interest in the investigation of criminal activity. John broke the silence, but not regarding the real matter at hand.

"I thought you'd be out of the law enforcement business by now, War. What's up with that horseless carriage franchise?"

"I can't believe you haven't heard," Tidewell replied. "Colonel Jim Gould stole the march on me. He locked up the rights to a Brunswick Ford dealership."

Le Brun pivoted and focused on the tall sheriff with a patrician's bearing. "Sorry to hear."

"But my friends up in New York are working on what may be a better deal for me," Warfield continued with enthusiasm. "A couple brothers named Fisher are building the bodies for several automobile companies. I might be the dealer for Cadillacs and Buicks."

Le Brun rose with a grunt and brushed off the seat of his pants. "Buick, you say? That would make it much easier to repair that contraption you bought in December."

"It would indeed."

"Willie Parker could benefit from such an agency. Doesn't he own a Cadillac?"

"Indeed. The first motorcar in Brunswick. Speaking of another Gould, there's a problem at the docks."

John walked past Tidewell in the direction of the city. "Do tell."

"Quite a puzzle." The sheriff came up beside the man who had been his superior for almost seven years and his mentor for ten. "Merriweather Gooderly's discovered a robbery in his warehouse. The Edwin Goulds, over at the Jekyl Island Club, like to have some of their art on display in their cottage when they winter."

"That mansion with the leaky roof and basement."

"Not anymore. He had it fixed when he bought it. Renamed it Chicota."

"You are still too much in awe of those robber barons," Le Brun chided. "Go on."

"Well, they had the club superintendent wrap the artwork up, secure it in a large crate, and transport it over to Gooderly's warehouse, for return to Oyster Bay. You know . . . your other stomping grounds . . . among the robber barons." He cocked an amused eyebrow as he delivered his return rebuke.

John declined to comment on his visits to New York and his occasional hobnobbing with the ultrarich. "The crate disappeared?"

"No. It's still there. But it's empty. It's a real skull scratcher, because Gooderly's is the most secure warehouse in the city," Tidewell declared.

John Le Brun continued his unhurried pace. "Was."

MERRIWEATHER GOODERLY'S SURE-TITE Warehouse stood beside the Brunswick freight house tracks and within shouting distance of Oglethorpe Bay. It had been built in 1900, following the massive fire that destroyed the B&W Docks and another half-dozen adjacent companies. Toward

the close of the nineteenth century, Brunswick had grown
into the fifth largest port on the Atlantic coast and ranked
number one in shipping lumber. Good money was being
made, even during the national financial crisis of 1907.
Gooderly owned two dock- and trackside properties. The one
near where the Brunswick River emptied into Oglethorpe
Bay served for shipping lumber north, exporting cotton to
Europe, and receiving European goods. The smaller Sure-Tite
Warehouse handled delicate and valuable items, particularly
for the local wealthy and the seasonal millionaires whose
families wintered on nearby Jekyl Island, the most exclusive
family resort in the world.

The warehouse was built as securely as a prison. There
were no windows in the brick walls. Natural illumination
was supplied by eight large skylights arrayed between the
massive roof rafters. The side facing west had two doors. The
standard-sized portal was solid, sheathed in steel, opening
into a corridor that led to the warehouse office. The other
was a massive rolling-door access for trucks and wagons, also
covered in steel sheeting. The first had both a regular lock and
a padlock; the second could only be opened from the inside.
A third door was set in the east wall. It presented a smooth
barrier from the outside, with neither keyhole nor handle. It
served as an emergency exit and closed automatically with a
spring mechanism above the inner side. The bayside wall was
completely solid. Opposite it, the fourth, trackside wall was
built without a docking platform. The warehouse instead had
three upward-rolling dock doors that nearly butted up against
a railroad freight car when it was positioned on the service
track. The structure's single floor was fashioned of thick, long-
leaf yellow pine planks and elevated to the height of freight-
car beds. During loading and unloading, a ramp was set down
between that floor and the boxcar.

John Le Brun knew the layout of the warehouse from

both firehouse blueprints and direct observations, as he did every other commercial building in Brunswick. He did not, however, have the same intimate level of acquaintance with Merriweather Gooderly that he did with the rest of the dock-area business owners. The word used around the port for this businessman was *standoffish*. Gooderly claimed to have come from Atlanta money and had moved to the seaport in 1900. His local associations were scrupulously limited to, as he claimed, "the better people of Brunswick." Seated directly across from the clearly aggravated man, John absorbed not only his words but also his facial expressions, his gestures, and the staccato cadence of his speech.

"Not even a five-year-old could slip between the boxcar sitting there and the warehouse wall," Gooderly asserted, mopping his temples and high forehead with his handkerchief. The warehouse office was cool, suggesting to Le Brun that the man's profuse perspiration came from a surplus of emotion rather than exercise or the room's temperature. "Even if somebody could, that door was closed overnight. I make my living on the very real perception that this place is virtually impregnable. A goddamned fortress for their belongings and products." He focused his furrowed stare through the pane of glass that separated his office from the storage areas. "I'll show you, if you care to take a tour."

"Not necessary on the outside," John replied. "Sheriff Tidewell and I perambulated the property before we entered the buildin'." He rocked back slightly on the rear legs of his chair. "But the inside is a different matter. This has the smell of an inside job."

The portly Gooderly wore a tailored three-piece suit. Menial duties were not part of his life. He was completely clean-shaven with not even the moustache that some two-thirds of Brunswick's prominent businessmen sported. "Virtually impossible," he came back. "The only ones who have keys are

Mr. Cate and myself, and for the past two days Mr. Cate has been at his mother's funeral in Valdosta."

"I already ascertained that," the current sheriff informed the former one. Warfield dipped his handsome head in the owner's direction. "And Mr. Gooderly has assured me that when the previous foreman left four years ago, he changed the locks and padlock."

John pushed himself out of his chair. "Let's have a look-see."

ON THE WAREHOUSE FLOOR were laid out more than two dozen squares of neatly arranged crates, barrels, and trunks. A single crate, some four feet square, sat in the main aisle. Its top was removed. The protective box, which had been fashioned with inside slots so that the artwork frames would not bang against one another, was easy to examine since all contents except some stray strands of packing straw had been removed.

"This was sitting alone on that pallet," Gooderly said, pointing. "It came in yesterday morning from Jekyl Island . . . on the *Kitty*. I was here all day, with a direct view of it from my office. Jimmy Galligan, Steve Moritz, and John Callahan were rousting, and they've all worked for me for at least five years. Excellent men." He paused to wave in a friendly manner at two laborers who moved freight from the warehouse through the open middle dock doorway and into a fifty-foot furniture boxcar. Each dipped his head in acknowledgment.

"You said the boxcar was parked there all night?" John sought to confirm.

"Since 3 P.M. yesterday," the owner of the warehouse replied. "The men came in with me at 8 A.M., same as usual, opened the dock door, and continued loading it. When they fetched the Gould's crate, they realized from the lack of weight that it had to be empty."

"And it was shut tight," John said.

"Pretty much the same condition that it arrived. No seals. Nail heads flush with the wood. Wood around the nails slightly chewed. A small cat's paw was used to open it."

"Who opened it a second time?" John asked.

Gooderly pointed to himself. "I was not nearly so neat."

"No large puddle of water under it," John observed.

"I don't understand," Gooderly admitted.

"If the crate looked pretty much undisturbed and yet the inside weight seemed to vanish overnight, meltin' ice might account for it. In which case, the crime happened before the crate was off-loaded from the *Kitty*. How can you be certain no one slipped into the warehouse and hid unobserved near closin' time?"

"Because I or Mr. Cate always do a walk-around before locking up the building."

John strode to the emergency exit door on the east wall. He bent slightly at the waist to examine the lock's latch bolt. He did not, however, handle the lock.

"Have you or anyone else touched this lock mechanism today?" he asked.

Gooderly said, "Not I. I'll ask my men if they have." He strode quickly toward the boxcar.

John faced Warfield. "Why don't you run and fetch your fingerprintin' outfit?"

"I have it in the wagon. I'll be right back."

While he waited for the two men, John removed the straw boater he had recently substituted for his habitual derby hat. He unbuttoned the casual jacket that had replaced the formalwear he had dressed in as a sheriff and still did when visiting other cities. He strolled up and down the long aisles, his hands clasped behind his back. With the point of his folding knife he checked floorboards, to be certain they were secure. He read the information on the sides of the Gould crate, as well as other

crates and trunks that were the same size or larger. At one point
he stopped, tilted his head, then nudged a small object with the
toe of his boot. He picked it up from the floor, examined it, and
placed it in the coin pocket of his trousers. He was observing
that nothing hung from the parallel rows of hoisting systems,
with their heavy chains, pulleys, hooks, and rollers when the
warehouse owner returned.

"Neither they nor I touched that door today," Gooderly
assured.

"That's a mercy," said Le Brun.

Gooderly followed Le Brun's eyes upward some twenty-five
feet. "Those skylights don't open. If you think I should get
somebody with an extra-long ladder—"

"I don't believe there is a need." Le Brun pointed to the
empty crate. "You're far more expert than I at the packin'
business. Accordin' to the label, the crate held thirteen paintin's.
What would you estimate the weight of the contents was?"

Gooderly shrugged. "Canvas weighs little, but the frames
are another matter. I'd guess between eighty and a hundred-
fifty pounds, depending on the various sizes of the artwork.
More bulky than heavy."

"When did the crate arrive?"

"Shortly before noon."

"How many crates the same size or larger came into the
warehouse yesterday between noon and closin' time?"

"I'd need to check." Gooderly hurried to his office.

Sheriff Tidewell entered carrying a box camera and the
fingerprinting kit that John Le Brun had created before his
retirement. Without a word, he went to the emergency door
and began working.

Gooderly returned holding documents. He handed the bill
of lading copies to Le Brun. "Six deliveries in the afternoon
and early evening. I personally closed up at six. Right after
we found the Gould crate empty, I had my men question

the workers at the surrounding businesses. A man from the Downing Company Rosin yard had put in overtime and was walking home at quarter to ten. He saw a fellow turn the corner from the wall with that door and move across the tracks toward town. Average height, average build. He said he was sure the man wore work clothes. But he couldn't identify him because the person avoided the lights. He was also sure that the man carried nothing but a tool belt. Our emergency door opens to a wide expanse of land. And several nearby buildings are in operation around the clock. Somebody would be insane to pull up a wagon and make several trips carrying those paintings out."

"Or very rash and extremely lucky not to be observed and reported," John replied. He whistled softly at the insurance document secured to the Gould shipping bill. The collective artwork had been evaluated in December in New York City at $16,900, roughly what Le Brun had earned in his last six years as sheriff of Brunswick. He walked to the empty space on the floor where he had found the small object. "I'm willin' to wager that a crate sat here last night and was moved into the boxcar this mornin'."

"Let's see." Gooderly led Le Brun to the boxcar. An electric cable ran from the warehouse into the car, and a strong light illuminated the space. A quick conference with the workers confirmed John's surmise. The crate stood behind two others, necessitating rearrangement. Presently, it sat isolated in the center of the boxcar.

John looked at the shipping marks on the crate and the paste-on labels. "Quinten Banks. He's the carpenter with the shop at the end of Union Street, if I'm recallin' rightly."

"He is," said Gooderly. "A custom furniture maker and repairman as well. He's in high demand."

"On Jekyl Island from time to time, I would suspect," said Le Brun. "But this says the crate is goin' all the way to Atlanta. Could his reputation stretch that far?"

Gooderly walked around the crate, which was about four and a half feet wide on each side and six feet high. Each side bore the stenciling: **THIS END UP.** A second stencil provided a good-sized arrow, for anyone who could not read. "I have no idea of his reputation. Something this high could be for a pair of armoires or chiffarobes."

Le Brun turned his head so that his one good eye looked at the crate straight on. "And yet the full weight, includin' the crate, was only two hundred fifty pounds."

"It ain't that heavy," Steve Moritz attested.

"Let's haul it back into the warehouse and put it on the scale," Le Brun suggested.

A cargo dolly was used to roll the crate onto the scale.

"Sho 'nuf," Gooderly exclaimed. "Only a hundred eighty."

Warfield Tidewell came up to the group. "I found some complete prints on the door handle."

"Admirable," said Le Brun. "Now hand me that little step ladder, War, and somebody get me a pry bar."

The ex-sheriff climbed the ladder, looked down on the top of the crate, and employed the pry bar on two sides. He relocated the ladder, remounted, and finished working the lid of the crate free. He pushed the wood halfway off, peered inside, and gave out a grunt of satisfaction.

"What's in it?" Warfield asked for the observers.

"Appears to be thirteen paintin's, nicely wrapped. Also a small ladder, a foldin' chair, and a milk can, all well lashed to one wall. Best you fetch a deputy and then pay a visit to the workshop of Mr. Quinten Banks, Sheriff."

"Not before I understand what happened here."

John returned to the warehouse floor. Before speaking, he fished out the object he had put in his trouser coin pocket. He held it up for everyone's examination.

"A common nail. Well, the head and half an inch of what was probably a three-incher. The bottom snipped or chiseled off." He pointed to the empty space where the crate had sat during the night. "I found it yonder. I assume there were seven others like it, all set in the top of the crate but not long enough to hold the lid against several sharp shoves from within."

"Within?" Gooderly questioned.

"Exactly. When y'all climb up here and look inside, you'll see that this crate is quite unusual. Not only was it outfitted to lash the ladder, chair, and milk can securely to one side, but it also has adjustable slots for securing the paintin's. However, the most unusual aspect is that the lid was actually held secure by inner screws and not by the outside nails. Accordin' to your records, this crate was delivered at a little past four o'clock in the afternoon. It had Quinten Banks inside it. Mr. Banks did not accompany the delivery of the crate, did he?"

"No," Gooderly confirmed. "It was brought here on a dray by a pair of Negroes."

"Be damned!" Tidewell exclaimed.

"I would estimate that Mr. Banks's weight," Le Brun went on, "accounts for the discrepancy between yesterday's scale readin' and this mornin's. I expect that Banks had done work recently in the Gould cottage. Perhaps he even fashioned the crate that originally held the Gould artwork. That's easy enough to check on, War. At any rate, he knew that a small fortune in canvas, wood, and paint was comin' to this warehouse yesterday for shippin' today. He contrived to have himself delivered in this crate. And then he waited patiently for the warehouse to close. He had his foldin' chair to sit on, his milk can with lid in case nature called, and I am certain he had a tool belt with screwdriver, cat's paw, hammer, nails, and a torchlight.

"When the warehouse became totally quiet, Banks removed the screws, unfolded his ladder, and bullied the lid up. Several of the shortened nails undoubtedly popped out and rolled around the floor. In the darkness, he lost the one I picked up. He opened the Gould crate, extracted the paintin's,

and moved them into his crate. His crate was to be off-loaded at
Thalmann Junction and put on a train bound for the Talmidge
warehouse in Atlanta. In a day or two, Banks would have
traveled up there, claimed his freight, and sold the paintin's to
patrons not too scrupulous to demand the sales certificates. I
daresay, for a man of modest means, those sales would finance
several years of retirement."

"The clever bastard!" Gooderly exclaimed.

"Not clever enough," John replied. "He had hours alone in
here to effect the transfer. As you stated, Mr. Gooderly, 'canvas
weighs little.' If he had carefully unpinned the canvasses from
the frames and left the frames behind, the slight difference in
weight would never have been noted."

"Please call me Merri," the greatly-relieved-looking
warehouse owner invited. "I certainly am merry at this moment.
We'll even get that boxcar packed on schedule."

"The only way he could have escaped with the office
entrance padlocked was through the emergency door," Warfield
reasoned. "I should be able to make your theory unassailable
with the fingerprints I found."

John clucked his tongue three times. "And so, I am no
longer needed and can return to my retirement."

Gooderly consulted his pocket watch. "Quarter to twelve.
A bit early for lunch, but I would be extremely honored if you
would allow me to host you at the Oglethorpe."

"As I am no longer collectin' a steady salary, I would be
extremely honored to allow your extreme honor," John returned.

THE ELEGANT OGLETHORPE HOTEL was in the midst of
closing its top floor and cutting back high-season services. The
1907–08 vacation period for Boston, New York, Philadelphia,
Chicago, and other Northeastern and Midwestern city families
of wealth had nearly come to its end. Interest in Brunswick as

a semi-cultured, clement relief from harsh winter and short days would not begin again until just after Thanksgiving. The luncheon menu had already been curtailed.

"I believe a Russian salad is all I require," Merriweather Gooderly said to the waiter. "That and a glass of Rhine wine."

Their waiter nodded crisply and set down a vase that contained woodland phlox and foamflower. Gooderly snapped off a sprig of the starry pink and white flower and pushed its stem into his lapel buttonhole.

John Le Brun had lost the sight in one of his eyes during his 1905 visit to London. His good eye focused but a moment on his host, then returned to his menu. He labored not to smile. He was convinced the man was making a statement of his powers to limit his appetite, but the extra twenty-five pounds around his middle that kept him at a distance from the table spoke otherwise. Gooderly was obviously a man who consumed too much starch, too many fermented beverages, or both. Moreover, the salad sacrifice was not too great on the warehouseman's part, since the celery, artichokes, string beans, and cucumbers on the bed of lettuce were liberally mixed with ounces of sirloin, ham, chicken, and seasoned mayonnaise.

To the waiter, John said, "Good day, Cassius. I might could want a cucumber and tomato salad with oyster crackers on the side. No oysters, though. And a pot of hot black tea."

When the waiter had departed, Gooderly said, "I've been waiting for the opportunity to meet you for some time, Mr. Le Brun."

"Do tell. And why is that?"

"Well, firstly because you are widely told to be a refined, intelligent, self-educated man who detests crime and injustice and works tirelessly to see that neither triumph. Secondly, because you are the unofficial chess champion of Brunswick."

The latter remark struck a particularly harmonic chord in John. He was indeed highly skilled at the game and always in search of partners equal to his talent. He caught sight of a hotel employee named Nicodemus Mason and nodded a greeting.

"I confess to every accusation. There goes one of my sometime adversaries."

Gooderly's eyebrows shot up. "That darkie?"

"Indeed. He's a much better conversationalist than a chess player, I must declare. Do you play then, Mr. Gooderly?"

"If you would do me the honor of calling me Merri, I could call you John."

"Fair enough. Do you play, Merri?"

Gooderly cocked one eyebrow. His slate-blue eyes seemed to twinkle. "I have defeated many others in my time. You and I share similar reputations, so that several competent players in Brunswick refuse to even discuss the subject with us. Have you played in the clubs of New York and London?"

"I'm afraid I did not have much free time," John replied.

"Due to solving some spectacular crimes, I would surmise." Merri leaned forward, slightly tipping the table. "I would like to proffer a proposition to you. I am the president of an exclusive club."

"Here in Brunswick?" John asked. He knew of religious clubs, sewing and quilting circles, garden clubs, card clubs, fraternal organizations, singing societies, and numerous other assemblies built around common interests and backgrounds, but he had never heard Merriweather mentioned as president of any of them. Unlike London, Boston, New York, and Chicago, residents of Brunswick did not manically join clubs merely to see who had assembled the most impressive lists in the annual Social Register. Nevertheless, they held them to be socially important. When the deceptively simple questions "Who is she?" or "Who is he?" were uttered, which clubs the one inquired of belonged to counted right along with family background, marriage partner, how much and where land was owned, profession or business owned, church affiliation, formal education or finishing school. If a woman belonged to the Daughters of the American Revolution or to the Colonial Dames, her standing was gilt-edged even if she was a harridan.

"Actually, every member but one lives in Brunswick, but we meet over at St. Simons Island. Distance aids privacy. It's called the New Century Club."

"I cannot admit to havin' heard of it," John confessed.

Merri smiled. "That is comforting to hear. The members do not want friends bickering for membership. I conceived of the club shortly after the turn of the century, you see. I was a club of one in 1900. The next year, I outlined my idea for the club to my friend Garland DeBrahm, and he became the second member. Each year thereafter, the members have elected and enrolled just one more, so that the total number is eight in 1908. One of our members, unfortunately, died last month of the cancer, and so we are spurred to determine a replacement. I would very much like to nominate you."

John dipped his head. "I must warn you, Merri, that I have an ingrained antipathy toward most clubs. My prejudice was reinforced when I was compelled to spend time over at the Jekyl Island Club solvin' a pair of murders."

"The story has become famous," Gooderly said.

"Notorious should be the word."

"Well, those *are* our country's robber barons wintering over there. I have heard a saying that 'Behind every great fortune are one or more great crimes.' I suspect the sentiment applies to a majority of their . . . what is it now . . . ninety members?"

"I suspect the same. However, I must admit that members of two clubs I was given run of in London and another two clubs in New York were largely decent gentlemen."

"And so are we."

"Who are your members?" John asked.

Merriweather waggled his forefinger. "We all agree that we wish to remain anonymous in relation to this club. You would need to meet our members and give them a sporting opportunity to put their best feet forward in your presence. We meet once a month." He removed from his inside jacket pocket a small appointment notebook, bound in leather dyed the color of claret. "The next meeting is by chance this Friday. Fridays seem best, as they give us a chance to unwind from the workweek but also do not interfere with the hours many members wish to spend with their families." Gooderly consulted his notebook. "Mr. Cate is scheduled to return tomorrow from Valdosta. This allows me to leave the warehouse at four o'clock."

The food arrived. Gooderly picked up his fork with his right hand and stabbed the first morsel of his salad. "So, what do you think?"

"I have one question at this time," John countered. "I am certain you did not hear of my personality, my exploits, or my skill at chess just this week. What kept you from seekin' me out earlier and havin' this conversation once your unfortunate eighth member expired?"

The question did not seem to offend or fluster John's host. He shrugged. "With the name Merriweather Gooderly, you can no doubt surmise that I am of British lineage. My family comes from semi-aristocratic London stock. Even here in America, our circle cannot allow themselves to strike up a conversation with another unless an introduction has been made by a common acquaintance. No one among my close acquaintances knows you well."

John accepted the reasoning, but not at face value. His family had come from good French stock, but they were small-time sea cotton planters. When he was tricked by a cousin into selling his parcel of Jekyl Island to the millionaire syndicate and took the position of sheriff, the respect afforded him was not for his societal level but rather his excellent record as the town's leading lawman. Only after he had rubbed elbows with the likes of Joseph Pulitzer, George Baker, J. P. Morgan,

Sir Arthur Conan Doyle, and a number of famous American actors and been lauded by all of them had his social standing increased in Brunswick. Those of wealth and high position talked with him but still did not invite him into their homes or elite clubs. Gooderly's strange invitation, the temptation of playing high-level chess, and John's native curiosity combined to neutralize his prejudicial antipathy toward clubs. Moreover, he knew the level of his boredom would only grow worse through the late spring and the summer, when there were no Yankee visitors to importune regarding chess matches.

"What have I got to lose?"

Gooderly relaxed his overweight frame back onto his chair. "What indeed?"

CHAPTER TWO

March 20, 1908

THE GATHERING FOR THE MONTHLY meeting of the New Century Club seemed to John Le Brun nothing so much as the clandestine movements of a cabal of anarchists. He, Gooderly, lumberman Claudius Tatnall, architect Irwin Jones, and banker Garland DeBrahm traveled the eleven miles down the Brunswick River, across St. Simons Sound, and up the Frederica River via one of the two operating ferries. Deepwater fleet owner Patrick Ebenezer rode over on one of his fishing boats, while cotton shipper Gilbert Reynolds sailed his thirty-foot yacht with maritime insurance magnate John White acting as mate.

Three carriages were hired separately at the pier as the three groups debarked, each heading from the tiny town of Frederica eastward toward the shore but staggered at intervals of a few minutes. A mockingbird welcomed John's carriage into the countryside.

"Did you know that there was once another club on St. Simons very much like ours?" Merri asked. Before John could reply, he added, "It didn't have my concept of adding one member each year, and outsiders were invited as guests, but in other aspects it was nearly identical. It was called the St. Clair Club, after the property rented out by Pierce Butler."

"We called the estate by the name of Sinclair, after the original owner," John said.

Merri dipped his head sharply, eager to continue his story. "It was made up of St. Simons Island planters. Like our meetinghouse, it also had a kitchen, dining room, library, and a game room. They also met monthly, began their meeting with a reading of a learned paper, and eventually moved on to cards and conversation."

John pushed his posterior against the outer edge of the landau's backseat, giving more room to the other man who occupied the same seat. Across from him sat architect Jones and banker DeBrahm. He asked, "To which plantation do we ride?"

"To Retreat," Jones answered. "The owner of it, Major Page, was a member of the St. Clair Club."

All three club members in the carriage began talking with animation about history on St. Simons Island, of the prolonged visits of Church of England priests John and Charles Wesley, of the origins of various plantations, and of the English actress and passionate antislavery advocate Fanny Kemble who lived there as plantation wife for a time. Swift as the words flew, each man was careful not to voice his opinion on the still-smoldering issue of slavery. For his part, John contented himself with listening. *It's as if they fancy me the learned don and them the students eager to impress him*, he observed with wonder. *Have I gained a far better local reputation in the last decade than I suspected?*

A teenage black postilion guided the landau with assurance

to the estate, which stood at the southern tip of the island, overlooking St. Simons Sound with the northern tip of Jekyl Island about a mile distant. The swollen sun hovered in orange-red over the trees to the west.

The plantation house had been abandoned and fell into disrepair during the Civil War. John was told that the King family owners moved back after the house had outlived its usefulness as the local Freedman's Bureau. When the father secured work as the deputy collector of the Port of Brunswick, the house was again abandoned. However, in front of a well-cared-for green lawn, on either side of the stately, tree-lined access road was a garden abloom with spring flowers and vegetable plants in various stages of growth. Inside the house, someone had set out fine linens and silver and provided fresh tapers for the many candlesticks and sconces. Only the first story was lit.

John learned that every member claimed skill at cooking and took a set turn at feting the club. He excelled at a couple dozen recipes and was encouraged by that fact to consider joining the club. The evening's host was Gilbert Reynolds, and he busied himself in a kitchen with a chimney stove already glowing and baskets filled with wheels of bread, chopped vegetables, a large soup tureen, and two ice coolers.

While Reynolds labored, John was invited to speak extemporaneously on the London clubs he had visited, on his chance friendship with Sir Arthur Conan Doyle, and the locked-room murders he solved with Dr. Doyle playing his Dr. Watson. After his brief, self-effacing talk, the floor was thrown open to questions. When asked about the motive for the murders, John paused for several seconds to organize his thoughts.

"It had to do with the Irish Question. Y'know, the concept of English colonization began in Ireland. As I have heard it told, the chief of one warrin' clan called on the British for help in conquerin' another Celtic king. Soon enough, the British reasoned that they might as well do the conquerin' on their own behalf. This would also protect their backyard from occupation of a Roman Catholic island by either the French or Spanish. It resulted in the Irish becoming their de facto slaves for the past five hundred years."

John paused to read the faces of the six men drawn into the semicircle around him. Although Le Brun was well aware that the plantation South, with its relatively poor soil and labor-intensive crops, could not have flourished without hundreds of thousands of cheap laborers, he nonetheless deplored the notion of slavery. His fundamental beliefs in freedom, equality under the law, and human dignity were, in fact, the reasons he had become a lawman. With his well-chosen words, he sought to determine if he could join himself socially to this group of men. He hoped that, since none made his living directly off of crops, their attitudes would be more liberal than most in the bitter, economically ruined Georgia Low Country. Reading no consternation or anger on their faces, he continued.

"Where we all work and play is quite a unique place concernin' slavery, is it not?" he asked rhetorically. "Although the importin' of slaves from abroad was locally outlawed in 1798 and by the federal government in 1808, the law was ignored for decades here. I am sure such learned men as you know of the illegal night landin' of Ibo tribespersons on the banks of Dunbar Creek just over yonder. Rather than live as slaves, they waded to a person into the water and drowned. Just across the inlet, on my home island, the *Wanderer* off-loaded 409 black slaves in November of 1858. It started from Africa with 600 souls, but such was the level of mistreatment that almost one-third were dumped lifeless into the ocean. Lest our fathers bear the burden of this crime alone, I emphasize that the ship was of Yankee origin and flew the flag of the New York Yacht Club, of which Mr. J. P. Morgan is currently president."

General laughter rang through the room. Again, Le Brun

read no sign of umbrage having been taken at his lengthy answer to the question of the London murderers' motive.

The meal was delicious if not overly complex. A fresh vegetable soup was followed by fillets of young rabbits, stuffed with mushroom purée and a half-glaze sauce, breaded English style and broiled over a low fire. Wheels of country bread accompanied with sweet butter. Declaring that opinions varied from country to country regarding red or white wine with rabbit, Chef Reynolds offered both a 1904 Jura Pinot Noir and a 1906 Saint-Maurice-sur-Eygues. When the meal ended, the men adjourned to the gaming room. The six who got into a spirited game of All Fours spent as much time talking business as playing cards. It was clear to John that a private businessmen's bureau operated monthly in the reclaimed mansion, with various moneymaking schemes being presented and either rejected or approved and underwritten. John and Merriweather sat at the opposite end of the room, at a table that had a chess board preset. Since his opponent had won white and the first move, John elected the Sicilian Defense. Gooderly was skilled, but not as much as he was cocksure. He made his moves more quickly than did John, with physical flourishes that suggested his confidence. On the twelfth move, Patrick Ebenezer quit the card table to refill his wine glass. He wandered over to the chess table and watched in silence for a minute, then retreated without comment.

On the twenty-third move, Gooderly placed the middle finger and thumb of his right hand on his remaining bishop and left them there for almost a minute. Then, suddenly, he conceded defeat by toppling his king.

"Those who speak of your prowess do not exaggerate," Merri declared.

"Not so good that you won't win many such matches, I assume," John granted.

"Does that mean you wish to join our exclusive ranks?"

"I believe so . . . dependin' on the dues."

The warehouseman nodded soberly. "Steep for the average club, but not nearly what the clubs in New York or London cost: twelve dollars a month."

A year earlier, the fee would have given John pause. However, with his New York detective agency income abetting his retirement pay and savings, he could afford the luxury.

"I can do that," John returned.

Gooderly turned to the other members of the New Century Club. "Good news, gentlemen: Mr. Le Brun has agreed to become Mr. 1908."

Noises of approval rose from around the card table.

"Hold on a moment," John said. "A major proviso of membership is one's cookin' abilities. How do you know I'm not a beans-and-pork-fat slinger?"

In a boisterous voice, insurance broker White replied, "That was the first thing I researched when Merri suggested you. You may well be the best epicurean amongst us."

WHEN THE RETURN FERRY dropped off five of those who lived in Brunswick, Merriweather suggested that he and John share a horse-drawn cab. Most of the town, with its grid of broad streets, was dark.

"Just how intensive was your group's check on me?" John wondered aloud.

Gooderly produced a cigar. "*Your* group now as well. Actually, it was casual . . . not to stir up undue curiosity. However, enough to learn that you smoke. This is Cuban. Want one?"

"Thanks, but I inhaled enough smoke at the club. I assume you learned not only my cookin' skills but also my ability to pay the dues."

"True enough. One fascinating fact I learned, purely by chance, is that you own a thriving New York detective agency, and that you travel up there several times a year." Before John could absorb the news and comment on it, Merri continued. "I make the same periodic trips. Half for pleasure and half business. I adore the theaters and music halls." He patted his large belly. "The restaurants as well. My day business is visiting art galleries, furniture galleries, department stores, and the like to convince them to move goods by ship and use my warehouses to distribute throughout the South. I also act as representative for Claude Tatnall's lumber and for plantation owners who ship some of their cotton to the Yankee mills."

John felt no need to respond to the information, so he remained quiet in the cab, with his arms folded across his chest.

"Will you be heading north soon?" the overweight businessman asked, after a series of coughs.

"At the end of April."

"I could arrange my schedule so that we might travel together. Of course, if you treasure your privacy, I understand."

John had done his own research on the club president. He learned that the man had no wife or children, leaving him free to alter his schedule at a moment's notice. John also appreciated the man's sensitivity to privacy, since Le Brun rarely allowed persons to venture beyond either his physical or emotional parlor. Poor experiences with random sleeping-car-compartment mates also tempted him strongly to consider the offer. His few hours with Gooderly had also proven the man educated and urbane. As John's father used to say of such persons: "He'd do to ride the river with." Moreover, in light of Gooderly's efforts to enroll him in the pleasurable St. Simons Island club, he felt a rebuff would be ungracious.

"Let's give it a try," John acceded.

"Wonderful!" Merri enthused. "Wonderful!"

CHAPTER THREE

April 29, 1908

"I KNOW YOU'RE A MAN of the world," Gooderly said to Le Brun as they followed the man lugging their suitcases off the Jersey City ferry, "but keep a careful eye on your belongings." He pointed to the unusual cityscape two blocks ahead of them. A great swath of New York City tenements and businesses had been leveled to make room for the new terminus of the most powerful railroad in the world, the Pennsylvania. Beyond the great open pit hemmed in by Ninth and Tenth Avenues and Thirty-first to Thirty-third Streets stood the framework of a structure whose proportions rivaled the ancient Egyptian palace at Thebes. The Beaux Arts train station had been designed by the firm of McKim, Mead, and White. Two years before, John had witnessed the murder of architect Stanford White at close range, on the rooftop of Madison Square Garden.

"The station is months from completion, but already the pickpockets are gathering, to fleece the gawkers," Gooderly went on.

"I am aware," John replied.

Merri laughed. "Ridiculous of me to mention, you being a master detective. Like warning a cavalry officer to be wary of red Indians."

"Then again," John observed, "Custer could have benefitted greatly from your caution."

They arrived at a hackney. While the cab driver stowed their luggage, Merri produced one of his Cuban cigars and set flame to rolled tobacco.

John watched the procedure in silence. It was, in his estimation, perhaps the sixteenth such immolation since he and Gooderly had left Brunswick by train. Because John was himself an occasional smoker, Merri's habit did not annoy. Nothing the man had done or said had lowered Le Brun's opinion of him. They had played three games of chess, and the warehouseman had won one, with all having been hard fought. It turned out that Merri read fairly widely and showed great curiosity about the world around him, allowing ample topics for time-passing conversation. Gooderly volunteered his opinions on national politics when the two traded newspapers. He was a declared Republican and, unlike John, favored the American imperialism that had grown unabated since the Spanish American War, declaring that "with the monarchs of Europe having gobbled up most of the world as colonies, it's far better that our democracy protect what's left."

Gooderly had made few personal inquiries of John's life and only seemed fixated on the detective's solution of the Metropolitan Club and subsequent New York City murders. He apologized for his fascination but declared that it was a setting with which he could most identify. He was especially effusive on the subjects of New York City dining and entertainment and had clearly spent great sums of cash to have had such experiences. He invited John to partake with him during their mutual stay, but the detective was noncommittal, using business and his eagerness to spend time with Miss Lordis Goode, to whom he had become engaged, as his excuses.

The cabman gestured for the travelers to enter the hackney. Merri clambered in first, tilting the conveyance. When John was seated, Merri asked, "To which hotel?"

"This time I'll be stayin' at the boardin' house of an associate of mine," John said. To the driver he called out, "Drop me off at 435 West Thirty-eighth Street, if you please."

"The Tenderloin is not the best of neighborhoods," Merri judged.

"Actually, this is just around the corner from mayhem," Le Brun rejoined. "Do you know how it got its title?"

"Tell me."

"It came from New York Police Department Captain Alexander Williams. He had the justly deserved nickname Clubber. About thirty years ago, he was transferred to the area and immediately raised the bribes for police protection, both for legitimate and illegal businesses. Lots of them brothels. He told his friends, 'I've been eatin' chuck steak ever since I joined the force; now I'm dinin' on tenderloin.'"

The blocks between Twenty-third and Fifty-ninth Streets from Fifth to Eighth Avenues, known collectively as The Tenderloin, were still a nursery and hotbed for thievery, pick pocketing, protection rackets, and prostitution. Mrs. Mary McMahon's three-story apartment house lay near the rough edge. John had met the petite woman with the straw-colored hair when investigating his first case in New York City. He realized only seconds after their introduction that her powers of observation were unusually keen. She was the manager, secretary, accountant, and sometimes investigator of the John Le Brun Detective Agency, with her home the headquarters. For

the seventeen months the agency had been in operation, she and
the other employees had booked almost twelve hundred hours
of time, at the exclusionary rate of nine dollars per hour per
hired employee. The other members of the group included Alice
Ainsworth, a member of New York Society with a sharp mind
and a longing to slip now and then out of its strictures; Kevin
O'Leary, a detective with the NYPD who served exclusively
as consultant and liaison with the police; and Stuart Hirsch
and Lawrence Wilker, both retired policemen with plenty of
experience and an abundance of free time. Mary's main source
of cash flow derived from the rental units in the building that
she and her husband, Martin, were paying off at a quick rate.

The cab shuddered to a halt in front of the address John
had delivered. The smell of horse manure wafted strongly from
the curb. John looked forward to the day when horse-drawn
conveyances would disappear from Manhattan's streets.

"Not so shabby," Merri judged, looking at the tenement
house. "If you find a night free and want someone to carouse
with, I'm staying at the Astoria Hotel. Ring me up."

"I shall," John replied, with more promise in his voice than
he felt.

The cabbie set John's luggage on the first step of the stoop,
accepted two quarters for the short ride with no word or gesture
of thanks, and hurried back to his seat to complete his trip.
John shook his head slightly. As a group, he observed that New
York City dwellers had a sardonic shell, which they did not
bother to conceal. John credited it to the hardened spirit of the
hordes of immigrants, cynical even in their hopes in the Land
of Opportunity. He knew that the state motto of New York was
Excelsior, meaning "Ever Upward," but he reflected that New
York City should have its own motto: What the hell are you
looking at?

As the cab's horse clip-clopped away, an alto voice called
down from a first-floor window.

"You'll need to drag your valise up yourself, John," Mary instructed, leaning out beyond the sill. "My old man's tiptoeing around on the Penn Station scaffolding."

John nodded and grabbed his single, oversize suitcase. He noted that Mary wore a flower print dress he had not seen before and had arranged her wavy hair up, like that of the Gibson girl drawings in current fashion. He also registered that, for the first time, he heard her say "my old man" instead of "me old man." When he first met her in the summer of 1906, he realized that the woman retained little of the brogue of her Irish birthplace. On each subsequent visit, he noted that she spoke a more secure neutral American English. She was a woman focused on grabbing her share of her adopted country's cornucopia, by dint of hard work, dressing habits, and a more acceptable accent. Although he had never spoken of the subject, John privately applauded her attitude.

"How is Martin?" John inquired of Mary's husband as he stepped into the front hallway and found his employee holding an opened envelope in one hand and a thickness of newspaper in the other.

"He's fine, but we have no time for idle chitchat. Come in, come in!" Mary stepped back to allow John into her four-room apartment. Just inside the front door sat a desk with a cubbyhole cabinet at the back. The perpetual neatness of the desk never ceased to amaze John. From the tiny space, the entire business of the John Le Brun Detective Agency was run. On the desk sat a candlestick telephone, whose purchase and operation cost as much as all the other nonsalary outlays combined. Beyond the indirect message to their clientele of modernity and success, the telephone allowed almost instantaneous response to emergency situations.

"Sit!" Mary directed, as she set the envelope and newspapers down on the desk surface.

John shrugged out of his coat and hung it and his straw

boater on a coat tree that stood on the opposite side of the door
from the desk. He sat and examined the outside of the envelope
first. In block printing were the words: JOHN LE BRUN DETECTIVE
AGENCY / 435 WEST 38ᵀᴴ STREET, NEW YORK, NY. He withdrew
a single sheet of stationery, which was cream in color and of
a high rag content, and immediately noted the letterhead. The
embossed name at the top was that of J. P. Morgan with his
Manhattan home address below. The typed message read:

> Herbert M. Moore, of 80 Washington Square North,
> murdered night of April 28. Expose the assassin without
> involving me. Burn this letter.

The letter was unsigned. Also inside the envelope were ten
new, sequential fifty-dollar bills.

"From the king of the pirates himself," Mary commented.
"Hand delivered by a young courier."

John made a deep, bearlike noise in his throat. "Did he
offer identification of employment by a Morgan firm?"

Mary's shoulders slumped slightly. "No. I didn't know it
came from old Strawberry Nose until I opened the envelope.
But I should always ask who a courier works for and from
whom he accepted the delivery."

"I'm sure you will from now on." John knew that she
needed no further lecture. He handed the letter and currency
to his associate. "We will not burn anythin' until the conclusion
of this business . . . if then."

"Do you doubt it comes from Morgan?" Mary asked.

"I have a piece of his stationery at home," John replied. "It's
from his yacht and also cream in color, but with an entirely
different letterhead. This might be genuine, but the words used
give me pause. Also, why would he not call? You sent our business
card to him and to a hundred other upper-crust folk that Mrs.
Astor invites to her ballroom." He pointed to the stick telephone.

"The card and business letter both included this number. A phone call would have been a more anonymous method of reachin' out than this . . . with no need for burnin' paper."

"But whoever it was felt the need to prepay. It certainly gets my attention." Mary nodded at the gold certificates with the engraving of U.S. President Grant's image. "If not Mr. Morgan, then it was at least someone of means."

John held up one of the bills and slowly angled it back and forth in the indirect sunlight, studying it with his good eye to be sure it was genuine legal tender. "At any rate, someone is willin' to pay half the cost of an automobile to have us pursue this case, and no murder should ever remain unsolved." He set the bill down and nodded at the newspapers on the desk. "I assume the murder actually occurred."

"According to the *World* and the *New York Journal American*. I am in constant awe how a murder such as this can happen at half past nine in the evening and yet appear on the pages of the morning papers."

"The minions of Messieurs Hearst and Pulitzer work around the clock," John said. "And those two lurid journals make the most profit from reportin' crime in the five boroughs. I imagine both publishers don't finish their mornin' edition layout until quite late, to include as many dramas of the night as they can." He accepted the newspapers, which had been turned to the brief articles on the murder, deemed in both publications of only third-page worthiness. Herbert Moore was reported to be a third-generation American of "some social standing," fifty-six years of age, and "owner of more than a dozen city buildings." He was found bleeding on the sidewalk directly in front of 224 East Twelfth Street, "a genteel block populated by citizens of quality." He suffered a knife wound to his back, was transported to Bellevue Hospital, and died en route without speaking. No suspects were in custody, but a "thorough police investigation" was in progress. Moore was survived by his wife of twenty-nine years, as well as a son, daughter, and two grandchildren.

"His home address is a goodly distance south of the place of attack," Mary noted, as John finished reading the second article. "What was he doing walking there alone and at such an hour?"

John consulted his pocket watch. The time was two minutes before noon. "Both important questions. Let's see if we can't earn this money the easy way. Call the 19th Precinct headquarters and ask for O'Leary."

Mary made the call while John trudged with his valise to the top floor and entered a room that had been occupied by a poisoned actor two years earlier. It was the reason he had met Mary McMahon. The same unevenly worn wallpaper that he had first seen in 1906 greeted him. Clearly, every spare cent was being channeled to pay off the tenement building. When he returned to the landlady's apartment, Mary smiled with triumph.

"Kevin will meet you over at the 17th Precinct. Don't go—"

"Inside," John interrupted. "Naturally. We can't compromise the integrity of a decorated officer of the law."

"Want some Mulligan stew before you set off?" Mary asked.

John knew from having accepted such an invitation on an earlier visit that the Irish stew consisted of whatever meat, potatoes, and vegetables had been left over from the previous days' cooking. Further, Mary was an unenthusiastic cook at best.

"Thanks," John answered, "but I'll find a sidewalk eatery near the precinct and wait for Kevin to collect the information. Why don't you ring up Alice and ask her what she can gather on Mr. Herbert M. Moore?"

Mary nodded sharply, sat, and picked up the telephone.

THE PLACE LE BRUN chose to wait for his detective friend and employee was a quiet saloon with several café tables out front. Although the checkered tablecloth needed replacing, the liverwurst on rye with onion confit was passable, as was the beer on tap. That the saloon was to the taste of the local police was evident by the presence of several of their number.

Kevin O'Leary spotted John from across the street but walked to him without any acknowledgment and sat down. He carried a folder in his right hand and a stylish Homburg hat in his left. John had not connected with the detective in months, and he saw that his thick, russet-toned hair had become salted with white. His close-set eyes were just as blue, though. He also wore what John recognized as a well-cut and fitted three-piece suit, the type from a department store such as Macy's, Lord & Taylor, or Abraham and Straus.

O'Leary set the hat on the table, offered his hand, and sat. "Welcome back to New York, John."

"You're lookin' more prosperous and happy than the last time I saw you," John observed.

"Right you are. Me missus decided I was gone too many hours each week and found herself a younger guy who sells musical instruments on Tin Pan Alley. Tells me on the way out the door that they make beautiful music together. This comin' Tuesday, we get officially unhitched, and I do a jig in fronta City Hall. I oughta buy the gent a motorcar for the favor he's doin' me." Unlike Mary McMahon, the immigrant from the Auld Sod had not lost a bit of his brogue.

Le Brun cocked one eyebrow. "A younger man, eh? And what happens if he tires of her and leaves?"

O'Leary shrugged. "That's her risk. She'll have to support herself." He had clearly said all he wished to of his personal life. With only a moment to draw in a new breath, he asked, "Who's payin' ta have Moore's death researched?"

"Ostensibly? J. P. Morgan. But that can be checked later. Whoever it is has laid out hard cash."

Kevin smoothed out his moustache. "Good enough. Ya seen the papers this marnin'?"

"The *World* and the *Journal American*."

"They're correct as far as they go. Moore was found with his head facin' 224 East Twelft'. As if he had reached his destination and just turned to mount the stairs . . . on his way to mount a classy lady of ill repute."

"It's a whorehouse?" John asked.

Kevin shook his head gravely. "The owner would be extremely upset ta have it called that. This class of establishment is referred to as an 'assignation house.' Swells with deep pockets only. It may simply have been a violent robbery of opportunity. The block is not well lit. Views obstructed by sidewalk trees. Moore's billfold was found at the left side of his neck, with no money inside. His pocket watch had been ripped from his vest. Moore wore his weddin' ring, and it would have disappeared as well, except that his finger had swollen around it over the years."

"How frequent are violent robberies in that section?" John asked.

"Quite rare, me fellow officers tell me. Twelft' as well as the block of Park Avenue just north of Union Square and a large house on Stuyvesant Street are all well patrolled."

"All with assignation houses," John understood.

"Two on Twelft', in fact. Almost directly opposite each other. Moore was probably a client. I've been told ta keep me nose out and warn whoever I'm inquirin' on behalf of."

John nodded. Protection was being paid. "So Herbert Moore's death will be written off as a chance robbery and the investigation quietly dropped."

"Exactly."

John took a sip of beer. "But how did this business come to J. Pierpont Morgan so soon? I find it difficult to believe he spends a minute perusin' any newspaper third pages, much less those of the *World* and the *Journal American*."

"Maybe he got the news more direct. But why would he care?" Kevin returned. "I can't imagine he has anythin' ta do with Twelft' Street. His women are all personal mistresses, as I understand it."

"All educated and beautiful," John added. "Two of them married physicians in this city when Morgan was done with them."

O'Leary eyed the untouched half of Le Brun's liverwurst sandwich. John pushed the plate in his direction. The detective murmured his thanks and then said, "The murder weapon was t'in but not small. It went all the way t'rough his chest and out the front. Had to have been like a stiletto but at least eight inches long. And shoved by either a man of at least average build or else a good-sized woman motivated by rage. Like a vindictive wife or betrayed mistress." O'Leary paused to take a bite.

"Any estimate on how long it took for him to die?" Le Brun asked.

The detective shoved the folder where the plate had been. John opened it and read in O'Leary's hand a summary of the emergency room physician's preliminary report of death. The dorsal entry wound was between the shoulder blades, just left of the spinal column. The ventral exit wound, however, was three inches off center, just under the right nipple. Estimated time of attack was 9:38 P.M.; official time of death was 9:58 P.M.

Kevin said, "I figure the knife struck a vertebra and glanced off, missin' the heart. Probably damaged his spinal cord, 'cause they found him lyin' in a heap like a rag doll. His lungs filled with blood, and he suffocated."

"So we've answered where, when, and how, but not who or why," John said.

"And the New York Police Department, leastways Precinct Seventeen, cares not a whit about the last two," Kevin said. "Naturally, they'll go t'rough the motions. Accordin' ta what I overheard, a Detective Dortmund went ta the victim's house mid-marnin', but the maid said the widow was out to the hospital and then her church and the mortician's. He left his

card and a note sayin' he'd visit again tommorah." His eyes
were following something as he spoke. John turned and saw
a pretty woman of perhaps twenty-five years sashaying along
the sidewalk and returning a saucy smile at her two admirers.
"Jaysus, they're everywhere . . . and I'm soon enough back in
the hunt," O'Leary declared.

"Maybe she'll return home soon," John said. "I mean the
widow Moore, not your wife."

"T'anks. Hey, I never heard none of it. Say hello ta Larry
and Stu fer me." Kevin shoved the last of the sandwich into his
mouth, chewed it down, and licked his fingers daintily. "Tell
Mary I'll collect what's owed me on Friday."

HERBERT MOORE'S RESIDENCE stood on the north side
of Washington Square Park. It was wider than the normal
townhouse, fashioned of brick and marble, four stories high,
with marble columns supporting an abbreviated portico. This
confirmed to Le Brun that Moore was quite well off but not of
the class of multimillionaires who were erecting urban palaces
along Fifth Avenue above Forty-fifth Street.

John waited until a man from Knickerbocker Florists
knocked on the front door. When a plump housekeeper of
middle age answered, he presumed to climb halfway up the
stoop. The elaborate bouquet of multicolored tulips and ferns
was delivered. When the man retreated, John hurried to take
his place.

"Good afternoon," John began, producing his best imitation
of a Northerner's accent. "I'm John Le Brun. I've been assigned
to investigate the death of Mr. Herbert Moore."

The housekeeper cocked an eyebrow. "We already had a
visit today. I was told by Detective Dortmund that he would
come back tomorrow morning."

John smiled broadly. "That is correct. I understand Mrs.

Moore was out all morning, at the hospital, her church, and the mortician's. But, given the social prominence of your former employer, we want to let no moss grow under the investigation. Please summon your mistress."

The housekeeper gestured to the parlor, which lay to the right side of the foyer. "Please have a seat. I'll announce you."

The wallpaper, tapestries, chandelier, furniture, mirror, and mantelpiece all were in good shape but harkened back to the end of the Victorian Age. John pegged the owners as comfortable with living in the times of their early adulthood.

John rose quickly from the tufted velvet couch when the lady of the house entered the room. He noted from its design that, unlike her home decor, her black silk mourning gown had been created within the last year or two. A lorgnette depended onto her chest from a black silk ribbon. She was a woman in her early fifties, of average features and build, thin-lipped and with a haughty air. Her expression was solemn but apparently not due to distress. Her cheeks and eyelids betrayed no hint of weeping. John immediately added her to his list of suspects.

"I am Heloise Moore," the woman declared.

John captured her extended fingers, bent formally from the waist, and brushed the back of her hand with his lips. "John Le Brun. I have been charged with solving the unfortunate matter of your husband's murder." He excused his disingenuous words in light of the seriousness of the situation.

"Sit, please. It's too early for tea."

"Don't distress yourself. I just ate," John said. "I am genuinely sorry for your loss, Mrs. Moore."

"Thank you." The widow reacted to the solicitation as if to the loss of a pair of gloves.

"Was it your husband's habit to be out alone late at night?"

Mrs. Herbert's mouth turned down and her eyebrows rose

slowly. "Would *you* say that a New York businessman being out three or four evenings a week is unusual?"

"Three or four evenings to clubs, the theater, sporting events, I would say not," John returned. "But not alone."

The widow lowered herself onto the front edge of a tufted chair placed opposite the couch. "Herbert owned more than a dozen buildings of some size, with multiple clients in most. Sometimes, matters could not be handled by a superintendent or building manager."

"Was one of these buildings on Twelfth Street?"

"Not to my knowledge. My husband did not feel a need to involve me in his business . . . and I confess that I had no curiosity in it."

John could not help glancing around at all that the husband's financial dealings had purchased.

"Did he speak recently about fear for his life?"

"Not at all." John realized the woman had not blinked since she sat. He felt as if he were talking to a life-size automaton.

"Did he ever mention anyone whom he might have considered an enemy?"

"No."

"Where is his main office?" John asked.

"On Carmine Street, near Hudson Park."

"South and west of here."

"That's correct."

John paused, hoping to elicit some look of guilt or at least discomfort on the woman's part. When she continued to sit ramrod erect, as if posing for a portrait, he asked, "So a stroll on Twelfth Street—more than ten blocks northeast from here—would be out of his way for virtually any business or leisure activity?"

"I can't say with assurance."

"Let's consider the day rather than the place," John went on. "Last night was Tuesday. Was he gone from his home most Tuesday nights?"

Heloise Herbert shrugged. "No more than any other night of the week. Except for Sundays. We entertain on Sundays. Most often my side of the family. Sometimes members of our church and the pastor . . . or a few neighbors."

"And his family?"

"He's outlived everyone in the city. His parents and his older brother."

"Your children and their families then?"

"They live in Chicago and St. Louis."

"Is there anything that I've failed to ask that you feel is important for the police to know?"

"I can't think of anything."

"Anything that I can answer for you?"

"Nothing comes to mind. Herbert was simply unlucky. I imagine the attack as the New York equivalent of an African stepping out of a straw hut and encountering a hungry lion walking by."

John had asked enough to know that Mrs. Moore was not especially focused on the solution of her husband's death. His many years of experience as a sheriff and detective suggested to him that she had had no part in her husband's demise. With him alive, she seemed to have all she could desire. Moreover, he found it difficult to imagine some ardent male encouraging her to free herself from her husband without losing half the fortune. However, since she seemed unreasonably unmoved by Herbert's death, he made a mental note to have Mary McMahon work her magic in exploring the financial angle. Between liquidated businesses and life insurance policies, Moore might well have been worth more to her dead.

John hoisted the watch from his pocket and consulted it. He produced his best approximation of a genuine smile for the widow.

"Thank you ever so much," John said as he stood. "We will be sure to report findings to you as we uncover them. In fact,

Detective Dortmund will probably stop by tomorrow morning to see if you have remembered any other facts that might be pertinent to the case."

IN LIGHT OF THE RELUCTANCE of top 17th Precinct officers to pursue the investigation, John elected to use both of his former NYPD employees. He telephoned Mary McMahon from an apothecary shop and asked her to summon them to her building.

Larry Wilker was waiting when John arrived, shortly after three. He was an amiable fellow, in spite of years of dealing with New York's hardened criminals. He had white bristle-brush hair, bright blue eyes, an abbreviated nose, and an infectious smile. When interviewing ex-cops for his agency, John had found him to be highly knowledgeable of his city and connected to its denizens on many levels. His passion was for the theater. Most of the theatrical houses, emporia, and roof gardens were in the 29th Precinct, where he had served his last nine years. Through lingering connections, he sometimes wangled gratis tickets for John and John's significant other, Lordis Goode.

Stuart Hirsch arrived a few minutes later, with a couple of newspapers under his arm. Bespectacled Stu was tall and burly without being fat. He was dark of hair and complexion, the pepper to Wilker's salt. Both men had sharply-honed senses of humor, but Larry's expressions of wit arrived like underhand pitches, while Stu's deliveries were clipped, like bursts from a Gatling gun. Each was dressed in a suit, ready to work.

John gave the group the information he had gathered from Kevin O'Leary and the victim's wife, then offered his own speculations.

"Mary has Alice workin' through the gentry, to learn the wife's attitude toward the deceased and if Moore caroused regularly with either sex at night, particularly on Tuesdays. I took away the conviction that the wife could not have cared less if her husband was frequentin' ladies of the oldest profession. He kept her in ample luxury, and she was apparently left alone to do whatever she wanted, whenever she wanted."

"Just like my wife," Stu quipped with a straight face, "minus the luxury part."

John turned his gaze on Mary. "If we can believe we were commissioned by J. P. Morgan, then it stands to reason he had a personal motive for sendin' us five hundred dollars. I want you to visit the Tilden or Lenox library and scan through the last three months of the *Times* and the *Herald Tribune*, business and society pages. See if there was any public connection between Morgan and Moore. In fact, any information on Moore's dealin's will be useful."

"And now for the shoe-leather assignments," Wilker invited.

"Tonight, I want you two to ghost the opposite ends of the block where Moore was murdered. When a john leaves 224 East Twelfth, you wait until he clears any police who may be patrollin', collar and cower him with a flash of badge, get his particulars, and pump him for information on the house. How many women work in it, who owns it, if they knew Moore. You know the drill. Before it gets dark, visit several of the conventions in town and see if you can find a shill who works for any of the assignation houses around Twelfth Street."

"Finally, some respectable work," Wilker added. "I'm tired of standing around weddings, acting like a poor cousin."

In truth, the bulk of the two ex-policemen's agency work was bouncing gate crashers and guarding gifts, billfolds, and purses at society events such as balls, cotillions, coming-out parties, weddings, and funerals. At other times, they investigated the backgrounds of would-be husbands and wives of rich daughters and sons to be sure they were not gold diggers, or shadowing wives and husbands to gather proof of infidelities. The entire team was abundantly aware that, on the whole, there was little glamorous or exciting about detective work.

Hirsch unfolded his newspapers. "I just picked up some afternoon editions. Both of these have society photos of Moore in them. We can show them to the Johns."

"That ought to discourage the patrons for a while," Mary remarked.

Wilker said, "We'll have to be cautious. Captain Treacy down at the Seventeenth will probably increase the number of flatfeet patrolling that neighborhood."

"What about you?" Mary asked of Le Brun.

"Lordis," was John's simple reply.

JOHN RAPPED WITH ONE of Whispering Hope's two oversize knockers. In spite of the fact that his fiancée had effective control of the Upper East Side mansion, she had never offered John a key; nor had he asked for one. The house at the corner of East Sixty-second Street and Fifth Avenue was one of infamy from its very creation, built by an eccentric, heartless Southern millionaire and christened Whimsey House. Like the room in Mary McMahon's apartment house, it had been the scene of a murder. Both locales figured in the same deadly scheme that John had solved two years earlier. Now it housed Lordis Goode and the two children in her legal care, while they awaited the release of their mother from prison.

Benjamin Topley, Jr., who was twelve, and his sister, Leslie Lordis Topley, ten, were at least polite in their antipathy toward Le Brun. He had been the one responsible for solving the crime that eventually killed their father and sent their mother to the recently built second iteration of the prison bearing the nickname The Tombs. They had never known life without Lordis's love, since she was Sally Topley's best friend and their godmother. Over the months, Lordis had made little progress in convincing the children that John had only done his duty as a lawman. Nor had the fact that he and Lordis had become engaged softened their attitudes. During the Christmas/New Year's holiday of 1906, John had hosted the trio in Brunswick, to enjoy the balmy weather and the festive tourist season. Le Brun had done everything in his imagination to entertain them and ingratiate himself, but their spirits remained as cool as the climate in New York.

So John resigned himself to visiting Lordis on his seasonal travels to the great Northern city and awaiting the coming time, now only a year and a half if Sally remained on good behavior, when the young people went back to their mother. By then, he trusted, Whispering Hope would have outlived a good part of its infamy and could be sold at a reasonable price.

Lordis answered the door, dressed in a receiving gown and looking as arrestingly beautiful as the first time he met her. Her light brown hair was piled high atop her head and pinned with a Japanese lacquered comb. She had subtly applied makeup, but John felt that she did not need it. Although she was forty-six, she looked to him no more than in her midthirties. She drew John into the foyer with elated energy and kissed him with passion.

"At last!" she exclaimed. "Imagine my surprise when Mary called and said you no sooner set foot on the island than you were hired for a case."

John set down his hat and shrugged out of his coat. "True enough. I am apparently once again in the employ of J. P. Morgan."

"Apparently?" Lordis came back.

John shooed away the topic. "That can be determined for certain after the case is further along." He looked through the first-floor archways and up toward the second-story hallway. "Where are Ben and Leslie?"

"They ate when I expected we all would have sat down.

They're doing their homework . . . or should be."

"I hope you're eatin' with me."

Lordis took John's hand and drew him toward the dining room. "Certainly. A crown roast. I hope it hasn't dried too much."

"Any more progress at reducin' me from ogre status?" he asked, speaking of the children.

Lordis answered with a shrug. "They're still not old enough to—"

"I was never good with children," John confessed. "Claire's death never gave me the opportunity. The son she carried would have been twenty-four this year. Once you get to a certain age—"

Lordis stopped and turned. "Let it go, John. It is what it is."

"Amen." John fished a small box he had carried from Brunswick out of his pocket. "A new charm for your bracelet."

Lordis broke into a smile. "Will you never stop spoiling me?" She opened the box and drew in a delighted breath. "A gold peach!"

"In truth," John said, "I was lookin' for a pomegranate."

After a year of courtship, Lordis had agreed to marry John. However, she said it would only happen after Sarah Topley left prison, and she would only live with him in Brunswick from the beginning of each year until after Easter and again from early August until the end of September. She loved her adopted family and New York City too much to abandon them completely. So John had agreed to play Hades to her Persephone and fill in the rest of each year with periodic trips north to oversee his detective agency, be with her, and enjoy the rich culture of the city. At thirty or even forty, the arrangement would have been untenable. At his age, however, he had long since learned the art of accommodation.

CHAPTER FOUR

April 30, 1908

JOHN LE BRUN'S SECOND business day in New York did not begin until almost ten o'clock. The long trip up from the Georgia coast, the immediate launch into an investigation, followed by thrashing in bed with Lordis after the children were asleep had combined to exhaust him thoroughly. Directly after greeting Mary at her residence, he made a telephone call to the editorial offices of Joseph Pulitzer's *World* and left a message for the head editor. Hopeful that his words would intrigue the man, he took only toast, marmalade, and tea.

Although they lived more than a mile from each other, Larry Wilker and Stuart Hirsch arrived as a team, clumping into the parlor-cum-office with a level of energy that immediately told John they had had success on the previous evening.

"Y'know, the captain of the 17th is a sharp character named

Errol Treacy," Larry began without the usual conversation starters. "He's got a reputation for managing both sides of the law with great dexterity."

"Legerdemain," Stu echoed.

Larry ignored the interjection. "For whatever reason, he had two plainclothesmen haunting Twelfth Street. We had to maintain our distance. Only able to nab four johns in three hours—"

"Two each," Stu expanded.

"But I got my hands on old Jeffrey Hobson. He was the principal in the law firm that handled Alva Belmont's divorce from Willie Vanderbilt." He laughed. "Won on the grounds of adultery. Ironic, no? I asked him what his wife would do if I made a formal arrest. He turned as white as Marley's ghost."

"My nightingale was Judge Ritter," said Wilker. "Must have been Legal Night . . . a lot of examining of briefs."

"So, what's the scoop?" Mary asked with impatience, saving John the need to focus the conversation.

Hirsch folded his arms over his chest. "The owner of the place is—was—the victim. Herbert Moore."

"Now ain't that a howdy-do?" Mary exclaimed, forgetting for a moment her efforts to Americanize.

Wilker added, "There's a husband and wife team that fronts it, keeps the women under lock and key and so forth."

"How many prostitutes?" John asked.

"Seven. All dope fiends, according to Ritter."

John turned his gaze upward, as if studying the ceiling. No one interrupted him for the quarter minute he pondered the news. Then he focused on the expectant group.

"How much per trick at a place like that?"

Wilker said, "Twenty to thirty dollars, depending on day and hour."

John nodded. "At just four tricks a day per female, with seven girls that's a passel of money. Seems to me the next logical place to investigate would be the competition directly across the street."

"If the murder was because of rivalry," Larry said, "then you could be putting yourself in danger."

"I'll have my revolver and derringer close at hand."

Stu handed John a folded sheet of paper and a business card. "From yesterday's late-afternoon work. It should help you. You should also carry an umbrella," he advised. "It'll start raining soon."

———————————

A FEW MINUTES AFTER the meeting dispersed, John left the tenement house. As soon as he arrived at Sixth Avenue, he was hailed loudly from a motorized cab. He saw that the passenger was Merriweather Gooderly. John's fellow Brunswickian opened the door.

"I was on my way to see if you were available for lunch today," Merri said.

"How nice," John dissembled, "but I have a prior luncheon date . . . at the Manhattan Club."

"Ah, yes. Your *second* favorite club," Merri said, winking. "Driver, the Manhattan Club, please." He fixed his attention on Le Brun again. "I had a cancellation of an appointment, unfortunately. The owner of a Persian rug gallery may have appendicitis."

"Sorry to hear."

"What about tonight?" Merri asked.

"Business."

"How late?"

"Maybe past the witchin' hour." John paused as a Sixth Avenue Elevated Railway train roared above them. "Actually, I will probably not have a spare moment for the next few days," John imparted. "My agency has been hired to investigate a murder."

Gooderly rocked backward, as if avoiding a roundhouse swing. "A murder! And what are the particulars?"

"A gentleman was stabbed to death outside of a house of ill repute."

"Sounds more like police business," Merri speculated. "How far along have you gotten?"

"Given that we've been on the case only one day, fairly far."

"That sounds like John Le Brun, the famous detective."

"But, whether I solve this case or not, I must devote time to my fiancée."

Gooderly threw up his hands. "Pity poor, lonely me. Perhaps I should lower my character and consider patronizing one of the better 'houses of ill repute.' " When John failed to respond to his attempt at humor, he said, "Well, if you do find yourself free . . . even for breakfast, call the Astoria and leave a message. I'm in room 404. To counter my canceled appointment, I have managed to open up negotiations with the owner of several metropolitan lumberyards, on Claude Tatnall's behalf."

"Good for you."

"So I'll be in New York until at least Sunday. It would be marvelous if we could ride back to Brunswick together."

"I'll let you know," Le Brun said.

JOHN LEFT THE CAB at the corner of Park Avenue and Twenty-sixth Street. A high-mounted, barrel-sized sidewalk clock told him the time was half past one. The Manhattan Club was the bastion of Liberal Democrats and Progressives, generally aligning with John's egalitarian views. He was elated to find himself among so many politically kindred souls. While membership was restricted by recommendation or sponsorship, the club number exceeded a thousand.

Waiting for John outside the club was Frank Cobb. He was

a tall man, with the clean-shaven and slightly lumpy features of a college pugilist. He had been the one who recommended John for membership. They had seen each other at the club several times in the past two years and even dined together once. John was, however, leery of spending too much time with the head editor of the *World*, lest he be maneuvered into visiting the owner of the newspaper, the infamous, highly opinionated, evil-tongued, all-but-blind, mercurial-tempered hypochondriac, Joseph Pulitzer.

"He arrives at last," Cobb said in a loud voice. "I'm sorry the trumpeters are on break, or I would have paid them to play a flourish."

John appreciated the man's wit, his extremely sharp mind, but most of all his Kansas accent. John liked not being seemingly the only American in New York City with a pronounced regional dialect.

"The only thing regal about me is that I'm a royal pain in the bottom," John returned, gesturing for Cobb to lead the way inside the club. "Speakin' of royal pains, how is Pulitzer?"

Cobb's face scrunched up. "Still meddling with the paper from home, choosing the stories, the headlines, red-lining my editorials. We have half a dozen fights every day by telephone. Four years of it is enough. I finally got him to agree to a face-to-face meeting over editorial policies two weeks from today. We'll see if I get what I need or if I go to a rival newspaper. I got your message about being hired to solve the murder of Herbert Moore," Frank said, abruptly changing topics. "We're quite keen on following that death, given the time, the place, and the man's reputation."

"Reputation for what?" John asked as they ascended to the dining room.

"Owning almost a score of outdated office and tenement buildings and being fined half a dozen times for slumlord antics. Who hired you?"

"He wishes to remain anonymous," John revealed. "But that, in and of itself, is a story."

"Which you'll give me?"

"We'll see," John cadged. "It won't be a story unless the murder is solved, and you may be able to help me considerably."

"Let's discuss this over lunch," Cobb said. "If I'm the deep well of information, then your wallet is the pump."

"Fair enough."

The gentlemen were seated off to the side of the dining room, at their request. Along with its prevailing political attitudes and a prodigious private library, the Manhattan Club's culinary splendor had provided the final temptation for the club-wary Le Brun to join. John ordered the famous Manhattan Clam Chowder with Original Trenton Crackers and a Greek salad.

After the waiter retreated, John opened the serious conversation. "Do you recall us sittin' out on the veranda two years back, lookin' out on Madison Square?"

"I do," said Cobb.

"And I pointed out a young woman who called herself Mornin' Mary."

"I remember that as well."

"You delivered a brief lecture on the topic of prostitution in the City."

"Did I?"

John smoothed his napkin across his lap. "Indeed. I also know from your editorials that this is a social problem you deplore. I'd like to hear more about it." John knew that, like himself, Frank Cobb was capable of gathering and remembering volumes of facts and figures on topics that obsessed him and then delivering protracted, soapbox-type harangues to anyone who expressed an interest. John also knew that few listeners to either Cobb or himself were impressed by the completeness of the answers; most were impatient or annoyed.

"Where to begin," Cobb started. "Well, the 1900 census for

New York City put our population at 3,437,202 inhabitants. The number must be up to at least 3.6 million by now. Of these, about 51 percent were women. The official police estimate last year was that some 12,000 females are full-time, professional prostitutes. That's approximately one in every 300 women."

"That is astonishin'," John marveled.

"And yet it doesn't tell the entire story. Another 6,000 or so augment their incomes by part-time prostitution. Barmaids, actresses, saloon singers, dime-a-dance girls. That reduces the ratio to one in every 200. And then there are the innumerable victims who have sold themselves into a more stable form of prostitution, by living with men or marrying them solely to survive, with no love or even respect involved.

"There are about 800 common houses of prostitution—or brothels—and about ninety assignation houses—or bordellos— in the boroughs, serving vice just as the opium dens do in Chinatown or the gambling houses in the Bronx, Queens, and Brooklyn. They cater to the lower instincts of men, not just their sexual lust but also their desires to control and demean others. And there's so much money in it that the police are happy to take their share and turn a blind eye. We've campaigned against it at the *World*, just as other city newspapers do. Every few years, the ministers and priests cooperate—with sermons, demonstrations, and even parishioner parades in front of these places. But to no lasting effect."

"But 18,000 women!" John exclaimed. "Where do they all come from?"

"Many from right here. The unwanted children, the orphans, the wives who have been widowed, abandoned, or divorced."

John thought of Kevin O'Leary's wife and her sad fate if the musical instrument salesman grew tired of her.

"But many are also from beyond state and national borders," Cobb went on. "There are the daughters from the farms that no longer need so many children, due to mechanization. They read the silly ladies' journals or romance novels of plucky girls making good in 'the big city.' They can't type or take stenography. They arrive to find no work except sweated shops. They're lured to brothels under the pretense of cheap accommodations and offered a bath. When they emerge, they find their clothes have been taken. They're made to use their bodies to pay for food and lodging. If they object, they may be beaten or turned submissive by being fed opium.

"Probably the largest source is the immigrants. Their families die of disease on the trip over, or they respond to advertisements and promotion men in their native lands, promising well-paying jobs in American kitchens, laundries, clothing factories, in ladies' shops, or as maids and nannies. They're met at the ferries and whisked right into the sex trade."

"They're imported slaves," John said. "Just like we used to do in the South."

"'Slaves' is the proper term for it." The editor shook his head ruefully. "The best looking are secured for the higher-class assignation houses, where the clientele is well off and made to pay three times the usual cost for a bottle of champagne or whiskey before they can even view the flesh merchandise. And another reason why these houses are not shut down is because many of the clients are local politicians, police captains, judges, lawyers—even religious leaders. Plus, the houses hire shills to prowl conventions and hotels and invite eager out-of-town husbands who have fantasized about such sinful escapades. If many arrests were made, the various national organizations would stop holding conferences and conventions in Manhattan."

"The place that Herbert Moore died in front of is one of these assignation houses," John disclosed.

Cobb's eyebrows shot up. "How do you know?"

"One of the city's detectives is in my employ. Not only that, another house across the street is a bordello too. On Twelfth Street, between Second and Third Avenues."

"I don't know the street, but given the location, it must be an otherwise dignified neighborhood," said Cobb.

"I was hopin' that during your various crusades, the *World* had learned who owns some of these places," John said.

Cobb's pinched expression showed no confidence. "We have tried. But the more high-priced the house, the more careful the true owner is to hide behind a straw owner or a dummy corporation. When we did uncover several, it was invariably not worth the repercussions to publish the truth. For example, one eight-story, so-called hotel near Times Square does nothing but rent rooms to whores. When we dug, we learned that the property is owned by the Catholic Church."

"Anythin' you can dig up about this place would be greatly appreciated," John said.

"As in 'the *World* gets the story first' greatly appreciated," Frank Cobb understood.

"Precisely. And what if the owner of this particular assignation house turns out to be a lower-ranking member of New York society?"

"As editor in chief, I would be inclined to publish the name." Cobb's eyebrows knit. "You know, when you mentioned Morning Mary, I realized I haven't seen her in several months. I'm going to ask around about her as well."

JOHN SPENT THE REMAINDER of the afternoon visiting two of the midtown hotels that hosted national conventions. Just before six o'clock, he downed another sandwich and a pint of ale in Union Square. Low, thick rainclouds shrouded New York in shadows. John turned off of Third Avenue onto East Twelfth Street with his umbrella canted forward against the spitting droplets of rain. A pair of brogans came into his view. He lifted the umbrella and caught sight of a beat cop. He smiled and the policeman smiled back. Someone on the block had evidently asked for patrol presence. John was certain that the petitioner was from neither of the houses of ill repute.

John climbed the steps of 223 East Twelfth Street and knocked, using a brass rapper shaped like an angel. The door was opened by a behemoth of a man, dressed in a formal suit but with a permanently misshapen head that suggested decades of back-room saloon brawling.

"Yes, sir?" the man asked in a gruff voice, barring the way.

John set down his umbrella and opened up his raincoat. "I'm in New York for the *In*surance Undawritahs Convention," he stated, laying on as thick a caricature of a Deep South accent as he could. He reached into his inside suit pocket and produced the business card ex-cop Hirsch had been given by a bordello drummer at the Herald Square Hotel. "A Mr. Richard Springer suggested that this address was the perfect place for liftin' one's spirits."

The bouncer glanced at the card. "Dick said that, did he?" His face curled into a lopsided smile. His eyes redirected to the convention badge affixed to John's coat. Le Brun had deftly liberated it from the lapel of one of the genuine insurance underwriter attendees an hour earlier. "Yes, we can provide spirits and elevate whatever it is you want lifted, Mr. Stone."

The bouncer unblocked the door, snatching up John's umbrella as he did. John shrugged out of his raincoat.

"I understand y'all have lovely hostesses," John said, maintaining his thick accent.

"We do indeed. Each one is delighted to pass time with an educated man such as yourself without asking a thing from you . . . except the quenching of their thirst. A bottle of bubbly costs thirty dollars."

John widened his eyes. "Gracious, that must be some special bubbly!" He reached into his billfold and produced three ten-dollar bills. The bouncer held out his large hand and received the cash.

"At present, four of our lovely hostesses are at liberty: Miss Lily, Miss Rose, Miss Daisy, and Miss Violet."

"What about Miss Pansy?" John asked, intending to joke.

"She and Miss Peony are upstairs entertaining. But surely one of these other flowers would be willing to open their petals wide for you."

All of the lounging women were fair of face, with tantalizing figures that were more than half-exposed by the diaphanous toile they wore. John judged that not one of them was older than twenty-five. The first three remained seated, but Miss Violet came off the parlor's piano bench as if it had springs.

"I heard a vonderful Southern drawl," she gushed as she advanced on him. Ironically, her English was tainted with an Eastern European accent whose exact placement eluded John. Her smile was artful, if too broad. Her cheekbones were prominent and her face more round than average, suggesting a Slavic heritage. He noted that her eyes were bright blue, but the skin around them was pinched, giving her a hardened look well beyond her years.

"Yes, ma'am," John said.

"I like the Southern gentlemen much. Vee go to a private place to know each udder better?"

Before John could reply, she cocked one eyebrow, then twice darted her eyes sharply toward the front windows, as if in silent signal.

"I would be honored," John answered.

"I get champagne and two glasses, und vee start evening." She disappeared into the back of the house for about half a minute. While she was gone, John listened to the subdued conversation among the three remaining prostitutes. What he heard was also accented. He had the ability to distinguish Italian, Spanish, German, and Scandinavian tongues, and he spoke a smattering of Russian and fluent French, but what they spoke was from more southeast in Europe.

With the brute watching him from his post in the foyer, John slowly climbed the central staircase. By the time he reached the first landing, Miss Violet had caught up. She carried a silver tray with two glasses and a green bottle with a fancy label. Violet nodded at the door nearest to Twelfth Street. John opened it for her. The moment she passed through, she set the tray down on a nightstand, shaking her head.

"Is garbage," she pronounced of the champagne in a soft voice. She locked the door, leaned back against it, and eyed Le Brun. "You are a man of the law," she declared.

John was caught completely off guard, particularly by the degree of her assurance.

"Ma'am, you are mistaken. I am from Georgia. I certainly do not work for the New York Police Department."

"Then you are a man of the law from Georgia. A man of plain clothes," she persisted. "I am guessing you come here to learn who killed man across the street."

John remained astonished at the woman's words. "Do you have something to tell me?" He replied, without making an admission.

The young woman rushed to the window and pulled the curtain aside. "You see here? That is place where man is killed. Two nights before this, I am just ended with client, and I look out. I see him killed."

John looked out the window. Much of the street was obscured by trees, but the view to the assignation house opposite was unobstructed. A lamp to the side of its door threw down just enough light to illuminate passing figures.

"I am . . ." The English word she sought failed her, so she splayed out all her fingers, raised both hands to either side of her head, and shook them, at the same time making her eyes as wide as possible.

"You were frightened?" John supplied.

"No. Vut I see is man who own this place come up to back of other man. He hold a cane. He pull a long knife from inside the cane and . . ." Violet pantomimed her description as she spoke, finishing with a vicious, left-handed stabbing action.

"You were surprised."

The woman jerked her head sharply in agreement.

"You're saying that man downstairs killed Herbert Moore?" John asked.

"No. He is not owner. Owner is Mr. D. Mr. D is not here now."

"What does the D stand for?" John asked. Violet shrugged her shoulders in confusion. "You call him Mr. D, but what is his real name?"

"I do not know."

"What does he look like?"

Violet raised her hand about two inches above her head. "Like so." She pantomimed a waist about sixteen inches larger than hers. "Brown eyes, brown hair. A little moustache." She pointed to a closed door in the sidewall. "Dis room is vhere he stay vhen here."

John tried the adjoining door. It was locked. He reached into his side jacket pocket and pulled out the lock-picking case he invariably carried when he worked. The lock was not complicated; within seconds he had the door open.

"You stay in here and make noise like we're havin' fun," he directed the prostitute. She immediately threw herself on the bed, bouncing and moaning.

John ventured into the small, dark room. It also had a window facing the street. The house was built in the gaslight era. The only electrification came via a channel running up the sidewall and halfway across the ceiling. From there, a cord dangled down, connected to a banker's lamp sitting on a desk. A candlestick phone sat on the desk as well, with its cord running in sight along the floor and into the sidewall. John pushed a small area carpet against the bottom of the hallway access door with the toe of his shoe, to prevent the light from leaking out. Aside from the narrow brass bed in one corner, the room had a swivel chair, the desk, and an armoire. The desk drawers had no locks. When he rifled through them, he found only a stack of bills and receipts, a letter opener and scissors, a collection of pens and nibs, a sealed inkpot, a few postage stamps, and a paper tube surrounded by cotton string. Nothing linked the owner to either the business of prostitution or to murder. The armoire, however, was locked. John applied his skills again. Inside the cabinet, he found an ebony walking stick with a brass handle. Using his pocket handkerchief, he lifted the cane carefully out and brought it into the lamplight. He found the locking mechanism and gave it a twist. Drawing up on the handle, he exposed a foot of thin steel, tapering to a lethal point. The end of the weapon had been wiped clean, but about an inch of it, just below the handle, showed a few dried patches of blood.

John relocked the armoire, turned off the lamp, pocketed the string from the desk, and returned the rug to its usual place. He retreated from the room, holding the handkerchief-wrapped cane gingerly by the top of its handle.

"Is this what Mr. D used to kill Mr. Moore?" Le Brun asked the wide-eyed prostitute. She nodded in answer, still bouncing on the bed. "I've got to get this to the police. Is there only the one man watchin' the house?"

"No. Two men. Live in room next to kitchen. Both not sleep now."

"Then I can't help you get away. But I will come back. Do you understand?"

Again, Violet nodded.

John sat on the bed beside the young woman. He realized for the first time that she smelled of violet. Her hand went to the buttons of his trousers.

"You have half hour until you must leave," she said.

John gently returned the hand to her lap. "I appreciate your attention, Miss Violet, but the sooner I leave, the better." He captured the wooden middle of the cane between his knees and carefully tied the string around the handle. He was disappointed to find that the string's total length was only about five feet.

Keeping his voice low, John said, "We can pretend that you were such a good lover that I did not last long." He held out his index finger, then let it sag toward his palm.

Violet laughed. "Yes, vee pretend."

John left the bed, went to the window, and opened it a crack. He saw that the rain had intensified. He hoped that the weather would dissuade would-be clients from arriving, at least for the next few minutes. He set the cane against the windowsill, with the string extended across the floor. Then he went to the bed and took Violet's hands, compelling her to stand.

"I will leave the house and raise my umbrella," John said, using pantomime as the woman had. "When I am sure no one is watchin', I will lower the umbrella. Like this. Then you put the cane outside the window, let it down as far as the string will go, and drop the cane the rest of the way." Again, he made the requisite motions. "Do you understand?"

Violet had fixed her lovely eyes on his. A sly smile slipped onto her face. "Yes, I understand. And you vill come back to help me and Lily and Rose and—"

"I promise," John interrupted, wanting to be gone.

Violet raised her hands, captured his face, and gave him an expert French kiss. "I think I vill thank you longer very soon."

"We'll see," John evaded, slipping from her grasp. He offered her a smile as well, then hurried out the hallway door and down the stairs, pretending to be a man focused on escaping the scene of his adulterous crime as soon as his passions were satisfied. He shook his head in wonderment as he came into the doorman's view.

"Woowee, that is a woman with a clever tongue!"

"I'm glad you were satisfied, sir," the brute said. While he fetched John's umbrella and raincoat, Le Brun glanced into the parlor. Another man, heavyset and wearing out-of-fashion, muttonchops-style facial hair, attempted to speak with Daisy, Rose, and another female John had not seen on entering the house. The last one was more girl than woman and somber-faced, seeming to John to deserve the name Miss Weeping Willow. Her upper lip curved too high to cover her front teeth, giving her a coquettish look that John associated with French women. Her hair had the color and luster of anthracite coal. *If she had been born to one of the wealthy families of New York City,* John mused, *she would be the toast of the town and besieged by dozens of eligible rich men. But for a whim of fate, she services any man who walks through the front door and desires her.*

John exited down the stoop. As he raised his umbrella, he heard the front door shut soundly. He looked up and down the street. A Hansom cab splashed through street puddles with pace, followed by a noisy motorcar. No one moved along either sidewalk. John turned and lowered his umbrella. The cane appeared from Violet's window. It descended to the full length of the string. A moment later, it plummeted toward the narrow garden that separated the house from the sidewalk. John caught it by the wooden shaft and immediately tucked it inside his raincoat. He turned westward and moved as quickly as his legs would take him.

UNION SQUARE LAY ONLY two blocks distant from the assignation house. All the while John made his way toward it, his mind worked furiously on his next moves. He had no legal authority in New York City for making arrests. He also feared that if he approached the captain of the 17th Precinct, the man would work far more diligently on protecting his job than on bringing the killer to justice. He settled on the power of the Fourth Estate. At lunch, Frank Cobb had handed John his private card, which supplied his address and home telephone number as well that of the newspaper. Le Brun found an open apothecary shop in Union Square and used the public telephone. At seven o'clock, Cobb was almost assuredly in the *World* building, supervising the pasteup of the morning edition. John connected with the switchboard operator and gave her the number.

Cobb's secretary answered and fetched the editor from the newsroom.

"John, I haven't had any time yet to—"

"Don't worry about that, Frank," Le Brun said. "I'm fairly sure I have the proof of who murdered Herbert Moore. If you want the exclusive, you'll bring a photographer post haste to 223 East Twelfth Street. However long you estimate that should take, have someone on your staff call the 17th Precinct five minutes beforehand, so you're sure to be there ahead of them."

"And where will you be?"

"Hangin' around Third Avenue and Twelfth, waitin' for you. It looks like the owner of the cathouse at Number 223 stabbed his competitor in the back. I have the sword and the cane that conceals the blade."

"I'm on my way," Cobb told him.

In the display window of the apothecary shop were rolls of what the signage called Cellophane, another wonder of the new century. The clear, waterproof wrap was described as being "perfect for protecting your tablecloths." Expensive as it was, John paid for a roll of the novel material and encircled the walking stick several times with it.

THE PERSISTENT, COLD RAIN encouraged John to walk briskly. He arrived at the corner of Third Avenue and East Twelfth in less than fifteen minutes. He sought shelter under the canopy of a maple tree and watched the foot and vehicular traffic. The area did not resemble the midtown night spots such as Times Square, where the electric lights were bright even on dismal evenings. Darkness had claimed many of the vistas around Le Brun. An abundance of horse-drawn wagons still dominated the avenue, moving apace to replenish Manhattan's daytime needs. There were also a goodly number of motorized vehicles, far more than were on the streets during John's first visit to New York in 1906. A large van moved with speed across the avenue, heading west. John noted that the driver was alone in the open-sided cab. He could not make out the figure's features, but his gaze lingered as the van passed because the dark shape was only as large as a young teenage boy.

Head editor Cobb also had the advantage of a motorized vehicle. It was one of the *World's* delivery trucks. Cobb's trip north from Newspaper Row, across the street from City Hall, took eighteen minutes. New as it was, the machine sounded like a collection of garbage cans rolling down a rocky hill. It had a tiny motor compartment attached to what looked like the body of an old English sedan chair, backed by a six-foot flatbed. The driver pulled close to the curb and shut off the engine. While Cobb conferred with Le Brun, the driver withdrew a bag that held a large box camera with a sliding lens and a canopied attachment for flash powder.

"How in thunder did you get your hands on the murder weapon?" Cobb asked.

"I had help from a woman in the house. I'm fairly positive she's one of those immigrants held against their will. What was said to the police?"

"I told an assistant to call after ten minutes and tell them a reporter from the *World* was on his way to get the story on who murdered Herbert Moore. He was to give them the address you gave me. They should be here any second now." He turned to the photographer. "Hurry up, Lester!"

The trio hastened along the soaked sidewalk. When they were only feet from the front stoop of the assignation house, two policemen galloped up on horseback. They dismounted and closed on Le Brun, Cobb, and the photographer. One wore wire-framed spectacles; the other's most distinguishing feature was a large gap between his upper front teeth.

"What's happening?" the bespectacled cop asked, using his forefingers like windshield wipers.

The editor stepped forward. "I'm Cobb, from the *World*. We just got here."

John broke in, saying, "I was inside earlier under the guise of a patron. I'm John Le Brun, a private detective registered with the City of New York. I was given this cane by one of the prostitutes." He passed it to the questioning policeman. "Be careful handlin' it; it has blood on the hidden sword and may have fingerprints as well. The woman said she witnessed the murder that occurred across the street two nights ago." He turned his face upward and fixed his gaze. "From that window."

A motorized police patrol wagon puttered down the street and came to a shuddering halt. Three men climbed out, two in plainclothes.

The policeman with the cane held it up. "We have reasonable cause for entry."

The older of the two plainclothesmen took the cane. He conferred with the bespectacled officer while the other horse patrolman tied their reins to the ornate iron post that stood beside an equally ornate boot scrapper. John offered him his New York business card. After he had received Le Brun's information secondhand, the man ordered the horse patrolmen, "Use that driveway to get around the back, and let no one escape!"

Quick introductions were made. The detective in charge was Lieutenant Kasper Bergman.

"You two will have to stay out here," Bergman said.

"I don't think so," Cobb shot back. "If so, the *World* will raise holy hell about you barring the very ones who advanced your case for you. Besides, Mr. Le Brun is needed to identify the woman who saw the murder."

Bergman sighed. "Very well. But stay right behind me. I want to be able to see both of you at every second." He did not wait for reply but climbed the stoop and banged forcibly with the door knocker. It remained shut. He banged again. Still, nothing happened.

The gap-toothed mounted policemen dashed out of the narrow alleyway and fixed his attention on the lead detective. "The back door was halfway open. There's a man lying on the floor just inside."

Bergman nodded at the two men he had arrived with. "Take cover and ready your pistols!" He jumped off the stoop and followed after the mounted cop, with Le Brun and Cobb trailing a few paces behind.

The rear of the property was poorly kept. Five garbage cans attested to the number of people living in the house and to the many entertained inside. The outer rear door was fashioned of iron. While its elements were decoratively curved, the bars were clearly meant to prevent passage when its sturdy deadbolt was engaged. However, it and the inner wooden door both stood partially open.

The room just beyond was a pantry and storage area, connecting to a kitchen at its side. A blond-haired, muscular young man of medium height lay on his back, his dead eyes seeming to study the ceiling. He wore a white, long-sleeve shirt and dress trousers that were held up by suspenders. His legs were straight and parallel, pointed toward the center of the house. John strode into the room with no hesitation. The man had been shot in the center of his chest. Within moments, Le Brun was surrounded by three officers of the law and the editor in chief, all engaging in animated conversation.

"Hush up!" John ordered.

Jolted by his authoritative tone, the other men fell silent.

"What do y'all hear?"

"Nothing," Cobb said.

"In a house filled with frightened women?" John doubted. The policemen had all drawn their revolvers. John removed his from the holster at the small of his back.

"God in heaven!" the cop wearing rain-smeared glasses exclaimed from the doorway that connected the pantry to the rear of the central hallway. "Somebody shot one. Maybe all of them."

Again, the crowd of men advanced and spread out. John was the last forward. He squatted next to the female corpse.

"Damn! It's Violet. The one who said she saw Moore murdered."

The woman had been shot squarely between the eyes. John pressed the back of his hand against her pale cheek.

"She was murdered right here," Bergman noted, pointing to one wall. It was covered with blood, strands of hair, and bits of brain matter.

"And it was a powerful piece of lead," John added. He lifted Violet's hands and examined both sides in turn. "Less than half an hour ago, accordin' to her skin temperature. Let's hope the entire house wasn't slaughtered."

Bergman led the way along the hallway toward the front of the house. He had taken only a few cautious steps when he paused. "Jesus! A third one."

As he moved into the foyer and the other two policemen fanned out, Le Brun was able to recognize the very large doorman. He lay partially on his side. When Bergman grabbed his upper arm and forced the body into a fully supine position, John saw that the man had been hit with three bullets, two in the chest and one through his right eye.

"Both men had nothin' in their hands," John observed,

squatting a second time, "but I see the tip of a knife sheath pokin' out from under his jacket."

"And the retaining snap is closed," Cobb said, as he lifted the hem of the coat. "How could one person get the jump on them both?"

"I don't think one did," John replied. "Look at the holes in this shirt. They're bigger than the one that killed the guy in the pantry."

"A pair of murderers?" Bergman wondered aloud.

"Makes more sense than one shooter with revolvers of different calibers."

"But were they from inside the house or outside?" one of the mounted policeman asked.

Lieutenant Bergman turned to Cobb and Le Brun. "It's time for you two civilians to leave."

"Are you kidding?" Frank shot back. "Hasn't Mr. Le Brun already proven himself to be a master detective? For my part, I promise to keep the details of this massacre and all of your names out of the *World* for twenty-four hours."

Bergman sighed again.

During the exchange, the bespectacled cop had ventured halfway up the stairs.

"It's just as bad up here," he called down.

A scouring of the three floors revealed two clients shot dead. The man found at the top of the first flight had his trousers unbuttoned and was missing his shoes. The one wearing muttonchops had tried to hide in an armoire and was shot dead while stark naked.

"Not a soul left alive," Bergman said. "Unless somebody's in there." He pointed to the only locked door upstairs.

"That's the office," John told him. "I went in through an inside door," he reported. "The sword stick was locked inside an armoire, and there are papers in the desk."

With three powerful kicks, Bergman had the door open.

The lieutenant entered with revolver raised, illuminated the banker's lamp, and began rifling through the sheets of paper.

"Just bills and receipts. Nothing indicating the owner of the place," the officer reported.

"But now you have the names of the companies that serviced this house," John said, "the items provided, the costs, and the dates. All you have to do—"

"Right," the lieutenant interrupted curtly. He went to the room's window. "That tree is blocking the view across the street."

"But the one in Miss Violet's room isn't," Le Brun said. "She could have seen Herbert Moore's murderer . . . as she said."

Bergman turned, saw the gap-toothed cop eavesdropping, strode across the room, and pushed the ruined door closed. Then he came up close to Le Brun, who had moved to the window. In a low voice, he said, "So, what's your take on this?"

"There are far too many possibilities at this moment," John replied. "One thing I do know is that no young women came runnin' by me from the direction of this place when I was waitin' at Third Avenue and Twelfth. Accordin' to the recitation of the big man near the front door, there were six women in the house an hour ago. That jibes, because I saw four, and the other two were evidently servicin' two johns." He smiled wanly. "I was only here for a matter of minutes."

"They couldn't have vanished into thin air," Bergman said, in an annoyed tone.

"The owner of this establishment—whoever that may be— allegedly stabbed his nearest rival to death two nights ago. He certainly had access to this house. I wouldn't omit him as a prime suspect."

"Maybe he came in right after you went out, realized the murder weapon was missing, and shot everyone who could testify against him," the lieutenant posited.

"Not beyond reason," John allowed. "However, how does that correlate with two shooters and two guns? And what happened to the other five prostitutes?"

"This is a goddamned mess!" Bergman fumed, kicking a corner of the desk in his frustration.

John stifled a snort of derision at the obvious statement. There was no way the head of the 17th Precinct could hide the fact of assignation houses in his corner of Manhattan any longer.

"You are correct, sir," John said. "So, it's best to solve the mysteries as quickly as possible. I'm sure that neighbors are gatherin' in the street right now. Perhaps you'll get as lucky as I did and find one who was lookin' out a window while all this carnage happened. And you do have that walkin' stick with the traces of blood."

Bergman nodded grimly.

"*Now* I think it's time for Editor Cobb and myself to bow out of this scene," John continued. "Unless you want to borrow his photographer for evidence."

"No, no. All three of you should go right now. And find some way into the next street through the back door. I'll have one of my men tell the photographer you're leaving."

FRANK COBB FOLLOWED Le Brun into the pantry where the blond-haired body had been covered with a sheet. No one else was in the room or the kitchen.

"Go back up the steps and engage anyone who heads this way," John directed.

Cobb retraced his steps, not bothering to question why.

From his jacket pocket, John again produced his lock-picking kit. Sandwiched between crudely fashioned rows of shelves was a wooden cabinet, its doors secured by a padlock. John had the doors opened in fewer than twenty seconds.

Inside, the top half held a crossbar, from which hung more than twenty of the newly invented wire clothes hangers that had become so popular. On the hangers were dresses, coats, and sweaters. When John examined a few of them, he found words written in a Latin language with accent marks and one example of Cyrillic writing on the labels. The bottom half of the cabinet had nine cubbyholes, all stuffed with clothing and shoes. Nodding to himself, John resecured the padlock.

"Let's go, Frank!" he called out.

"What were you doing?" Cobb asked as he followed the Georgia native into the rain.

"Gatherin' a bit more evidence."

"Do you have it solved already?" Frank asked.

John kept walking. "Surely you are havin' me on."

Frank pointed to a low spot in the wall that separated the property from another on East Eleventh Street, then replied, "Not in the slightest. After what you accomplished at Jekyl Island Club and the Metropolitan Club, I'd say you were the Harry Houdini of detectives."

"Say it after my work solves this case. Bergman sent your photographer packin'."

Cobb vaulted the wall with no trouble and held out a helping hand for John. "Lester had better have gotten a few pictures of the cops standing out front with their guns drawn. This slaughterhouse is worthy of coverage in the rotogravure section."

CHAPTER FIVE

May 1, 1908

SINCE THE WALDORF ASTORIA'S dining salons were perpetually reserved for dinner by New York's upper crust, John invited his fiancée to breakfast instead. Lordis made no secret that she enjoyed the better things in life. She was the live-in chatelaine of a mansion overlooking Central Park; she drank wines of excellent vintages; she had for years spent much of her salary on clothing from the finest shops. She did not disappoint John with her latest display of daytime wear. She stepped out of one of the shiny, red, mechanical "taxi-meter" cabs that had been introduced to the city from Paris the previous year. He had not seen her outfit before. She wore a Paris import, a Worth navy worsted twill edged dress and jacket with black moustache net and machine lace vestee. As they promenaded along the Thirty-fourth Street carriage drive into the hotel, John complimented her on the matching hat with dyed feathers and her white blouse with a double row of brass buttons. He deemed himself prodigiously lucky to have the smart, urbane, considerably younger, tall, thin woman with high cheekbones, bright blue eyes, and a crown of light-brown hair on his arm.

"I picked up four different newspapers this morning," Lordis announced, even before they passed into the hotel foyer. "Only the *World* had an article on the horror on Twelfth Street, and that was disappointing in the extreme. Whoever Benjamin Penn is, he should be fired."

"There is no such reporter," John told her. "Frank Cobb, the paper's editorial director, did not want his name associated with the article."

"Why not?"

"Because he promised to be vague, in exchange for an exclusive on future discoveries."

John wondered how much two breakfasts would set him back as he viewed the French wall tapestries, the Germanic paintings, the authentic eighteenth-century furniture they passed. He had never dined in America's most famous hotel, known as The Hyphen after the older Waldorf Hotel was joined to the Astoria. According to the awed reports of his former deputy, Warfield Tidewell, John and Lordis were moving along the thick carpet of the new Peacock Alley, with its elegant stuffed chairs and sofas and enormous mirrors, which allowed society to check itself every few paces.

"So, *you* tell me what happened," Lordis invited.

John rolled out a dispassionate detailing of both his visit to the brothel and his subsequent work with the police. He knew that his companion was made of stern stuff and never blanched nor swooned at the sight of blood, in photographs or in person. When he spoke of the bullet between Violet's eyes and her brains on the hallway wallpaper, Lordis did not even lift an eyebrow.

They entered the main dining room, designed in Italian Renaissance style, with carved pilasters and columns of midnight-sun marble imported from Russia. Through a large archway, he could see the equally chic Palm Court.

The waiter took an order of pastry crescents with preserves from Lordis and waffles with Vermont maple syrup and a coddled egg from John. They elected to share a plate of seasonal fruits and a pot of coffee.

"Now tell me what you learned from these facts," Lordis said.

"Neither entrance was broken in. Both guards were surprised. Naturally, any man with a password or the right business card could have gotten through the front door. A second later, that man could have raised a revolver and put three bullets into the big man from a range impossible to miss.

"The other house warden was, in my estimation, murdered by a second shooter. I was the first one inside the back storage room. The floor was filthy, hadn't been mopped in days. I observed a semicircle like a spread-fan pattern, cleaner than the rest of floor. The body had been swung around 180 degrees, and the backs of the trousers scoured the dirt."

"In order to seem as if the shooter from the foyer had also killed the second man," Lordis said.

"Exactly. Which was not the case unless a single man brandished two different caliber revolvers. As I said, the front door could have been opened by the bigger victim to any one of a thousand men. The back door was most likely opened by a key or in response to a secret knock. I would guess the report of the gun in the hallway was the cue for the second shooter to dispatch his victim."

"Why was the woman who called herself Violet the only woman murdered?" Lordis asked.

"The logical reason would be that she was the most likely suspect for the disappearance of the cane. Until I saw her on the floor, I thought perhaps she might have been the mastermind of the two murders, livin' inside the second bordello and workin' with a person who wanted to take over both."

Lordis poured coffee into the scalloped porcelain cups. "From what I've read, such women are virtual slaves. Are they ever allowed to leave those houses?"

"Not accordin' to Frank Cobb. But a man could always visit her as a fond john and present her a plan that would seem to be her salvation." John shook his head. "No use wanderin' up that dark alley. I initially thought she might have murdered one or both guards, then been murdered herself by whoever took away the other women, but she had no sign of gunpowder on either hand."

"You've told me more than once that the most logical and simple solution is usually the right one," Lordis said.

John nodded. "That would be Violet's Mr. D enterin' his office shortly after I left. Perhaps he sees somethin' askew. He checks his armoire and finds the dagger cane missing. His two male employees know of the murder of the house's rival. Mr. D also knows that Violet may have observed that murder, as she told me. He may have suspected her of aidin' in the removal of the cane. Mr. D telephones an accomplice. When he knows the accomplice is at the back door, he shoots the man in the front hallway. The second man is shot. Violet tries to escape and is the third victim. Two johns upstairs are hunted down and shot to ensure their silence. Mr. D and his accomplice herd the other women out of the house in a hurry, without takin' their street clothes . . . which I found in a locked closet in the storage room. That seems—"

"How did they move half a dozen women through the city in their unmentionables?" Lordis interrupted.

"They used a motorized truck. Remember, I said a van sped by me while I was waitin' at the corner?"

"Yes. And it had no markings?"

"If it did, the street was too dark for me to see them. I did notice a small person drivin'. It's difficult to imagine that a single person of that size could have pulled off the massacre inside that house and cowed a crowd of panicky women into a van alone. Rain was comin' down like a steady drumroll yesterday evenin'; before I left the place, I found the definite marks of van tires in the house's driveway."

"So, how do you use all that to further your investigation?" Lordis asked.

John rolled his eyes and shrugged. "I can't. I don't have the power to pursue these murders. Especially with the boys at the 17th Precinct involved up to at least their kneecaps in this prostitution business."

The lines disappeared from Lordis's brow. She allowed herself to smile.

"Well, I can't say I'm disappointed. This visit was supposed to be a cursory visit to your detective agency and then hours and hours with me." Her eyes drifted to a couple at a nearby table. They were in their thirties and stylishly dressed. Good as the service and food at the Waldorf-Astoria might be, John knew the patrons were happily paying a premium to see and be seen. Beyond the younger couple, a man about John's age had his attention riveted on Lordis.

He's probably wonderin' how a man of my years has the company of a beauty like Lordis, John thought. *And if he thinks it has somethin' to do with money, he's only half wrong.* Much as she would protest that John need not spend lavishly on her, since she had moved up from the South as a young woman, she knew only good living in an expensive city. Such thoughts had months before made him relieved that he would not be with her twelve months a year, buying frequent gifts, feeling obliged to take her out to dinner every night, keeping her entertained. In 1898, Warfield Tidewell had convinced him to take insider information found onboard J. P. Morgan's yacht and invest in a market-cornering scheme. John had retired more than comfortable. His detective agency further allowed him to live rather lavishly on his New York visits. However, he was far from rich. Also, he was set in his ways and admitted it. Lordis got what she wanted, and so did he. He daily acknowledged his immense good fortune that he and she had developed a mutually desired arrangement. He sometimes felt as if he and Lordis were characters in a Henrik Ibsen play, defying the honored strictures and mores of Victorian life and leading the charge of more broad-minded Americans.

John said, "I'm sorry about this turn of events. Naturally, I would much rather spend my time with you." In spite of his apology, he was sorely frustrated and would gladly have dogged on in the investigation had it been possible.

"But it ended quickly. So, we can take in a moving picture show tonight," Lordis said with enthusiasm. "You can't imagine how the new art has exploded since you were last here. I understand there are now more than one hundred houses in the five boroughs."

"It's become a mania," John judged. Unlike Lordis, he was unwilling to call the phenomenon 'art.' "Before I even met you, the Strand on Forty-seventh Street opened with three thousand seats. I wonder if it's a passin' fad."

"Not at all," Lordis replied. "Two theaters in Longacre Square—I mean Times Square—are now showing two-reelers . . . more than twenty minutes to a story. One is showing *Romeo and Juliet* and the other has *Dr. Jekyll and Mr. Hyde.*" Her corn flower-blue eyes went even wider. "Oh! And they now insert cards in between the moving pictures with narrative and dialogue. So clever, and all for just ten cents!"

"We live in an astonishin' time," John agreed, thinking of the Victrola, the radio, aspirin, the vacuum cleaner, electrocardiograms, the automobile, the telephone, the moving pictures, and even wire coat hangers and Cellophane.

A couple walked by their table. The man reminded him of his traveling companion from Brunswick. "We should go to an early show so the children can come with us," he suggested.

"Only if it's *Romeo and Juliet*," Lordis replied.

John understood his fiancée's reasoning, that the murder count might be the same on the screen, but at least Ben, Jr. and Leslie would be spared the undoubtedly hideous makeup of Mr. Hyde. "The fellow I spoke of the other night—Merriweather Gooderly—he's been pesterin' me to spend some time with him up here. I'd like y'all to meet, since you'll surely bump into him when you stay with me. He's a bit of a strut fart, but not too overbearin'. If we invite him to the picture show, it will just be one more seat."

John could tell immediately that Lordis was not enthusiastic. However, she agreed with feigned delight. The waiter arrived with their food, cleverly presented.

"Now, when you eat well in Brunswick, Savannah, or Charleston," Lordis said, "you can say with authority: 'It's just like dining at the Waldorf.'"

AFTER PUTTING LORDIS in a Hansom cab, John walked back to Mary's apartment building. She reported that a desk officer had called to request that Le Brun pay a visit to the 17th Precinct. He thanked her, left a message for Merriweather to meet his group at the movie theater that evening, and ambled to the corner to hail another taxi. He noted that the profit margin on the money paid to his agency to investigate Herbert Moore's death was rapidly dwindling.

AFTER WAITING LESS THAN a minute, Le Brun was escorted into the office of Lieutenant Kasper Bergman. Bergman had dark circles under his eyes from the double pressures of

earning his salary and protecting his payoff system. He gestured
to the two chairs placed on the far side of his desk. John set his
business card on the man's desk, then sat in the closer chair.

"You were right about the papers in that desk leading to an
identification," Bergman began. "The owner of the house was a
man named Dietrich Diefendorfer."

John nodded and tried not to look self-satisfied. "Mr. D.
You said 'was.'"

"That's right. He was unmarried. Lived in a fancied-up loft
on Perry Street . . . almost on Hudson. We paid a visit and
found him hanging from an iron crossbeam."

John adjusted himself in the chair. "Was there a dark-
colored van parked nearby?"

"Not that we noticed. He must have realized that no amount
of killing could hide him from us."

"Did you estimate the time of death?"

"He was cold when we got there."

"What time was that?"

"A little before six o'clock."

"Did you find evidence of his sexual slavery business . . .
perhaps that he operated more than one house?"

"There was nothing."

"Strange. What was he wearin'?"

"A lightweight nightgown."

"Strange also that he got ready for bed and then changed
his mind and hanged himself."

"Maybe all the holes in his plan came to him as he
undressed." The lieutenant flipped open a folder that lay in
front of him and wrote two lines of notes in an unhurried
fashion. Le Brun recognized both that he had given the man
things to think about and that Bergman was also intent on
demonstrating that he was in charge. He took the moment to
pluck one of the officer's business cards from a tray on his side
of the man's desk.

The instant the policeman stopped writing, John asked, "What happened to the prostitutes?"

Bergman shrugged. "Maybe he killed them all and dumped them in the East River or the Hudson. We get female floaters almost every day. We'll find them eventually."

"But you don't know who you're looking for," John pointed out.

Bergman hunched up his shoulders. "True. But any young women who we find without identification in the next few days, we'll be sure to call on you for a visual identification. Eventually all of them will turn up. In their line of work, they're about as unremarkable as horses on the streets. Both die there. Except now, with the motorcars and trucks, the dead whores may one day outnumber the dead horses."

"That is truly sad," John said, gripping the arms of his chair to prevent himself from launching over the desk and thrashing the unfeeling younger man. "These women were so young and so pretty. What happens to them when they age and get hard looking?"

"You mean 'used up,'" Bergman answered, "That takes about three years. Then they're thrown out with the clothes they arrived in. Until then, their food and shelter are taken care of. Once they're discarded, they have to pay all their earnings for both. For a while the better looking of them work the streets around hotels and entertainment areas. At places like the Buckingham Palace dance house on West Twenty-seventh, Cremorne Garden, or the Haymarket. The beat cops get wise to them soon enough because most cruise the same streets hour after hour. We cart them to court and jail by the paddy-wagon load, but the citizens of the city don't want to pay for their upkeep. They pay what they can in fines, and soon enough they're out on the streets again. If they survive three or four more years and have lost their charms completely, they migrate down to Soho and Hudson Park . . . Greene Street, Leroy,

Houston, and King. There are flophouses where they gravitate."

John wanted to say, "If you know all this, why don't you shut those places down?" but he knew the answer. The lieutenant had either been born with a distinct lack of humanity or else become inured to the suffering and habituated to the bribes.

Bergman continued, "The last stops are the Bowery and near the piers. Water and Front, just in from the South Street Seaport, have plenty of taverns with rooms upstairs. Or what they call bed-houses. By that time, the women are nothing more than sexual garbage pails. Most of them have social diseases. Not just of the private areas but the lungs from constant smoke and the livers from constant drinking."

"No doubt in search of oblivion," John said.

Bergman shook his head and sighed dramatically. "They die from booze, or beatings, or abortions. Some are rescued by the Midnight Mission on Greene Street, the House of the Good Shepherd, the House of Mercy, or the Magdalen Society. The ones who have families sometimes find their ways back, like the Prodigal Son. Or the families send somebody looking for them. Appetites, legal or otherwise, always pursue satisfaction."

Bergman picked up John's business card, leaned forward over his desk, and narrowed his eyes. "While others were waking tradespeople in the middle of the night to solve this case, I was researching you. You're the one who solved the murders of those two wealthy brothers on the Upper East Side."

"That's me."

"And you've solved some other thorny cases, both here and abroad," Bergman went on. "What prompted you to nose around these secret houses in my precinct?"

"Money," John returned. "Pure and simple. I was hired to learn who killed Herbert Moore."

"Now you know." The lieutenant glanced down at the open

dossier, then back up at Le Brun. "And what do you intend to say to the newspapers?"

"I have nothin' to say in public. Your concern is with Frank Cobb, of the *World*. He's a social progressive. I suspect that New York's prostitution is something he wants to curb . . . and my friend Joseph Pulitzer wants to exploit. This affair should provide a tall soapbox."

Bergman said, "You were the sheriff of a small city not long ago."

"More like a big town."

"Okay. A big town that provided all sorts of diversions to vacationing Yankees. How did you deal with prostitutes?"

"I stuck 'em in the cooler for several nights. Made 'em sweep the sidewalks durin' the day. Then I walloped their shapely butts hard with a big oak paddle, so they wouldn't be inclined to lie on their backsides, and put 'em on a train back to where they came from."

Bergman laughed. "Small city, small problem. So, now that you learned who killed Moore, your business is concluded, right?"

"That remains to be seen," John said, after giving the policeman a long, hard stare.

"What else do you need?"

"The satisfaction of the one who hired me."

"And who is that?"

In reply, John reached into his jacket pocket and produced the letterhead with J. P. Morgan's name. "Here's what was delivered to my agency."

HAVING BOUGHT A DEGREE of respect by showing the sheet of letterhead, John thought it most prudent to check with J. Pierpont Morgan. When he called the business titan's office at the corner of Broad and Wall, he was told that Morgan had just left for The Players Club in Gramercy Park. The club was the country's premier men's organization concerning those who loved good theater. Almost half the members were not actors or producers. They were architects like Charles McKim and Stanford White, authors like Booth Tarkington and Mark Twain, painters like Childe Hassam and Frederic Remington, military men like William Tecumseh Sherman and Andrew Russell. The occasion was a farewell party for Club President Timothy Hutton, who had announced his resignation due to business demands on the West Coast. Morgan was a long-time member but not a frequenter. John had been made an honorary member in 1906.

John climbed the front steps to the former home of the great Shakespearean actor Edwin Booth, brother of the notorious John Wilkes Booth. He reacquainted himself with the plaque that held the club's symbol, the twin masks of Comedy and Tragedy. He was recognized by Walter Oettel, the club superintendent, and warmly welcomed. The rooms above and below in the openly designed structure buzzed with members assembled for the occasion. John took a hitch in his step when he looked downstairs and his glance fell on an old man with a wild wealth of white hair and a startlingly white suit.

John found Morgan in the front sitting room, speaking with club board members. John took his place at a distance, leaning casually against one of the columns but keeping his gaze fixed on the most powerful financier in America. Morgan saw him almost instantly but made no move to hurry the conversation in which he was engaged. As a lure, John withdrew the piece of letterhead, opened it, and held it up at chest level with the writing facing Morgan. For a moment, the famous, piercing eyes focused on the sheet of paper. Then he returned to his conversation. Another two minutes passed before he excused himself and moved with ponderous dignity to Le Brun. His misshapen nose, turned into an enormous strawberry by rosacea, begged in vain for John to lower his line of sight. Le Brun was content to study the flesh around the man's intelligent eyes.

Morgan looked older, less indomitable than during John's last encounter. The year 1907 had been very difficult on American banking and finance. A spate of wild but successful speculations had tempted the board of the Knickerbocker Trust Company and allied institutions to try to corner the stock of the United Copper Company. The venture failed; investors made runs on the banks; panic spread across the country as savings were withdrawn and stashed under mattresses. With no central Federal bank to shore up the withdrawals, a major depression seemed imminent. Morgan had pledged his own fortune and convinced many of his financier friends to take the risk in stabilizing the situation. Eventually, they had prevailed. But two results were clear to Le Brun: the country needed a reserve bank, and J. P. Morgan had been exhausted by the ordeal.

Le Brun raised the paper to the level of Morgan's neck. "I need to know if you sent this to me."

The robber baron flinched immediately, but he continued to read the typed words.

"That is most definitely not my stationery," he proclaimed. "Furthermore, I would not call the murderer of an ordinary citizen an assassin. Assassins are those who kill persons in political office."

"You are absolutely correct, sir," John said. "I knew you would not use the word loosely."

The praise from Le Brun brought a faint smile to Morgan's soft face. Then, just as quickly, it hardened again. "Who is Herbert Moore?"

In as succinct a manner as possible, Le Brun recounted the tale of multiple murders and disappeared prostitutes, as well as his part in the events.

Morgan listened without any expression of emotion. When John paused, he nodded sharply. "Burn the letter indeed! To destroy the lie of it."

"Embossed," John noted. "Someone went through considerable expense to convince me I had been hired by you."

Morgan harrumphed. "I had no idea you were even in New York. You wasted hours of time without checking with me on its authenticity?"

"I wouldn't say my time was wasted. The envelope this came in had ten fifty-dollar bills. I made no assumption that you were the sender. As such, I spoke your name to no one . . . until an investigatin' police lieutenant demanded to know how I came to be involved in the case," he dissembled. "Now I shall tell this man you had no interest in Mr. Moore."

Morgan nodded again. "Indeed not. I would have expected no less of you." He set his hand lightly on Le Brun's shoulder. "Let's go out to the piazza and have a drink."

The two men began walking.

As they moved toward the man in the white suit, John said, "Mr. Hutton's send-off looks to be a big wingding. I saw Mr. Samuel Clemens as I entered."

Morgan's expression darkened. "The once and present member. He was drummed out of the club for nonpayment of dues several years back, but he later expressed contrition in private, and several influential members spoke up for his reinstatement. Not I."

"As I understand it, he lost the fortune he had made writin' his wonderful stories by investin' in unwise inventions," John said.

"Correct. He lost $300,000 on the Paige compositor. Too many flaws in the prototype. It lost the march to the Linotype. The lesson is that just because one is a literary genius, that does not make him a financial one as well." Morgan issued his last sentence as he came to a halt less than six feet from the author of *The Adventures of Tom Sawyer* and *The Adventures of Huckleberry Finn.*

John had heard that Mark Twain was opinionated,

irascible, and sharp-tongued in retort, but the tall, thin man did not choose to respond to the rebuke from the heavyset man in the black suit. The detective was sorely disappointed that a gratuitous insult had deprived him of meeting one of America's most famous figures.

Morgan walked out onto the ornate porch that looked down on a small garden with a tree and a fountain in the center. From the hovering waiter, he ordered two glasses of Burgundy.

"I think it best that you hang onto that letter," the capitalist said. "As I believe you know, I hold nothing higher in life than my good name. It has annoyed me into wanting you to continue on the case. My interest, however, is in learning who sent that and why it was worth five hundred dollars to involve me and you."

"From my dealin's with the officers of the 17th Precinct, I can tell you that I am persona non grata in this affair," John said.

Morgan managed a half smile. "No doubt. However, I will speak with Mayor McClellan and Police Commissioner Bingham on your behalf. You *will* be accommodated, Mr. Le Brun."

DURING THE EVENING'S ACTIVITIES, Ben, Jr. and Leslie were warmer toward John than he expected; *Romeo and Juliet* was quite affecting, although John found the constant insertion of white lettering on black cards counterproductive to the pacing for someone like himself who knew Shakespeare's drama intimately. Since it was Friday, with no school the next day, the group hunted down one of Italo Marchioni's sidewalk carts and partook of scoops of ice cream in edible waffle cones with rounded sides and flat bottoms. John felt that Merriweather was ridiculously solicitous of and flattering toward Lordis, but she did not seem to share her fiancé's opinion. Before they parted company, Gooderly took out his ever-present wine-colored notebook, consulted it, and recited several blocks of time when he would be free in the next two days. John knew the action was a waste of time, but he said nothing.

John counted the entire evening a success. All those around him expressed their delight. But as he fell asleep in Lordis's bed, Le Brun decided that not even novel diversions could have driven from his head the thoughts of the many murdered victims and the fates of the missing prostitutes.

CHAPTER SIX

May 2, 1908

AS SOON AS HE RETURNED to Mary McMahon's apartment house, Le Brun made a call to NYPD Detective Kevin O'Leary. He asked if it was possible to get a copy of the autopsy report on Dietrich Diefendorfer and any identifying information on the two assignation house guards who had been shot. O'Leary answered in the affirmative, if John was willing to spend up to one hundred dollars. They agreed that if that much did not produce results, then a thousand would not either. Clearly, in light of the revelation of two assignation houses operating on one street, the status quo of the 17th Precinct was in jeopardy and, as Kevin put it, "they'll be circlin' the wagons like Buffalo Bill's Wild West Circus."

The report on Heloise Moore had come in from their socialite associate, Alice Ainsworth. The woman and her

husband were only seen together in public for social events and
Sunday church services. They had a small group of friends. Alice
determined the term should more accurately be acquaintances,
due to the so-called friends' relative lack of knowledge of the
intimate details of the Moore marriage. Heloise was known to
shop for clothes at least twice a week and was rarely seen in the
same outfit more than twice. To a Washington Square neighbor,
she had the day before announced that she would be moving
from New York City to London, once all burial, business, and
realty affairs were settled. As Alice had put it, "She's fleeing
the city just like Mrs. Bradley Martin did in 1897." When John
admitted he had no knowledge of Mrs. Martin, Alice explained
that the simple-minded but rich woman had decided she could
revive the entire nation's economy during a depression by
throwing a huge masquerade ball whose extravagances would
trickle down to seamstresses, florists, wig makers, bakers, and
the like. Stirred up by several mocking reports of her plans
in city newspapers, ranks of the unemployed met her and
her guests at the hotel doors, hurling profanities and rotten
vegetables.

Alice further reported that her research at the Tilden
library had revealed nothing public of any joint business
ventures Moore might have entered into in the past six months.
Nothing in any of six newspapers suggested that an associate
might have had reason to murder him.

The insurance policy on Herbert Moore had been twelve
thousand dollars. In John's estimation it was not enough to
inspire the degree of complex carnage that recently befell
Twelfth Street. He was convinced that Heloise Moore knew
about her husband's bordello but had no involvement with his
death. Having him killed in front of the house he owned could
do nothing but destroy her social reputation. When such news
inevitably broke, no social-elite clique in any American city
would welcome her. Flight abroad was the only alternative.

A surprising call came from Frank Cobb via the agency telephone. The editor in chief had found time to track down Morning Mary. The brazen young streetwalker had been found strangled in a dark subway station corner the previous November. The contents of a couple bundles of her belongings concealed her corpse, evidently picked apart for anything of value. Cobb guessed that she had been murdered by one of New York's legions of beggars on the off chance that she might have a few dollars and perhaps some trinkets worth pawning. Not surprising to John was the news that she had had sexual intercourse shortly before her murder.

"She received a quarter column on page five of our paper," Cobb reported. "Too common a death to merit more. And, of course, no obituary. No one claimed the body."

Le Brun listened to the bitterness in Cobb's voice. "By the way," he added, "I forgot one more class of abused women when we spoke. Probably the most pathetic. They're the flower girls found all around City Hall and Wall Street. They're always twelve to sixteen years old. They're allowed in the buildings because they're too young for mischief, dress cleanly, and appear to be selling paper nosegays. They're invited into closed offices, spend ten to fifteen minutes—either under an occupied desk or bent over it—and leave with the same number of blooms they arrived with."

"Truly monstrous," John replied.

"Too monstrous to allow to continue," Cobb said. "In the next week, count on daily articles in the *World*. I want this cleanup campaign to succeed where all the others have failed."

"I've been pretty well hog-tied by the police," John said, "but if I can learn more about these assignation houses, you'll be the first to hear from me."

Out of frustration, John decided to take a stroll around the streets of Hell's Kitchen. He passed a newspaper stand and saw a headline in the *Herald* stating that carbon monoxide had been found among the chemicals in cigarettes. Even the pleasures of tobacco, it seemed, were deadly.

John thought about the large, dark van driven away from the massacre by the small person. He had no idea even of its company of manufacture. All he knew for sure was that it moved directly west, as if in a hurry. Toward the Hudson, not the East River. Dietrich Diefendorfer's loft lay in that direction from East Twelfth Street.

LE BRUN CAUGHT A TAXI to the corner of Perry and Hudson Streets. He asked a half dozen people about the police visit the previous morning. Only one had seen anything. An unmarked car and a police wagon had been parked on the sidewalk when the witness came to work at the warehouse across the street. He had looked down from the third floor from time to time, out of curiosity, and seen several electric lights on at a little past six in the morning, which was unusual. Half an hour later, four men in suits had removed what looked like the shape of a corpse wrapped in sail cloth and loaded it into the back of the wagon. Their movements had been, to the witness's way of thinking, quite matter-of-fact.

John thanked the man and pressed a silver dollar into his hand. He wasted no time in crossing the street and entering an alley next to the building the man had pointed to. He swore under his breath as his aging body was forced to drag a garbage can under the fire escape, climb on it using a tightrope-walker's balance, leap up to grab the lowest rung of the iron fire escape ladder, drag the ladder down, and haul himself skyward.

The rear windows of the second-floor loft were bolted and backed by thick wire. Using repeated kicks, John was able to smash one apart. He reached through the bent-wire mesh to coax open the lock with his forefinger. A sloppily applied layer of paint resisted his efforts to raise the damaged window, requiring several more kicks.

Inside, the loft was elegantly furnished, as Bergman had mentioned. The German owner had evidently had a penchant for things oriental. Black lacquer cabinets were filled with jade, ivory, China red stone, coral, and porcelain objet d'art. Large bronze and porcelain urns stood on the polished oak floor. A beautifully carved Japanese tea table showed twin dragons emerging from a tempestuous sea, with Mt. Fuji rising in the background. Even the man's rosewood desk had an East-Asian style. Two of the walls were filled with large, framed photographs of young, naked women, either posing lasciviously or engaged in unnatural sex acts. When John lifted several from the wall that faced the street windows, he noted that the difference in paint hues indicated they had been there for some time. They had not been put up recently to frame an innocent man.

John explored the desk and then every inch of the loft. While not one item of furniture, lamp, writing implement, or piece of clothing seemed to have been disturbed, there was not a single piece of paper in the entire loft. All desk drawers and a two-drawer file cabinet were conspicuously empty. A free-standing safe of medium size had been drilled open. Nothing remained inside it. Diefendorfer's corpse had not been the only thing removed. John checked the pockets of three suits that hung inside an armoire and found only a dry-cleaning tag. No stray slip of paper appeared when he lifted the desk blotter.

Le Brun dragged two lacquered chairs over to the first of the iron crossbeams, arranged them so the seats faced each other, forced an ornamental cabinet between their arms, and climbed up. He saw where a layer of dust had been disturbed. The pattern was in keeping with a loop of rope, moved during the dead man's final struggles or else by the police cutting it down.

Clucking his tongue repeatedly in exasperation, Le Brun restored the loft apartment and quit it by his means of entrance. Intended or not, the police had done a perfect job in denying him any clues to the lives of the abuser of women or his victims.

JOHN CALLED THE 17TH PRECINCT, identified himself, asked for Kasper Bergman, was told the lieutenant was not on duty until two o'clock, then asked if any young female corpses without identification had been found in the city. He heard the duty sergeant riffle papers, but he was not sure the act was genuine. The reply was that no young Jane Does had been reported in the past twenty-four hours. And then the desk sergeant said that he remembered a note directly in front of him. The note asked John to come to the station to fill out a witness report concerning the evening of April 30.

Le Brun ate a light lunch, then took his time wending his way through Greenwich Village, walking east by northeast to a personal wonderland he had discovered on his second visit to Manhattan. It lay two blocks south of Union Square, mostly on Fourth Avenue, and was called Book Row. Eleven bookstores stood within sight of one another, calling to John as the sirens did to Odysseus. Each time he visited, he never came away with fewer than a half-dozen volumes. After visiting each shop, he barely had time to walk to the 17th Precinct.

Kasper Bergman had arrived punctually. John made his presence known and waited ten minutes. When he once again entered the lieutenant's office, he found a man seated in the farther chair with a large, lined notebook. He recognized the preliminary jottings as Gregg shorthand.

"I apologize," Bergman began, as his eyes darted to the bulging cloth bag John had purchased to hold his newly bought books. "We should have taken your testimony the first time you were here, but it was a long night and my brain was like cottage cheese."

"I understand," John said, even though he did not. He wondered if the words were genuine or if Bergman had needed to clean up other business or destroy case evidence before dealing with John's testimony. He lowered his bag to the floor and sat in the one remaining chair.

The lieutenant allowed Le Brun to detail the evening as he saw fit, and John rewarded him by speaking with the thorough yet concise professionalism of a long-time lawman. The moment he finished, he said, "I might could be of further value if your offices were to share information with me. J. P. Morgan is still very interested in the total solution of this case."

Bergman's head swung slowly back and forth as he said, "But we all now know who murdered Herbert Moore. The whore told you it was her employer . . . or captor or whatever you want to call Diefendorfer. And he, too, is dead. So that ties everything up with a neat ribbon."

"Actually, it does not," Le Brun countered gently. "Because the fates of the remainin' prostitutes are unknown and the identity of Diefendorfer's accomplice was not determined." Bergman opened his mouth to respond, but John hurried on. "Since there were so few records in the house on East Twelfth, there must have been stacks of paper in the suicide's loft. Surely, diligent combing and footwork—"

"We will begin that process on Monday," Bergman interrupted.

"And will you labor as well to determine how the sex slaves in that house came to be there?" John shot back. "The one who called herself Violet was from somewhere east of Austria or Italy."

"I'm sure we will."

John looked at the shorthand clerk, then back to the lieutenant. "I have several free hours right now. If you provide me a desk and the papers collected from Diefendorfer's loft, I would be happy to offer my experience to look for promisin' leads."

Bergman's jaw tightened. "We can't do that."

"Evidently, Mayor McClellan and Police Commissioner Bingham have yet to call you or Captain Treacy regardin' my value in support," John said in a soft but measured tone.

Bergman turned red. "If they indeed wish you to participate further in this case, I will be in touch with you, Mr. Le Brun." The lieutenant put just the faintest hint of emphasis on the word *Mister.*

John stood. "Thank you. I trust you still have my business card from my first visit."

Silence reigned in the office as Le Brun left. He knew that any piece of paper that might reflect poorly on the men of the 17th Precinct would have long since disappeared before he was allowed to nose around. As to other written or typed clues that might lead to a complete understanding of what had happened, he could only wait impotently. Le Brun had never been involved in a murder case where he did not have free rein. His severe limitations redoubled his determination to learn the whole truth.

JOHN AND LORDIS WERE ABLE to spend Saturday night alone due to a phenomenon on the Upper East Side that Lordis had dubbed The Lepers' Club. There was no clubhouse, no official membership or dues, no recognition of the title beyond Whispering Hope's walls. According to her, it consisted of those neighbors who had no dignified forebears in their lineage (whether real or invented) but possessed *nouveau riche* money from a family-member genius in real estate speculation, inventions and patents, or perhaps a talent for pleasing the public by writing a play or musical. Because of Benjamin Topley, Sr.'s one-time profession as theatrical entrepreneur, several of the latter group had become known to Lordis's adopted family. There were also those who were unscrupulous scalawags who made money by barely legal means who were financially well off but social pariahs.

Lordis explained, "Those without live-in maids or governesses ask me to take in their equally unpopular children overnight so they may get out to the theater, the moving pictures, or those few parties that will have them. When you visit, I call in their debts to me."

Thus, the couple was able to get away to Oscar Hammerstein's Paradise Roof Garden atop both the Victoria Theatre and the adjacent Theatre Republic, both of which Hammerstein owned. Located at the corner of West Forty-second Street and Seventh Avenue, the combined spaces allowed seating for almost one thousand persons. The best seats sold for one dollar each. The fare was called vaudeville. As a speaker of French, John knew the origin of the term was *voix de ville*, or "village voice," low-brow entertainment in comparison to the city's dramatic plays and operas. This was their second visit to the Paradise Garden. The singing waiters were still there, but the monkey near the bar who did tricks was not.

The opening act of the evening was a beautiful woman with an hourglass figure and a lovely singing voice named Grace la Rue. She sang "I'm a little maid, dark, demure, and dreamy" and "A poplar tree in the forest stood, her head the highest in the wood" from *The Blue Moon*. The musical had had brief success two years prior and told the improbable tale of a British child born in India who was stolen from her parents and raised as a native.

The main act was the very popular Harry Houdini, who, Lordis revealed, lived on 113th Street in Harlem. As a solver of real-life criminal puzzles, John had long been a fan of magicians. Houdini was doubly fascinating to him because the performer was constantly escaping from handcuffs and prison cells. Only hours earlier, John had purchased a new book by Houdini entitled *The Unmasking of Robert-Houdin*. The book jacket promised that the author, who had idolized the French magician in his youth, would prove the man a liar and braggart concerning his claims of inventing many illusions.

The slightly-but-powerfully-built Hungarian immigrant, whose real name was Erik Weisz, began his act with fairly common sleight of hand tricks, swallowing of sewing needles and a spool of thread to regurgitate them united, and moved on to a sword box and a levitation illusion. However, the second half of his act was built around ever more astonishing feats of escape. He invited a member of the audience to handcuff him. Le Brun had his own handcuffs ready and thrust up his hand as a volunteer. After giving the Georgian an assessing glance, however, Houdini selected a younger, bumptious gentleman. The magician was out of the cuffs before his volunteer could count to ten.

Houdini next allowed himself to be put into a straitjacket and suspended upside down. As other volunteers fastened the many belts and straps, John moved his mouth to Lordis's ear and whispered, "I think he has learned how to dislocate his shoulders. It is indeed an astonishin' feat of contortion."

The final element of the evening was an escape from a giant milk can filled with water and secured by several locks. As Houdini emerged dripping wet with his chest heaving from lack of air, Le Brun rose to his feet along with the rest of the crowd and offered his frank admiration by clapping his hands together so loudly that they stung.

As the audience gave the magician/escape artist a prolonged final round of applause, Lordis observed, "His skill at misdirection is as good as his contortions. So quick. Do you know the term 'drag artist'?"

"Yes," John answered. "It's a male role done in women's clothing, where he pretends to be a woman. The opposite of a pantaloon role for women."

Lordis squeezed John's arm as they slipped into the crowded aisle. "No wonder you beguiled me: a man's man who knows the theater. At any rate, the reason I asked you is because I saw a musical several years back where they slipped a young man in drag into the middle of a female dance number without the audience knowing it. I actually went to the show a second time, just to see how it was done. Even though I knew it was coming, I almost missed it. There was a flash of light on stage left just as the man slipped into the line at stage right. Houdini does it without any such bold distraction."

While he descended to street level with his arm protectively around Lordis's waist, John reflected that even the most diverting entertainment of New York City could not prevent him from his fixation on the brutal events on East Twelfth Street. The song selections from *The Blue Moon* reminded him of young girls torn from their families; Houdini's illusions spoke of mysteries appearing before his sharp eyes that he could not explain. He wondered as well if some form of misdirection was being played on him and for what purpose that would be worth five hundred dollars to his unknown employer. He knew that if he lived another twenty years and continued to visit the city every few months, he would continue to poke and probe until he found the split in the onion skin that would allow him to peel away all the protective layers of the Twelfth Street murders. He would not rest until he exposed the well-concealed truth behind why he had been hired. Relentlessness was, after all, the very bedrock of his nature.

CHAPTER SEVEN

May 3, 1908

JOHN, LORDIS, AND THE CHILDREN in her charge
attended the late service at the Church of the Heavenly Rest on
the corner of Fifth Avenue and Ninetieth Street. The Episcopal
reverend had clearly been following the news and heated
editorials on the issue of, as he preached, "rampant prostitution
in New York City." He spoke of Jesus' compassion for the
woman found in sin and exhorted the congregation to follow
their master's example. John looked around the filled pews and
found no heads nodding. To him the worshippers expressed the
collective non-emotion shown by the *Syndics of the Drapers' Guild* in
Rembrandt's monumental painting. He looked at hands folded
quietly on laps that might easily pick up stones to cast, given
the slightest opportunity. He was little surprised. For the past
decade, immigrants had been flooding into the city through

Ellis Island—the biggest influx since before the Civil War. Unlike the first settlers from the Netherlands, Great Britain, Germany, and France—many of whom had at least a degree of wealth but who sought more in the land of opportunity—the current immigrants were truly "the wretched refuse" of teeming shores. They were penniless Italians, Greeks, and Polacks and a second major wave of the reviled Irish. What made them even worse was that they were either Roman or Orthodox Catholics. John imagined the conversations opening within view of the church after the mass of "good Christians" were blessed and sent on their justified ways for another week:

"Nobody asked them to come here. There are so many that of course they're taken advantage of. Supply and demand, pure and simple."

"They were no doubt whores in Italy, Sicily, Greece, Ireland, Poland. I don't believe for a minute that they were tricked into lying on their backs."

"I feel badly for them, but the lazy and the stupid are exploited and killed. It's Darwin's survival of the fittest in action."

"These farm girls coming into the city are products of liberal, atheist families. No unaccompanied child of a good Christian home and community would leave it to live in a city with more and more godless human trash streaming in every day."

From actual comments overheard in the church, on the street, and from letters to editors and editorials in the newspapers, far more emotionality was being generated over the murders of six persons within three days on East Twelfth Street than on sex slavery. Although the neighborhood homes dated back to before the Civil War and had seen better times and although commercial enterprises were rapidly encroaching the area, that part of the Lower East Side was still considered rather genteel among the city's law-abiding citizens. Le Brun realized with dismay that fears for personal safety had by far trumped concern for the plight of prostitutes.

In the afternoon, John settled into one of Whispering Hope's easy chairs to peruse several of the most successful New York newspapers. Like rats following the Pied Piper, they all had paid indirect tribute to Frank Cobb's Friday *World* front-page article on the Twelfth Street murders, to the accompanying information piece on prostitution in the five boroughs, and to Cobb's impassioned editorial "The Shame of a Great City." Le Brun envisioned the scrambling at every precinct to show their earnest efforts to remove both male and female purveyors of sexual gratification for money from streets and brothels alike. He pictured the public posturing from City Hall and the redoubled efforts by missions and churches to save the bodies and souls of the fallen. At the same time, he knew with a heavy heart that upon his next visit to New York little to nothing would have changed.

John forced himself to relax and try to enjoy "God's Day." In the afternoon, he accompanied Lordis and the children across the street to Central Park, visiting the zoo and watching miniature sailboats glide across The Pond. Although he replied to all of his fiancée's comments, his mind worked hard at assembling his plan of action for the next day.

In the early evening, he left a message at the Astoria for Merriweather Gooderly, apologizing for needing to stay in Manhattan "a little longer to try to solve the case for which I've been engaged." His second call, to Mary McMahon, detailed his plan of action for the morrow.

CHAPTER EIGHT

May 4, 1908

WHEN LE BRUN ARRIVED at Mrs. McMahon's apartment house, only she and Stu Hirsch waited for him. Larry Wilker had other agency work to attend to, and Alice Ainsworth's part in the case had been satisfied.

"I been thinkin' that people in the assignation house business probably don't need a van on a full-time basis," John began. He handed Hirsch a drawing he had made. "I want you to find out who rents motorized trucks with that shape in the lower half of the island and who they rented to on the day of the murders."

Hirsch whistled softly. "Yeah. Okay. As soon as I figure out where to start. Could be any one among dozens of stables."

John handed Mary a second piece of paper with the addresses of the notorious houses on East Twelfth Street. "I want you to go to the Bureau of Records and see if you can get a fix on the true ownership of these two houses. And when they're eventually sold, I want to know to whom."

"What will you be doing?" Stu asked.

"I'm thinkin' of sniffin' around on that street and see what the neighbors know. Also, to find out just how much leeway the mayor and commissioner of police want me to have. And then I'll meet up with Kevin, to learn more about Mr. D, bein' as how we don't know who the survivors of this debacle are or where they've gone to."

"What about the stationery supposedly from J. P. Morgan?" Mary asked.

"Y'know, in my hometown or even in a place like Savannah or Charleston, we might could have a chance of trackin' down the printin' press. But the Topley case proved to me that there must be a hundred legitimate print companies and a hundred more illegal ones in this city. It's likely an expensive wild goose chase."

"Have you ever had a case this difficult?" Mary asked him.

John puffed out his cheeks. "Can't say as I have."

"Perhaps a bit of prayer is in order," she said.

"Couldn't hurt," Stu chimed in.

ONLY A SINGLE NEIGHBOR in the middle of the East Twelfth Street block was cooperative. In fact, the doors to the houses flanking the notorious residences remained closed, even after John rapped long and hard with their knockers. The one respondent was a woman of advanced years. She used an ear trumpet but nevertheless asked that half of Le Brun's questions be repeated.

"My ears don't work anymore, but my eyes do," she said in a loud voice, giving John a moment of hope. "But I'm asleep by eight o'clock, so I couldn't have seen that murder in the street. I have a boarder"—she paused tantalizingly—"but he's a traveling salesman. Only here six or seven days a month. He was gone."

"What about last Thursday evenin'?" John asked, using his reinforced stage voice.

"The other house? Well, it was raining, and I was doing needlepoint." She laughed. "I honestly didn't know anything had happened until my next-door neighbor told me the next morning. I'm afraid if Judgment Day arrives, I won't hear it."

"Did your neighbor see anythin' before the police arrived?" John asked.

"She and her husband were climbing their front steps when a truck pulled out of the alley next to that house. They paid it little attention until it was past them . . . when it made that noise such contraptions do when they start to go fast."

"A backfire?" John said.

"What?"

John attempted to duplicate the sound with his voice.

"Yes, like that. Mr. Appelmann said that he noticed the handles on the back doors had a chain wound around them with a lock."

"When do you think Mr. Appelmann will return home?" John asked.

The woman pushed out her lower lip and shook her head. "Don't waste your time. He told me that if anyone outside of our street asked him any questions, that he would swear he had seen nothing. He wants no trouble."

John brought his mouth closer to the ear trumpet. "You and your neighbors must have known somethin' illegal was goin' on in those two houses."

The old woman straightened up and erected a self-righteous face. "Of course we did. But they kept their properties clean and their shrubs trimmed, and the police patrolled often. We never had to worry about our safety." Then she smiled broadly. "And the house on our side of the street gave every other household a beautiful dressed turkey for Thanksgiving and a cured ham for Christmas."

John bowed slightly as he offered his thanks. Nothing of their conversation had surprised him.

LE BRUN MET WITH Detective O'Leary a bit north of Union Square, out of the territory of the 17th Precinct. He knew the Irishman's penchant for bangers and boiled potatoes and ordered two meals before O'Leary appeared. He produced his notepad from an inside jacket pocket.

"The boys in the fourteen precincts between Houston and Forty-second are howlin'," he began. "Did ya see the *World* this marnin'?"

"I did not," said Le Brun.

"Well, your buddy Cobb published the names and locations of no fewer than t'irty-nine dance halls, bars wit' upstairs bedrooms, bordellos, whorehouses, and assignation houses. A note below the list said that many had been reported by readers of the paper . . . people 'tired of the trouble that slinks alongside prostitution.' I love that verb, 'slinks.' The bloodlettin' on Twelft', he wrote, was merely the most violent example of what goes on day after day in the sex trade. The good citizens are tired of the police doin' nothin'. All t'ree of the Union Square fancy cathouses we spoke of were listed. Imagine the drop in protection money for the boys in blue over at the Seventeenth! I saw a lot of sober faces there today."

"Then your offer to pay for the Diefendorfer autopsy report must have been welcome," John surmised.

"I didn't need to make an offer. The clerk handed it ta me straightaway."

"Which means they know you're moonlightin' for me and that the mayor, the police commissioner . . . or both . . .

ordered them to cooperate. Unless what you looked at wasn't the genuine article."

O'Leary flipped the pages of his notebook back. "Let's see. The autopsy report on Herbert Moore was twenty-one numbers earlier. Autopsies for Precincts Ten, Eleven, T'irteen, Seventeen, and Eighteen are done at Bellevue, so that seems reasonable for a t'ree-day period. Of course, most of the others had been lyin' on ice for at least a week, patiently waitin' their turn. Automobile tenpins and bridge jumpers don't rate special treatment."

Le Brun leaned closer to the notepad. "What did the autopsy say?"

"It was the briefest such document I ever seen. Death by asphyxiation."

"Not snapped neck," John said.

"Not accordin' ta the report."

John glanced at the pitifully few lines of writing on O'Leary's pad.

"Down in Brunswick, we call that 'pullin' hemp.' Were the rope marks deeper on the right or left side?"

Kevin said, "Again, it didn't say. It did say he was five foot nine, had brown eyes and hair, and was two hundred t'irty pounds." He tsked. "That's a lot of dead weight to deal wit'. Coroner probably moved him around wit' overhead pulleys and a hook."

John threw up his hands in frustration. "Ridiculous! The ink on the man's blotter indicated that he was right-handed. Which side the noose was on is important information."

"And what makes you t'ink they care about important information?" O'Leary replied.

"Naturally no mention of signs of a struggle, no defensive marks on his hands."

"Correct. You t'ink he didn't kill himself?"

"Until the possibility is eliminated. What did he use to accomplish the hangin'? Chair? Folding ladder?"

"Report didn't say."

"Time of death?"

"Estimate is midnight."

"Type of rope mentioned and whether it had been previously used?"

Kevin laughed. "Are ya jokin'? It says his toenails and fingernails were clean, if that'll help ya."

"Somethin' used to cut the rope and whether there were other pieces?"

O'Leary had grown tired of the rhetorical questions. "Nobody but you cares, John. Not the police, not Mrs. Moore, not the public."

"Apparently, not even the person who sent me the five hundred dollars under J. P. Morgan's name," John added.

"Yeah, I can't feature what that was all about," said the city detective. "I mean, if you hadn't spoke with that Violet woman about Mr. D or the second killin's hadn't happened, nothin' would have got in the papers. Which is the only way somebody who gives the wrong name for contact and provides no address or telephone number for your report could learn who stabbed Herbert Moore."

John downed the last of his ale. "Exactly. It's as if some wealthy person wanted me runnin' all around New York just for the hell of it. I tell you who cares besides me, Kevin: those vanished prostitutes. The whole affair seems like a wicked, slap-dash mess. And yet I can't help feelin' there is careful plannin' behind it."

"Then it's a mighty devious plan," Kevin decided. "Somethin' that looks like a cuckoo clock on the outside but runs like one of them Omega Swiss watches. What grand pieces of machinery! Won the Grand Prix for personal chronographs at the 1900 Paris World Fair, don't ya know?"

"Do tell," John said absently, as he digested his employee's report.

"I'm thinkin' of rewardin' meself wit' one after the old ball and chain has been severed from me ankle tomorra."

"What about the blood type on the sword cane?" John asked. "That report said it matched with Herbert Moore's."

"And fingerprints? I hope they at least took Diefendorfer's prints."

O'Leary shook his head vigorously. "They did, and they compared them successfully ta prints in the cathouse's upstairs office. But the cane had been wiped clean . . . or so the report reads."

Le Brun drummed his fingertips on the tabletop. He seemed to be idly watching the street traffic, but O'Leary knew better. His Southern employer said, "I can't imagine why the police would wipe the cane clean. It's not to their advantage to have both sets of crimes unsolved."

"I agree," Kevin said.

"But if Diefendorfer had already wiped his prints off the thing and it was not found inside his assignation house by an officer of the law, he should have been happy to find it gone. Instead, the theory is that he panicked, killed those in the house who knew what he had done . . . along with the innocent witnesses . . . and packed off the remainin' girls. Does that seem reasonable to you?"

Now O'Leary thought for several moments. "No. Not if he was payin' protection money. And not if he had enough left over for a good lawyer. If the murder of Moore came to a trial and he was the accused *and* a rebel up from the South and a foreign whore were the only testifiers, he could pretty much count on gettin' away with nothin' worse than runnin' a house of ill repute. Reasonable doubt, I mean."

The waiter came up to the table and looked at Le Brun. "Another mug, sir?"

"No, thank you," John returned. "My stomach seems to be turnin' sour."

WITH LESLIE AND BEN, JR. not due back from school
for an hour, Lordis and John crossed Fifth Avenue to Central
Park through the Children's Gate and walked beyond the
Outset Arch, where one of the stone benches with patterns
of chessboards cut into them stood vacant. Lordis opened her
cigar box and set out the thirty-two chessmen, giving herself
the white side. John was silent as she arranged the pieces in
their proper starting positions; his unblinking eyes seemed to
be focused on the center four squares.

"A lovely day," Lordis commented. "The shadows are so
sharp and dark, it almost seems as if I could pick up some of
the leaf shapes."

"Indeed," John said, shifting his attention to a young
woman struggling with two small children who were fighting
over an elephant pull toy on a rolling cart. She wore a uniform
that identified her as a nanny. He dipped his head in their
direction, causing Lordis to pause and study them as well.

"She thinks her life is hard," he said. "Everything is
relative."

Lordis moved her pawn out to king four. "You're not
staying, are you?"

John moved his pawn to king four. "No. Mrs. McMahon
has the agency in order, there are no upcomin' events that need
my attention, and this business with the houses of prostitution
has tumbled down a hole too deep for me to dig out."

Lordis did not reflect on her opening but instead moved
her knight to king's bishop three, causing John to counter with
knight to queen's bishop three.

"But I've come to know you well, John. You don't believe
it came to a proper conclusion." Her third move was bishop to
bishop four.

"Maybe it did. My misgivin' might simply be a product

of the pro forma work and nothin' more that the police are doin' to end it as fast as possible." John sighed. "At any rate, Mary will be checkin' up periodically on what happens to the two houses. O'Leary will keep his ear to the ground inside the NYPD, and Stuart and Lawrence will informally patrol the area from time to time. I'll give Frank Cobb a call before I leave and ask him to be alert to any city sex trade that might link to what happened. It's just those poor five young women who disappeared that really disturbs me." John moved his knight to bishop three.

"You seem to have arrayed your forces well before quitting the field," Mary observed.

"Better than I've done battlin' you here."

"We'll see. What about you and me?" She advanced her knight to knight five.

"I don't know how you're feelin' about me, Lordis Goode, but you're still my white queen."

"That's good to know. But if you attack me in a public park, might we not be arrested?"

John's pawn moved to queen four. "That's another game you're thinkin' of. You're still plannin' to come to Brunswick in the middle of June, with Ben and Leslie?"

"I am." For half a minute silence ruled as Lordis contemplated the board. "Two knights defense?" Her pawn took John's.

"More people to meet. More plans to make for our eventual Georgia weddin'." John's knight took the offending pawn.

Lordis set the black pawn at the side of the board. "We haven't decided which wedding comes first, the New York or the Georgia one."

"It also feels like my first major defeat as a criminal investigator, and it don't feel good," John admitted, shifting his mental focus.

Lordis tapped on the chessboard. "If you allow it to become

a distracting obsession, you'll experience other things that don't feel good . . . like losing this match to me." Her knight took his pawn, causing his eyes to dart up with surprise. "Beware, Le Brun!"

CHAPTER NINE

May 5, 1908

JOHN LOOKED DOWN from the train's moving course along the railroad bridge. He looked at the Raritan River flowing past New Brunswick, New Jersey. The train had traveled about halfway across the state on a northeast-to-southwest diagonal, and Rutgers College's buildings climbed the hill on the river's south side. John was about to return to one of the new treasures in print he had found in New York when a familiar voice boomed from the far end of the parlor car.

"As I live and breathe!" Merriweather Gooderly made his way up the aisle toward his fellow Brunswick, Georgia, native, watched by the two dozen other riders whose activities had been halted by his booming voice. "I thought I had left you behind in New York!" He collapsed into the seat beside Le Brun.

"And I thought you had left two days ago," John returned.

"Well, I had every intention of doing so, and then the importer of Persian carpets came home from the hospital only three days after having his appendix removed. It is astounding how quickly medicine is advancing. He insisted we work a deal before I left." Merri shrugged. "And who am I to turn down the disbursal of an expensive product through the Deep South?"

John nodded politely.

"Well, if you're on this train, it must mean you solved your case quicker than you expected," Gooderly surmised.

John closed his book, resigned to at least a few minutes of conversation. "There are still loose ends, but the police are satisfied."

"And what about the person who engaged you?"

"That's one of the loose ends." John saw that Gooderly was genuinely interested in hearing about his past week's efforts, so he made a snap decision to repeat most of it in detail. Several such spoken reviews in years past had required him to be clear and thorough and had exposed points that had led to later arrests and convictions. Sometimes, an innocent question posed by the listener made him reconsider an assumption made without sufficient thought. Given the length of the trip back to Brunswick and the fact that he would have more than enough time to read, he elected to lay out the business of the two assignation houses and the murders, event by event.

When John had finished, Merri asked, "So, you never found that van?"

"No. My associate learned it was an impossible task, given the little I saw. Garages and stables all over the city have one or two they rent out. The men who work for moving companies sometimes moonlight. It could have been stolen and returned."

Gooderly nodded soberly. "And did the houses indeed belong to Mr. Moore and Mr. Diefendorfer?"

"Moore's we were able to confirm. The other house was signed for by a Cordell Solomon, with an unlicensed front company listed as the owner. The only Cordell Solomon the city census revealed was a bartender who evidently moved to Cuba a few days after signing the papers."

"That sounds shady," Merri judged.

John snorted his derision lightly. "When it comes to shady, New York City resembles Kentucky's Mammoth Cave."

"So that's that," Merri said.

"Unless one of the prostitutes survived and wants to blow the whistle."

"Unlikely."

"Indeed," John agreed.

"Ah well," Merri sympathized. "Then look on the bright side: You're a mature man with his health, a magnificent woman who doesn't demand all his time, and enough money to enjoy a retirement that few ever experienced before our generation. On to better things, my friend. Like a drink. Care to accompany me to the club car? We can hold an informal meeting of the New Century Club."

"I fear we do not constitute a quorum," John returned.

Gooderly rose from his seat. "Then I shall catch you later. After all, how far away can you get on a train?"

CHAPTER TEN

June 19, 1908

"THERE WILL COME A DAY when all these men's clubs fall out of fashion," Lordis Goode pronounced, as she and John crossed the corner of Gloucester and Newcastle Streets, heading in the direction of Brunswick's Queen's Square. They carried wicker shopping baskets, which were being steadily filled as they visited various consumables shops. "Smoking clubs, hunting clubs, boating clubs, travel clubs, and now these ridiculous motoring clubs that encourage dangerous speeds on the roads."

"If you expect I'll be devastated when that day comes, you got another think comin'," John replied. "I believe that clubbin' is a mania that has proliferated way out of proportion. But the services clubs like the Elks and Rotarians or the religious ones like the Knights of Columbus shouldn't vanish. They do too much good. In the meantime, resign yourself to the fact that not only am I a member of a men's club down here, but that I am also the host for this evenin'. Resign yourself as well to the fact that not even a woman who is as marvelous a cook as you and who promises to stay in the kitchen the entire time is welcome."

"Fiddle faddle! And a secret club to boot. Like a bunch of boys in a tree house, giggling over their exclusivity."

"Exactly. We actually have a sign posted on the door of Retreat. It reads: No Girls Aloud." He spelled out the last word for his fiancée.

Lordis laughed, but then her eyebrows quickly knit. "Do you really?"

John rolled his eyes. "Pshaw! For a woman of the world, you are the most credulous creature."

"Which is one more reason why you love me."

Lordis had arrived with her young charges eight days earlier. Because of the limited room in John's one-story, shotgun home, he had arranged for the group to enjoy the amenities of the Oglethorpe Hotel, reduced as services were for the summer season. To Leslie and Ben, Jr., the enormous resort structure with its many hallways and sets of stairs was the combination of a palace and a maze. The evenings and nights were spent at the hotel, but days were filled either on John's property, with its mature trees and its carefully tended flower and vegetable gardens, or else exploring the countryside, the bays, the marshes, and the beaches. As children of a steel, concrete, brick, and stone world, Ben and Leslie delighted in the freedom of a leafy domain designed by Mother Nature rather than by landscape architects. However, they were doubly delighted to find that, since their last visit, a new family had moved in two doors down from John. They were the Owlsleys. The mother and father were Beecher and Wallis, a handsome couple in their midthirties. More important, they had a son and daughter. Regina was eleven—a year older than Leslie. Philip was twelve—

only two days older than Ben. They were intelligent, well-behaved children and fascinated to befriend a boy and girl who hailed from "the greatest city in the world."

For their part, the Owlsley parents were delighted to have the Le Brun group relieve them of a pair of bored almost-teenagers. On the previous five days, Regina and Philip had accompanied their neighbors on outings or else played with Ben and Leslie across one of the two shady backyards, chasing badminton shuttlecocks, using the joggling board John had built, throwing horseshoes, jumping rope, or the like. This Friday, Wally had volunteered to mind the four while Lordis and John shopped for the event of John playing host at the New Century Club's monthly get-together.

Lordis stopped short at the display window of a bridal shop. She pointed to a nosegay holder that trailed a profusion of light-blue silk ribbons. "Now that should go into my hope chest," she said.

"Your Whisperin' Hope chest," John quipped, playing on the name of the New York mansion Lordis lived in and managed.

"Shopping here is so much more relaxed than in New York. Each time I come down to Brunswick, I feel increasingly at home," Lordis revealed.

"That's a mercy," John replied. "As I've said before, comfort and companionship are what I crave. Your touch, your wise words, your smiles, you little indulgences." He doffed his straw boater at a passing couple that he knew slightly. They seemed to approve of the woman who had caught their attention.

At the butcher shop, John selected a rump of beef, which he intended to roast as soon as they returned to his house. His plan was to create a cold meal to suit the warm weather, something that was delightful to the eyes and the taste buds but which would free him of his chef's duties so that he could listen to the evening's lecture. Banker Garland DeBrahm had returned from a grand tour of northwestern Wyoming only a week earlier. John's bill of fare consisted of barley soup with celery, egg yolks, cream and fine butter, followed by cold rump of beef bourgeoisie style with side dishes of peas and asparagus. The pièces de résistance, however, were his lovingly fashioned pastries—a Neapolitan cake and an angel cake with strawberries and whipped cream.

"I do so enjoy cookin' and bakin'," John said, not the first time he had told Lordis so, "but I lack the space at home for entertainin'. We'll see what my fellow epicureans think."

Lordis carried a cornucopia of vegetables, including peas, celery, carrots, and onions. The parsley, thyme, bay leaves, and mace for his recipes came from John's garden and his dried stores. "I suppose this club is good for you," she decided. "Something other than voracious reading and hoping that Sheriff Tidewell will call on your expertise."

"That hasn't happened since I solved the warehouse case for Merriweather Gooderly," John said glumly.

"No more news about the assignation house murders, then?" Lordis dared, without looking directly at John.

Le Brun paid the butcher and tucked the large piece of beef into his basket. "Zero, *rien*, *nichego*. The John Le Brun Detective Agency has returned to party guardin' and wayward spouse investigatin'." He was frankly surprised that Lordis had avoided the question for so long. Like the figurative elephant in the room, it had long needed acknowledgment. Not a day passed without John regretting that there was no news at all to add to the spectacular set of murders. "I assume the righteous demands for actions to control the city's prostitution have lessened."

"Considerably," Lordis said, as they quit the shop. "Leastways, as far as I can glean from the drop in newspaper articles on the subject."

"Naturally. Other events pop up and shove even the most outrageous doin's to the side. What is the suffering of thousands of misused women compared with a major oil find in the Middle East or the *Lusitania* crossin' the Atlantic in fewer than five days? Ah, well. We'd better get back to my place before Addis arrives with that block of ice."

WITH THE BACKSIDE GROUNDS of Retreat abutting the southern shoreline of St. Simons Island, John had deemed it most expeditious to borrow his fishing friend Iley Rutledge's sixteen-foot catboat and sail his provisions to the clubhouse rather than to wait for the ferry and then seek out the rental of a wagon for the fairly long ride. Moreover, he could keep much of the food cold by tying waterproof bags to the gunwales and hanging them just below the waterline. The sky had been cloudless and the mid-June sun hot all day.

The edge of St. Simons Sound touched the bottom of the estate through about twenty feet of thick marsh grasses before washing onto the land. An all-but-useless, listing dock was enveloped in vegetatlon. John had dressed in waders and rough clothes and stowed his evening apparel in another waterproof bag. He raised the boat's dagger and hopped overboard into knee-deep water.

After tying the boat to the dock, John moved all his baskets, bags, and the box containing what remained of the block of ice up close to the house's well. He stripped off his waders and made his first trip to the cookhouse. Fires had burned down so many mansions in the South that a common practice was to build a cookhouse a short distance away and transport the meals to a back "warming room." John elected to move the food inside first, to keep it from predatory insects and rodents. He did not linger long indoors, but when he returned for the ice, he was astonished to see that the catboat was no longer tied to the dock but moving out into the sound. A slight figure sat in the rear, right hand on the tiller.

"Hey!" John shouted as he dashed to the water's edge. "What in tarnation do you think you're doin'?"

The figure turned briefly to stare at him. A moment later, it returned its attention to guiding the boat away from land. In those few seconds, John was able to focus on the thief's face. It was a young woman, older than a teenager but certainly not into her thirties. She wore a dark-brown skirt and an ecru-colored blouse. Her brown hair was mostly concealed under a scarf, which was dark blue and appeared to be covered with white polka dots. He could not make out any subtle, distinguishing marks other than pronounced cheekbones and eyebrows thicker than the current women's fashion. He noted as well that she was Caucasian, but her skin was bright pink. He knew that the hour was four o'clock, and he figured that she had been out in the sun for much of the day and might have the early signs of first-degree burns. He also noticed that the woman had failed to lower the dagger board, which made the little sailboat much more unwieldy in the gusting wind.

"Get back here!" he yelled. "You won't get away with this!" He suspected, however, that she might.

Cursing under his breath, John hurriedly finished transferring his things from Retreat's back lawn into the cookhouse. As soon as he had finished chipping wedges of ice, filling a couple of kettles, and arranging the food inside them, he rushed around to the front of the mansion. His bitter expectation was that he would be hoofing half a mile along the live-oak-lined entrance road, then north by northwest on King's Road until he could catch a ride into the village of Frederica.

To John's great relief, he came upon Esau, the teenager the New Century Club had engaged to tend the orchards and the vegetable and flower gardens. The groundskeeper had a wagon filled with tree branches and air moss and a mule hitched to it.

"Esau! Come into the house with me!" John ordered.

In rapid fashion, John wrote a letter to Warfield Tidewell,

detailing the incident of the stolen catboat. He folded it and pressed it into the hand of the thin, tall youth.

"I want you to get this to Sheriff Tidewell, just as quick as you can. You know where the jail is over in Brunswick."

"Yes, sir."

"I don't care how you get there . . . ferry or a friend's skiff. Just do it fast." He dug into his pocket and produced a silver dollar. The piece was what the groundskeeper made for an entire week of work.

"I is on my way!" Esau proclaimed, loping toward the wagon.

John shook his head as he watched the wagon jostle down the rough dirt road. The weather was fair. All kinds of vessels were out on the sound. Plenty of people in Glynn County knew Iley Rutledge's catboat, *The Tabby*. If a sailor lacked the curiosity to heave alongside the little sailboat and question the woman, surely one or more persons would see the path the thief took over the water. She would not get far, whoever she was.

THE EVENING WENT AS WELL as John had hoped. His meal was highly praised, and he was able to catch the last two-thirds of the lecture on Yellowstone National Park and the adjoining Grand Teton range. DeBrahm's photographs were passed around with great admiration, and, to a man, the desire was expressed to witness personally such unspoiled natural beauty. Garland gave much credit to the Kodak Model 4A camera he had purchased precisely for the trip. As John had noted with numerous rich persons, the price of items and what they paid were especially important to them. Garland was not shy about telling the group that he had purchased the camera for $100 but saved $9.50 off the list price.

Directly after the photo presentation, John played chess with Irwin Jones, trouncing him in twelve moves.

The architect insisted that the ex-sheriff learn the game of backgammon, so that he might return the favor of "abject humiliation."

Several times during the evening, John was tempted to reveal the strange theft of his friend's catboat that afternoon. He feared, however, that his reputation as a sharp-eyed lawman would be diminished if he was forced to say how easily a lone woman was able to steal his transportation. He judged that the affair was, after all, not sufficiently interesting to interrupt the evening's activities.

When the time came for the eight club members to disperse, John said to Merri, "I'm hopin' to hitch a ride with you back to Brunswick."

"Arranged transportation here but not back, then?"

"Exactly."

Gooderly looked over his shoulder at the owner of the deepwater fishing fleet. "Patrick and I planned to spend the next few hours on one of his boats, night fishing."

The remark caught John off guard. "Really? I always heard that you should start out before the sun goes down."

"No need to look for the best spot. We'll be chumming. Let the fish use their sense of smell and come to us. Shall I ask Cappy Ebenezer if it's all right for you to come along?"

"Don't impose on him," John replied. "Lordis is visitin' with her two godchildren, and—"

Merri shook his head so sharply that his double chin bounded. "Ah. You mentioned that last month. They're staying at the Oglethorpe Hotel."

"Durin' the nights," John clarified. "The rest of the time, they're with me."

"Why not ask Gil?" Gooderly suggested. "He and White sailed his yacht over to Frederica. I'm sure they'd be happy to carry you back to Brunswick."

Gooderly spun around to search for Gilbert Reynolds. A

moment later, however, a thought caused him to turn back. "By the way, John, how is it that you transported that delectable meal and a block of ice here by yourself?"

"I thought you knew," John replied. "I practice white magic."

Gooderly smiled broadly. "And magicians never reveal how they perform their astounding tricks."

"Exactly."

CHAPTER ELEVEN

June 20, 1908

LE BRUN STARED DOWN at the naked corpse. Behind his left shoulder stood the director of the Miller Funeral Home. Because Brunswick did not operate its own city mortuary, those who died of unusual circumstances were usually kept at Miller's. Past John's right shoulder stood Sheriff Tidewell. The men waited in silence for Le Brun to speak.

Finally, he said, "She wore a dark-brown skirt with a light-brown blouse."

"That's right," Warfield said.

"And a dark-blue kerchief."

"There was nothing on her head," Sheriff Tidewell reported. "It probably washed off in the sound."

"You say *The Tabby* was found near the mouth of Long Creek?"

Warfield moved around to the side of the embalming table. "That's right. Lying on her port side, the sail and mast caught in marsh grasses." He nodded to the corpse. "She was farther out toward the ocean, floating facedown."

Le Brun gently lifted the young woman's head and turned it left and right. "Nasty whack," he commented, of the split skin on her left temple. "But no swellin'."

"Her lungs were filled with water," the director said. "She was no doubt dead before her system had a chance to swell the wound."

"Looks consistent with a strike from a boom," said Tidewell.

John examined the woman's arms and hands, then moved methodically down the length of her body. "The land was hot when she stole the boat. A sea breeze was blowin'. All she had to do for quite a while was hold the tiller steady. She may have known nothin' about operatin' a sailboat. That boom can come around smartly when the wind changes sudden-like. Sure could have knocked her out before she had time to avoid it. Help me turn her over, gentlemen."

"I never saw her before," Warfield said, as he lifted the corpse's legs.

"Me neither," Director Miller agreed.

"That makes three of us," John said. "I've lived in this area my entire life. I reckon I know at least eighty percent of the folk in Brunswick and St. Simons by sight. For all three of us not to recognize her, the chance that she's local is nil."

"Then where in Tophet did she come from?" Tidewell asked.

"Not from inside anybody's house for sure," Le Brun answered. "Unless she was a very unwelcome guest who they recently threw out. She's got a small scrape on the inside of her wrist. Could have been caused by the gunwale. Iley needs to sand and paint that boat before she goes to rot."

"Along with a bunch of scratches. She was also out in the sun probably all day yesterday . . . until she died," said Tidewell.

"And maybe the day before. Her skin is still pretty pink, even with the blood drained to the backside. All those little bites on her skin I figure to be from mosquitoes and no-see-ums."

Le Brun had already been told that a pair of fishermen returning to port had discovered the body and that the time was about two hours after the woman had stolen the boat.

"She wasn't very wrinkled when you picked her up," John said to Warfield.

"No. She couldn't have been in the water very long."

John noted, "Her facial features are delicate, but her cheekbones are high."

The sheriff's eyes narrowed. "Like a Russian girl."

John shot his friend a doubtful glance. "How would you know what Russian girls look like?"

Warfield returned the look. "Because I subscribe to the *National Geographic Magazine*. They had an article on the many types of people living in Russia."

"Could be she was part Injun," the funeral director said. "They've got pronounced cheekbones."

"But not grey-green eyes, light brown hair, and a pale face," John countered, as he gestured for the other men to help him put the corpse once more on her back.

Warfield said, "She's a pretty thing, even dead. Not that that makes this tragedy any worse. Nobody should drown."

"Nor be stared at naked by three male strangers," John added. John wrinkled up his face. "No offense, but this embalming fluid and whatever else you use here is gettin' to me. Let's have a look at the clothes someplace else."

The trio left the preparation room with the wooden box filled with the corpse's clothing. Once he determined that the two shallow skirt pockets were empty, John wasted little time with the items of cloth. He lingered, however, on the shoes, turning them over and over.

"This is pretty crude work," he said. "And not in any style

I've seen our ladies wearin'."

"From where, then?" Warfield asked.

"Maybe homemade." John raised his eyebrows and stared at Sheriff Tidewell. "So, if we can't identify her, what should you do next?"

Warfield snapped his fingers, then pointed his forefinger at Le Brun. "Just like you did with that Jasper who turned out to be from St. Mary, I'll get a photograph of her face after it's made as natural as possible. Once the picture is developed, I'll have it run onto posters and spread them around town and over at St. Simons. *Somebody* around here has to know who she is, right?"

CHAPTER TWELVE

June 21, 1908

THE BREEZES WERE STRONG across the Golden Isles on Sunday. After church, John, Lordis, Ben, Jr., and Leslie packed a picnic lunch and took an old buggy John had hired onto one of the ferries that crossed to St. Simons Island. On the way, Le Brun stopped briefly at the city jail and picked up two dozen posters. The posters carried the photograph of the dead young woman, as well as descriptive information and the announcement of a five-dollar reward for information leading to proof of her identity. Moments after he handed the posters to Lordis, the children besieged him with questions. While he told them of the capsizing of *The Tabby*, he avoided mentioning that the boat had been taken while in his possession.

"I suspect that the poor lady had never handled a sailboat before," John told them, intending to turn the mishap into a cautionary tale. "Not only was she out on a big body of water alone, but she was also clearly not aware of how quickly the wind can change and bring around the sail boom. Whack! Splash!"

"Then the boat wasn't hers," Leslie said as she adjusted the poke bonnet John had bought her several days earlier.

"It was not."

"Whose boat was it?" Ben asked.

The horses had slowed, requiring a slight snap of the reins from Le Brun. "A man named Iley Rutledge."

"And he lives over on St. Simons Island?" Ben continued.

"No. Here in Brunswick," John answered.

"But those posters are for putting up on the island?"

Leslie elbowed her brother. "Just because the boat was from Brunswick doesn't mean she had to be. Maybe she was trying to get back to St. Simons for free."

"And maybe you're stupid," Ben said, jabbing his sister harder than she had poked him.

John concentrated on the avenue ahead, happy to merely drive.

JOHN GUIDED THE HORSES southeast from Frederica, along King's Road. His voiced excuse for the route was to show the others Retreat and its surrounding plantation, mostly gone to disuse and decay. He stopped three times before they arrived to tack posters to opposite sides of trees that encroached the road.

It was not until after the picnic lunch had been consumed and the youngsters were running up and down the fine-sand beach, each in command of a kite, that Lordis spoke of the drowning. As she shook the sand from the corner of John's old blanket, she said, "The only reason the woman would have to steal the boat would be if she started on this island and wanted to get to the mainland without using one of the ferries. She didn't start from Brunswick."

"I agree," John said. "*The Tabby* was over here. And I'm pretty certain she didn't come from the southern tip . . . the populated end." His gaze had been fixed on the gently lapping waves of the Atlantic as they rolled onto the beach, then retreated, creating dark patterns in the sand that swiftly faded. "That's why we're gonna cover St. Simons with posters."

Lordis smoothed the blanket out. "But what if she didn't come from the northern end either? Then where did she come from *before* she was here?" John opened his mouth to reply, but she supplied her own answer. "Maybe she was running from the law farther north. It couldn't have been from the south. You told me about how well the millionaires have the shores of Jekyl Island patrolled." Lordis lay back and stared up at the sky. "She could have come down from Savannah . . . or at least Darien. When she figured she no longer had a sufficient lead on the law, she abandoned the roads and took to the islands."

"With what?" John asked. "She obviously didn't know how to sail."

"With a raft or a canoe. All you need to know for those is how to pole or paddle."

"So she gets through the marshes at the top of this island and walks south until she's stopped by the St. Simons Sound," John supplied.

"Right. You said she was sunburned and covered in insect bites. My theory also explains why you, Warfield, and the funeral director had never seen her before." Lordis's eyes opened wide. "Or she could have been running from her family. An arranged marriage she couldn't abide. Or she was pregnant without benefit of marriage and afraid of her father's wrath. You should have a doctor cut her belly open and see if she carried a fetus."

"I'm not the sheriff anymore," Le Brun reminded his beautiful companion.

Lordis smiled. "I'll bet, among those three ideas, that one of them is the answer. Mary McMahon isn't the only female who makes a fine detective."

John smiled at his fiancée. "I'll transmit your ideas to Warfield. It certainly wouldn't hurt to send a few posters up to Darien and Savannah."

A sharp gust whipped Lordis's skirt up past her knees. John twisted to capture it, then rolled himself down until he was suspended inches above Lordis.

"Very sneaky," she said, cocking one eyebrow. "Pretending to save my dignity even as you attack me. There are children watching."

"Are you tellin' me to 'go fly a kite' as well?" John joked.

"Tomorrow. When they are at the Owlsley's house." Lordis stretched her elegant neck upward and planted a kiss on John's lips. "Tomorrow you may plunder and pillage to your heart's contentment. And then you will take me back to that bridal shop I discovered yesterday. Sally won't be in prison forever."

THE PARTY'S RETURN ROUTE to the Frederica ferry was long, describing a rough counterclockwise rectangle about two miles east-west and three miles north-south that followed between the plantation boundaries of St. Simons Island. By the time they had reached the ferry dock, only two posters remained, and Ben was given the task of tacking those prominently in the boarding area.

"Around here used to be called Gascoigne's Bluff," John lectured as Ben labored. "It was here that the lumber from some 2,000 Southern live oaks was gathered and shipped north for the buildin' of the USS *Constitution*."

"Old Ironsides!" Leslie chirped. "We read about it in our history book in school."

John asked, "Did your history book mention how it got its nickname?"

"No."

"Well, that great ship was heavily involved in the War of 1812. Sailin' out of the port of New York, she came upon the British frigate *Guerrière* and sank her. The enemy's cannonballs kept bouncin' off the *Constitution's* plankin' without causin' any damage. So somebody in her crew shouted, 'Her sides are made of iron!' Indeed, St. Simons live oak is as dense and durable as iron. Six months later, she took on *two* British ships in one day and captured them both! She's still afloat in Boston harbor. When your Ma comes home, y'all should visit the old gal."

Several curious bystanders, originally drawn by Le Brun's lecture, moved closer to view the poster's photo and words. If any of their number recognized the drowned woman, they said not a word.

CHAPTER THIRTEEN

June 28, 1908

A PASSENGER SHUTTLE TRAIN left Brunswick each morning at a few minutes before noon. Because so many of the city's winter-season tourists came from Philadelphia, New York, and Boston, its departure was timed to deliver travelers to inland Thalmann Junction only twenty minutes before a northbound express arrived from Jacksonville.

Lordis, Leslie, and Ben, Jr. stood toward the back of the platform so that several older ticketholders might board ahead of them. John had his hand on Ben's shoulder, and the boy allowed it with no sign of discomfort. Likewise, Leslie had smiled at Le Brun several times on the platform. John credited the softening of their hearts to the pleasant companionship they had experienced with the Owlsley youngsters, as if John had methodically planned and executed the arrival of the

family on his street solely for their benefit. Whether his surmise
was right or wrong, he gratefully accepted what the diplomats
called détente.

"Sometime in September, I assume," Lordis said to him,
meaning the next of John's quarterly visits to New York City.

"Unless somethin' unanticipated happens beforehand,"
he replied.

"The business with the missing prostitutes," Lordis
understood, nodding.

The conductor snapped shut his pocket watch and nodded
at the ex-sheriff to indicate that the train was about to leave. A
column of white steam pouring out of the locomotive's escape
valve signaled the same message.

"All right," John said as he passed Lordis's valise and
carpetbag to the conductor. "Time to get a move on. I'll see y'all
soon enough." He shook Ben's hand and kissed the two ladies.
Then he watched with his hands shoved into his trouser pockets
as they climbed the metal steps and, soon after, appeared at one
of the coach's windows. He waved; Lordis blew him a kiss; the
engine's whistle tooted once, and the train began to move with
the chuffing of expelled steam.

As John's eyes followed the trailing car, he caught sight of
Merriweather Gooderly standing at the far end of the platform.
The warehouseman's face carried an amused expression. He
sauntered up to Le Brun, drawing a handkerchief from his
jacket as he moved, mopping the sweat from his brow.

"A handsome trio," Merri remarked.

"I think so," John allowed.

"Something of a ready-made family for a confirmed
bachelor. I admit to a touch of jealousy."

"I am indeed a fortunate man," John replied.

"In relationships, leastways," said the warehouseman.
"What I mean to say is your work on behalf of justice has not
achieved its former platinum standards of late. I understand that

you've been assisting Sheriff Tidewell in solving the mystery of the woman who drowned. Yet still no identity revealed."

While Gooderly's voice was warm and overly mellifluous to John, the words carried a veiled rebuke. He wondered just how deeply his nine-to-four record over his fellow club member at chess matches had begun to rankle the ever-eager opponent.

"Nothin' revealed."

Gooderly mopped his brow once more. "Hmmph. Then certainly there is no way to guess her reason for stealing the sailboat."

"Right again."

"And since you're here in Brunswick and not off to New York with your group, I must assume that no further progress was made in learning what happened to the women who worked in the second whorehouse."

"Assignation house. The police have always had charge over those two cases," John said in a voice made to indicate that his emotions were imperturbable. "I was engaged only to determine who had murdered Herbert Moore, and I succeeded in that regard."

Merri looked toward his warehouse, then back again at John. "Good on you. But, as a longtime man of the law, surely you long to learn the unresolved details of the incidents."

"Right a third time." John turned away from Merri, looking for an excuse to take him from the annoying conversation.

"It's almost noon, John," Merri said. "I still feel deeply indebted to you for saving my company's reputation with that business of the Gould paintings. Your genius for detection was surely on display that day."

"Thank you. Now, I must—"

"Ah, my words have set you ill at ease," Gooderly hastened to say. "Forgive me if I seem to be riding your professional reputation."

"Like George the Fourth on his horse," John replied.

"George of which country?"

"England."

Merri shrugged. "I know nothing about him . . . or his horse. At any rate, any offense was purely unintentional."

John was not convinced. He was, however, convinced that portly Gooderly indeed had no knowledge of King George IV or his face would have shown it. The monarch was by far the fattest the British Isles had ever known. His horses were said to become sway-backed within a season of his riding.

"Allow me to make amends if needed by taking you to lunch," Merri said, lightly touching John on the shoulder and guiding him toward the center of the city. "And we shall speak of future trips to New York. Perhaps one or more where we may travel together."

"Much as I would enjoy spendin' your money," John replied, "I have a previous invitation over at the Minahans. Very gracious people." Then he started off with long strides, leaving Gooderly's familiar hand dangling in midair.

CHAPTER FOURTEEN

September 15, 1908

LE BRUN ARRIVED IN New York City without Merriweather Gooderly. He had not, in fact, alerted the Brunswick businessman that he was making the journey. Two weeks earlier, his generally favorable opinion of the man had taken a negative turn. Purely by chance John had learned that rather than a rental agreement, Gooderly had signed a purchase contract with the heirs to the Retreat plantation. Ten percent of the securing funds had come out of his own pockets with the balance deriving from the pockets of depositors in Garland DeBrahm's Brunswick First Savings and Trust Bank. DeBrahm, flattered to have been chosen as the second member of the ultra-exclusive New Century Club, had offered an attractive loan rate. Unlike the rental agreement Gooderly had described to John, one-third of the group's steep monthly dues went

directly to pay down the loan he had taken. The property had
been so depressed by abandonment, misuse by the Freedmen's
Bureau during Reconstruction, and lack of funds to refurbish
it that the price was a veritable steal.

Gooderly's conniving had sat particularly badly with John.
Years before, one of his DuBignon cousins had convinced
him to sell his parcel of Jekyl Island to him at a pittance.
Not a month later, the cousin had sold the entire island to J.
P. Morgan and his closest multimillionaire friends for many
times what he paid, only to be himself flabbergasted when the
syndicate sold memberships to the newly formed Jekyl Island
Club for more than ten times what they paid.

John had learned about Gooderly's chicanery from a young
man staying a week at the Oglethorpe Hotel who liked to play
chess. The man's name was Donald James Ross. The profession
of the recent immigrant from Scotland was the designing of golf
courses. He had been engaged by Gooderly to survey the Retreat
Plantation, envision an eighteen-hole course, and estimate the
cost. The rage for using golf clubs among the American rich
roughly equaled the level of mania that men's clubs had. More
and more speculation was taking place on St. Simons Island
and Sea Island for resorts and posh vacation properties, and a
good golf course would be high in demand.

When John had asked Ross the approximate cost of the
course, the man had also let on that his employer's plan
was also to take the mansion on the property and expand it
into a clubhouse. And then he had delivered what to John
seemed an astronomical figure. While John could not fathom
why Gooderly had wanted him in the New Century Club, he
realized that all the other men except him were among the
wealthiest in the county. Commercial schemes and deals were
discussed every month at Retreat while the men played cards,
backgammon, and chess. Thus, it would not seem strange when
Gooderly would choose to sell them on the grand concept. The

talented club member Irwin Jones could no doubt be drawn into the scheme as the clubhouse architect. Tatnall would have an inside track on all the lumber used; Ebenezer could get a sweetheart deal providing the seafood. Once again, John would be cheated.

For a brief time after the opening on Jekyl Island of the most exclusive wintering club in America—a club whose one hundred members controlled one-sixth of the nation's entire wealth—one local family had been allowed membership. Soon afterward, when pointedly not invited to any activity during the high season, the DuBignons had given up the membership and retreated to the mainland with their tails between their legs. They were far from the only Glynn County family who lusted to rub shoulders with the likes of the Vanderbilts, Morgans, Goulds, Bordens, and Rockefellers and to partake of the golfing, picnics, fabulous clubhouse meals, postprandial smoking and sewing circles, hunting, fishing, and cycling. Le Brun understood that what Gooderly had conceived was a reasonable facsimile of The Jekyl Island Club for the native rich and mere millionaires from around the country. It would be a resort just across the St. Simons Sound that could be mentioned in the same breath. John admitted that the man had a great idea; how he conspired to realize it and keep himself in charge was another matter.

The more he reflected on Gooderly's underhanded methods, the more annoyed he became. He searched his mind for ways to give the warehouseman the benefit of the doubt but could find no scenario where the man did not come off as less than an "Up-country scalawag." By the time the train reached Philadelphia, he had determined not to renew his membership to the New Century Club the next spring.

Following what had become his routine, John visited Mary McMahon directly after he arrived in Manhattan. She went over the agency ledger with him and showed great satisfaction at the increase in their business. She regaled him with Larry Wilker's successful defense against burglars at the home of a family attending the father's funeral. Regarding one of the two houses of prostitution on East Twelfth Street, she reported that, in spite of the elaborate front company obfuscations surrounding its last ownership, Mrs. Herbert Moore had been able to prove easily that it was, after all, part of her husband's estate. She had sold it for a decent price.

"And she must have sold off the rest of his holdings just as quick," Mary imparted, "because I saw a column in the *Herald* about her taking that elegant Holland-America liner, the *Nieuw Amsterdam*, to Plymouth. From there, she intended that she and her belongings would head to London's Belgrave Square district. I hope she gets robbed by highwaymen along the way."

"You're a century or two too late," John told her.

Mary grinned like the Cheshire Cat. "Never mind. She needed to hustle her bustle after I got finished with her. I sent the intelligence to Frank Cobb about Moore's wife coolly selling the property her husband owned and got killed in front of. He used it to good advantage. It kept the flames against prostitution fanned for a couple more days. She also got her townhouse egged the night after the story broke."

"Good for you," John praised. "Who bought the place from her?"

Mary shoved papers in John's direction. "A well-off, middle-aged couple. The house across the street is being subdivided into two apartments."

"So that ends the prostitution on that block," John said. "At least for a while."

"I hear that many assignation houses . . . you know, the ones in the better districts of town . . . have had a bad time of it since you and Mr. Cobb stirred up the hornets' nest," Mary let on. "But the traffic around the Lower East Side and Hell's Kitchen is livelier than ever. You win some; you lose some."

"I had no illusions that 'the world's oldest profession' would wither and vanish from such a diverse city," John said. "Any other news?"

Mary looked away for a moment. "Well, myself and Martin finally got enough money together so that we could afford to bring our girls over. Molly and Moira will be living in the room you sometimes use, until they can get themselves on their own feet."

John had seen photographs of the McMahon daughters, made all the plainer by their sober expressions. They were now twenty-two and twenty and had been left with relatives in County Kildare for the past six years so that Mary and her husband might accrue money all the faster in their dream to grow well-off in America.

"That's wonderful news," John said, privately thanking God for the sacrifices of his forebears. Crossing the wide Atlantic as a foreigner had been unnecessary for him. "I'll be stayin' with Lordis for the foreseeable future anyway. Allow me to keep my travel bags with you, however, until I secure a few gifts for Her Ladyship and the children."

AS A SEASONAL TOURIST RESORT, Brunswick was richer than most other small cities in curio and gift shops. However in comparison to New York—and particularly to Fifth Avenue— it was a backwater. John's goal was to purchase Christmas presents to carry back to Brunswick for the Whispering Hope trio's scheduled visit. Although Le Brun's home chimney was in his kitchen and hardly big enough for St. Nicholas's magic, fine gifts would nonetheless appear under the decorated fir that, although small, necessitated the rearrangement of John's parlor. Lordis would buy with John's money whatever winter dress Leslie expressed interest in, wrap it, and hide it in her luggage. He himself shopped for Ben, Jr. The gift was a Märklin

German toy locomotive with coal tender and two passenger trains, plus a large oval of track. With that boxed present under his arm, John walked up Fifth Avenue to the corner of Thirty-seventh Street. Tiffany & Company had moved there from Union Square two years earlier and was one of Lordis's favorite haunts.

As John entered the store, he recalled reading a 1906 newspaper article on the history of the iconic New York establishment. The firm was renowned for confirming the authenticity of every piece they sold. A *Times* reporter had written in 1870 that "a 50-cent pin can't enter or leave the establishment without its history being fully known and recorded." The store owners were not, however, so successful in preventing some pieces' physical exit. In 1871, a thief had entered Tiffany's through an unbarred upstairs window and would have made off with bags of booty had he not literally bumped into a night watchman. A few years later, a salesman named Henry E. Murray went to prison for stealing at least $10,000 worth of Tiffany's goods, and, in March of 1903, Alfred "Toothpicks" Britton had been arrested for stealing silver plate while an unnamed accomplice diverted an employee's attention.

John was well aware that, like banks, jewelry stores were prime targets of the clever and brazen, who were too lazy to use their talents to live by honest means. He had learned the technique of accomplices diverting attention in stores with glass cases while a light-fingered companion reached over and scooped out expensive items. Sometimes three criminals worked together, the third watching the other employees and looking out for possible plainclothes security personnel. Voracious reader that he was, John had learned this and much more about the ploys of American criminals from a book called *Thirty Years a Detective*, written by the celebrated Allan Pinkerton and published in 1884.

John's goal was to purchase a gold-edged broach Lordis had admired during her May visit. As he waited his turn to speak with a salesperson, he became aware of a theft in progress, using a technique neither described in the newspaper articles nor in Pinkerton's book. An elegantly dressed and bejeweled woman stood before a glass case that held scores of rings. Some were only gold wedding bands, but other trays displayed rows of mounted diamonds, rubies, pearls, sapphires, and emeralds against varying shades of velvet cloth. Although she looked almost straight down, the customer's small black hat decorated with white feather wings did not move even slightly from her crown of hair. Her search had evidently been protracted because four trays had been moved from the protection of the long glass case to its countertop.

The patron pointed to yet another tray that rested below, speaking rapidly as she did so. The instant the employee bent to retrieve the tray, the elegant woman picked up her long leather purse and relocated it atop the exposed tray farthest from the saleswoman. The purse did not come to rest atop the tray, as another patron would have expected, but seemed to devour it. John put on his bored face and turned as if to scan other items in the store. He saw a man who stood farther inside the showroom, alertly watching the movement of other people rather than being focused on the store's contents.

John ambled across the room to a tall salesman in his fifties who stood behind another set of showcases with his arms folded. John came up in front of him and placed his business card on the countertop.

"I don't see a guard on duty," Le Brun said softly.

The clerk's head reared back. "You want me to divulge that information based solely on a piece of paper, sir?"

"I can understand your caution," John returned, "and it is well founded. The man in your back aisle is workin' with the woman at the counter opposite us. Try not to look surprised. She has just boosted one of your ring trays with her false-bottomed purse."

"Our guard is allowed half an hour for his lunch," the clerk reported in a near-whisper.

John pointed to the case in front of him but kept his eyes locked on the salesman. "I would guess the same time every day. That is undoubtedly why this pair is workin' your store right now."

"What should I do?" the clerk asked.

"Why don't you wander toward the front door? I will get behind the man. They should be ready to leave very soon."

The clerk sighed in resignation and moved as John had directed. Le Brun set down his toy-train purchase and continued his perambulation, clasping his hands behind his back in a relaxed posture, even as the fingers of his right hand stole under the hem of his jacket to the revolver hidden there.

"Sir! Sir, can you help me?" a woman called to the salesman approaching the front door.

"I'm sorry, madam," the flustered man called back. He pointed toward the farthest recess of the room, where a second employee was engaged in arranging a display. "Please ask—"

At the first sounds of his raised voice, the well-dressed female thief lifted her purse from the counter, delivered a quick thank-you to the woman waiting on her, and headed with haste toward Fifth Avenue. Her accomplice also moved toward the front, but at a less-urgent pace.

"Stop her!" Le Brun cried out as he closed the distance on the male thief.

The lookout whirled counterclockwise, raising his right arm as he did, his fingers curling into a fist. He aimed a punch directly at Le Brun's head, but the ex-lawman ducked under it. When John came up, so did the revolver in his hand, striking the lookout smartly against his temple, causing him to collapse to the floor.

A female shopper screamed at the sight and dropped the bag she had been carrying.

The male clerk set himself squarely before the front doors and held out both hands in a halting motion. In response, the female thief reached up to her hat, pulled out a long securing pin, and jabbed it at the man's face. He succeeded in blocking the thrust with his hand. The pin went deeply into the flesh of his palm, causing him to yelp in pain. He did not, however, give up his blocking position.

A moment later, John had captured the screaming thief from behind and wrestled the tiny weapon from her grasp. As if by magic, two more male Tiffany employees were by his side a few seconds later. Then the store guard entered from Fifth Avenue into the noise and confusion.

John identified himself, released the struggling woman, and pried the booster bag from her iron grip. He opened the bag, ripped out the hidden-claw mechanism, and extracted the tray of glittering rings. He coolly placed it on one of the counters. Snatching up his toy-train purchase, he declared that he would return as soon as possible with a policeman.

"AS A TOKEN OF OUR IMMENSE GRATITUDE," the Tiffany & Company manager said to John, "we would be pleased to offer this broach to you *gratis*."

"You won't get in trouble?" John asked, as the man selected a presentation box and passed it to the saleswoman at his side for wrapping.

"Not after I assure the owners that you saved them an entire tray of engagement rings, Mr. Le Brun."

John returned the manager's broad smile. "Well, that's a very kind favor, sir. Y'know, you would do this fine business a favor as well if you let the guard go to lunch at different times."

"We shall indeed from this time forward. Miss Atherton will have your present ready for you in just a moment."

While John waited, a glow of satisfaction suffused him. He

realized that it was the first time since the stolen Gould paintings that he had directly succeeded in thwarting a crime. He silently pledged to give the affair of the missing prostitutes at least a few days' attention while he was again in New York City.

CHAPTER FIFTEEN

September 16, 1908

AS SOON AS LESLIE and Ben were dropped off at their schools, Lordis and John took the IRT subway line down to visit Sally Topley inside The Tombs. In 1906, thanks to a favor granted to Le Brun by J. P. Morgan, one of New York's best lawyers had been engaged to see that Sally would not have a trial by a jury of her peers. Instead she faced a judge who was known to be in Morgan's pocket. Sally had not been responsible for the crimes of her husband and, as her lawyer argued, could not be found guilty beyond a reasonable doubt that she even knew of his crimes until well after they had been committed. Clearly, however, she had aided and abetted him once she had become aware. For this, she received the law's minimum sentence, which was five years, with as much as two off for good behavior.

For months, Sarah Pinckney Topley had blamed Le Brun for putting her in prison and taking her from her children. Gradually, with most of the credit due to Lordis Goode, she had softened in her attitude. When Lordis had returned from the June trip to Brunswick and related how much the children had enjoyed themselves, she at last allowed that he might visit her. John knew that she was a smart woman, understanding that continued animosity toward him would only place Lordis in a perpetually awkward position regarding divided affections.

"She's no doubt able to see the end of her misery," John said to Lordis as they exited the train at the City Hall station, with its barrel vaulting, multicolored tiles, and ornate skylights.

"Counting the days, I assure you," Lordis replied.

"They would be more bearable if she allowed her children to visit her," John judged.

Lordis shook her head rapidly. "I agree, but she is dead-set against it. She does not want them seeing her inside a prison, nor seeing the other women around her. She fears the images will scar them for life." In her lap she held a basket containing jarred preserves, tins of cookies, several bananas and apples, needlepoint materials, toiletries, and bars of chocolate favored by the guards and matrons.

For his part, John held a metal vase filled with Mme. Caroline Testout roses, Sally's favorite pink Hybrid Tea variety. He carried as well a clutch of books bound by twine.

The six-year-old replacement of the original Tombs loomed before them. The prison had cost one million dollars. Its eight-story Châteauesque façade with conical towers faced Centre Street. The structure was so huge that it occupied an entire block, bounded by Centre, White, Elm, and Leonard Streets. Lordis informed John that only fifty cells, located on the Leonard Street side, were built for women. One subdivision housed the more incorrigible prostitutes. The other section housed the ladies convicted of arson, burglary, confidence, defrauding, embezzling, forging, grand larceny, and the rest of the alphabet of nonconfrontational crimes. Sally had confided to Lordis that she and her cellmate, a woman who had had sex with various married city officials and tried to blackmail all of them, were known by the titles Queenie and the Duchess. As former members of a more privileged life, they were scorned by the other women, who would try to do them petty injuries if given the opportunity. But for her gender, Sally would have merited one of the six special cells looking out on Centre Street, reserved for white-collar criminals.

Lordis and John were patted down and then allowed to take an elevator to the seventh floor. They entered a whitewashed room being mopped by a boy inmate and sat at one of the metal tables.

The prisoner appeared in a cotton day dress. She carried three books and a colorful length of linen. She offered John an immediate smile. He rose quickly, wondering if he should extend his hand or even embrace her. Lordis rushed forward and did the hugging for both of them.

Over her friend's shoulder, Sally said, "Thank you for coming, John. And thank you for looking after my children so well. They wrote that they adored their summer visit."

"My pleasure," he replied. He set the vase on the table. "For you."

"How beautiful! A touch of beauty inside this hellhole."

"I'm sorry you have to endure it," John said.

"I know how hard you worked on my behalf to lessen my sentence. I think I would have slit my wrists now if the sentence had been any longer."

Lordis dragged her friend to one of the tables. "Never say that! Think of all the life ahead of you and of how much your children need you."

Le Brun had been made aware that all but three of Sally's former female friends had abandoned her. Lordis visited twice a week. The other two came, on average, every three months. John also knew that Sally survived by doing elaborate needlepoint and by reading voraciously. He knew her life was basically one interminable day of boredom and isolation after the next.

"You want me to take away those books?" John volunteered, pointing to the two volumes.

Sally's pale face reddened slightly. "If you would. I was not unaware that you have been supplying me with quite a few of the books Lordis delivers."

John rocked on his heels. "Well, not the chapbooks, but things I read and no longer have room for that I believe might entertain you."

A mischievous smile lifted Sally's cheeks. "Like Mary Shelley's monster, Ibsen's plays, and those intrepid but crazy Englishwomen who jaunt all over the globe?"

Now it was Le Brun's turn to blush. "I thought perhaps—"

"I'm only having you on," Sally interrupted. "They are much appreciated."

John carefully set down his twine-bound books. "In that case, here are the collected installments of Ida Tarbell's *History of the Standard Oil Company, The Troll Garden* by a talented young woman named Willa Cather, and Edith Wharton's *House of Mirth.*"

"How wonderful! Thank you."

Sally's eyes began to shine with the onset of tears, causing John to remark, "As the British say, 'Stiff upper lip and all that!' I know Lordis has things to share with you that are best said out of my earshot, so—"

"Oh, no! Don't leave on my part!" Sally hastened to exclaim.

John took two steps backward. "And, as a former lawman and current detective, I really do wish to see more of this formidable structure. Lordis, I'll meet you in the street lobby."

Before other less-than-totally-sincere expressions of disappointment could be voiced, John turned and strode to the barred door, where a female matron stood watch.

"May I leave unescorted?" John asked the matron.

"Unless you want to pay for one of *those* 'escorts,'" the woman said, nodding down the length of the corridor, whose walls were punctuated by evenly spaced doors fashioned of sturdy wood with barred openings. Having pronounced her witticism, she chortled with glee.

Le Brun slowed his pace, steering his path close to the doors on his good-eye side. He looked through the succession of window bars at the bedraggled women of the street.

"I was just having you on, y'know," the matron called out cheerfully. "You'll have to wait until your choice does her time."

At the third door, John's pace faltered. He turned around and went up to the bars as closely as possible.

"I'll be switched!" he exclaimed. He glanced at the matron. "Can you come here and tell me who this is?"

"I can't leave my post until your lady friend parts company with the Duchess."

"Fine," John said. "Tell my lady friend that I need to visit the warden, and then I'll be back up here." As he loped toward the elevator, he heard the matron muttering about his slim chances.

WARDEN CARNABY PRECEDED John to the cell door, followed by the Sister of Charity on duty.

"It's time for their daily exercise walk anyway," the warden said. "We'll just isolate the one you want in the visitation room."

The nun inserted an iron key in the door. The warden pulled the door back and pointed to the nearer of the two women occupying the cell. "Is that the one?"

"She is," John confirmed.

Carnaby snapped his fingers at her, then jerked his thumb backward over his shoulder.

There was no doubt in Le Brun's mind that he was looking at the young prostitute whom he had thought of as Weeping Willow. Her face, with its Cupid-bow lips and frame of jet-black, shoulder-length hair, was just as stolidly sad as when he caught a glimpse of her on the way out of the assignation house. What was different was that she wore a high-necked shirtwaist blouse with a long skirt intended to narrow her silhouette instead of a negligee that revealed the pink circles of her breasts and the dark vee of her lower torso. Her clothing looked remarkably new if not clean.

"That's the woman," John said. "Or perhaps I should say girl. They called her either Pansy or Peony at the house."

At the mention of the two names, the young woman's eyes widened and then quickly narrowed. She was obviously trying to remember his face and not succeeding.

"Where was she picked up?" John asked the warden.

"Where *wasn't* she picked up?" Carnaby returned. "She's not like so many of the girls, working a few blocks. She's been plying her wares from Forty-fifth down to Eighteenth, from Second Avenue to Madison."

"Never down near East Twelfth?" John asked.

"No. Her class needs hotel rooms. She's still too pretty. She's a couple years from the flophouses and saloon traffic." His words sounded like echoes of Lieutenant Bergman's. "She knows two English phrases for sure: 'Going out, honey?' and 'Five dollars.'"

"And you got this from various precincts?"

"Indeed. This is the third time she's been a guest of the city."

"She's in for how long this time?"

"I believe three weeks. When she's loose, she never seems to sleep. I'm told she's brassy bold about bothering men, considering she knows so little English. She's arrested much more often than the usual streetwalkers."

"Whatever it is she speaks," Sister Agnes said to Le Brun, "it might as well be Martian."

John executed a Continental bow and swept his arm out to invite the girl-woman to leave her cell. She continued to eye him with rapt curiosity as she moved into the corridor. The warden gave her a shove on the posterior to keep her moving. His gesture spoke volumes to Le Brun about the prison attitude toward prostitutes. He understood that they were an unending societal problem and that some among their number were not total victims, actually content to make money on their backs. However, he had no doubt that the female walking down the corridor was one of society's victims and worthy of respect.

As the group entered the visitation room, Lordis stood. Sally had been removed for her morning period of exercise.

"Why don't you wait downstairs, dear?" John suggested.

Lordis shook her head. "No. I'll stay if I'm allowed."

"I don't care," Warden Carnaby said, this time pushing on the prostitute's shoulder to steer her toward one of the tables.

"I'd be grateful if you didn't do that," John said, in a low, even voice, causing the man's eyebrows to raise in surprise.

"You have five minutes to get something out of her," Carnaby said.

John took the girl's hands gently and guided her down to the metal bench opposite where he sat. He smiled again.

"Peony?"

She shook her head. "Pansy." With her accent, the word sounded like Pan-see.

"You speak English?"

She shook her head again.

He pointed to himself. "I was with Violet." He knew that she was trying valiantly to understand him. He made his right hand into the shape of a gun, pretended to fire twice, and said, "Bang! Bang!" She jumped slightly. "Violet." He pointed his finger gun directly between Pansy's eyes and softly repeated, "Bang."

Pansy inhaled deeply, then burst into tears. Her hands flew to her mouth. He nodded several times.

"*Parlez-vous français? Vy govorite po-russki?*" he asked.

"Sister Agnes told you," the warden said. "She speaks no language a white woman might. What have we tried, Sister?"

"Italian, French, Spanish, Greek, Yugoslavian." The nun folded one hand over the other as she regarded the prostitute. "We thought we had finally succeeded when we brought someone in who had spent some time in Croatia. This one's face lit up, and she started babbling. But the man couldn't understand her."

"She does look like she might come from that part of the world," Lordis interjected. "Perhaps she speaks a regional dialect."

The warden looked doubtful. "How different could a dialect be that she couldn't understand the basic language?"

"But you said the man you brought in was not a native speaker. What was his native tongue?"

"Turkish."

Le Brun wanted to scream. No doubt the self-proclaimed translator was an immigrant eager to make a few dollars and exaggerating his knowledge of languages. If John felt frustrated, he could imagine how upset Pansy was.

"We've done pretty much everything we could," Sister Agnes said. "When we failed to understand her, I brought in a map of Europe. She was unable—or unwilling—to put her finger on where she came from."

John drew in a long breath. "All right. I might be able to help her speak, given a day or two. How much longer is her sentence?"

"Until the end of the week," Carnaby said. "She's got three strikes now. The Immigration Service would like to deport her for moral turpitude, but they can't do that if we don't know where she came from in the first place."

All the while the group talked among themselves, Pansy's eyes darted back and forth. Her expression approached that of mild terror.

John lifted the young woman's hands and squeezed them lightly. "This is one of the women I saw in the assignation house. She is a figure of great interest. I would further remind you that the one woman I talked with spoke with a heavy Eastern European accent. We will return," he promised Pansy. He lifted his forefinger and waggled it, then pointed to Lordis and himself and gave her a thumbs-up sign. This she seemed to understand. She recaptured John's hands, and covered them in kisses. Tears started from her eyes and streamed down her cheeks.

Warden Carnaby, clearly embarrassed by the display, worked his fingers gently under her armpit and encouraged her to rise.

"We'll take care of her until you return," he promised.

John was not completely convinced. "This is not merely my concern. I feel strongly that she is the key to the solution of those assignation house murders last May. I can produce documents from Mayor McClellan, Police Commissioner Bingham, the chief editor of the *World*, Mr. J. P.—"

"I'm sure you can, sir," Carnaby cut in. "You have my word she will be kept safe."

John's head jerked up and down several times. "Good, good."

The city official, the nun, and the inmate left the room.

"Poor creature," Lordis said.

"Very much in need of our help," John added.

LE BRUN SEPARATED FROM LORDIS at the IRT Twenty-eighth Street stop and walked west toward Mary McMahon's apartment house. As he came to her block, he was still concentrating on what could be done to tap Pansy's mind while simultaneously protecting her. His attention was not so diverted, however, that he failed to see the little man propped against one of the tenements on the opposite side of the street, tucked into the angle formed from the outer wall and the top of the stoop. John gave him only the slightest notice, but he registered that the character had basically one long eyebrow—like a caterpillar crawling across his forehead—the smallest of goatees, and deep-set eyes. He was built in perfect proportion, but John estimated that he could not have stood higher than five-foot-one in his stocking feet. The tiny character's eyes definitely had fixed on Le Brun's movement.

John continued without slowing his pace and took the steps from the street two at a time as he entered Mary's building. He rapped on her door and received no reply. Cursing under his breath, he knocked louder.

"Keep your trousers on!" Mary bellowed from two flights up. The wooden steps creaked with her rapid movement. "Who is it?"

"John."

"John Le Brun! I didn't expect you today."

"I didn't expect to see you either," John called up through the stair rails.

"I was just giving the girls' place a lick and a promise. They're at work." Mary descended the remaining steps, a white cleaning cloth waving in her right hand like a flag of truce. "And what brings you to the John Le Brun Detective Agency, sir?"

"It was one thing, and now it's three," John answered, as he followed Mary into her living room. "I found one of the prostitutes from the massacre." Mary's eyebrows remained raised all the while he related the story of Pansy.

"So, I have this suspicion that she's from an interior country somewhere in the Balkins," he finished. "Didn't you say a man lives on this block who came from Rijeka?"

"Yes. Mr. Luppis. It's a seaport at the top of that ocean on the east side of Italy. He goes by the unlikely name of Johnny. Just trying to fit in, I suppose."

"The Adriatic, yes. It would make great sense for a number of the city's prostitutes to come from that area. It's had nothing but fighting and poverty in the past thirty years. Control by the Ottoman Empire, some kind of peasant revolt, takeover by the Austro-Hungarian Empire, and recently some new revolts against them. I believe the so-called police translator from Turkey knew precious little Croatian." He paused. "Or maybe she speaks Serbian. Anyway, we must start somewhere, and I'm hopin' we can get Pansy and your neighbor together for a parlay."

"I'm sure I can," Mary said. Her button eyes glowed like backlit amber with the anticipation of personally participating in the hunt. "And what's the two other things?"

"There's a fellow standing in the shadows across the street. He put himself so's he could watch your front stoop." John nodded toward the room's two windows. "Without movin' the curtains, can you make him out?"

Mary went close to the lace curtains and narrowed her eyes. "Yes, I see him. He's not from this block, I'll tell you."

"Well, his gaze locked on me," John said. "This big nose of mine is rarely wrong, and it smelled vermin. I think that might just be the little man I saw drivin' the van away from the assignation house."

Mary's neck craned forward. "The devil you say!"

"I'm almost certain he wasn't there yesterday morning when I first arrived."

"Nor was I aware of him," the agency coordinator shared.

"Here's what I need, Mary. Whatever Stu and Larry are doin', they need to drop. I need them here in two shakes of a lamb's tail. But they must come in from the back alley."

"And what else?"

"You need to do a little shoppin'. Take your basket, but visit a few neighbors before you do. Ask how long the little bugger has been hauntin' the neighborhood."

"Sure. Somebody will know. We got nosey fishwives up and down this street." The telephone rang. Mary excused herself and answered with the agency greeting. Then her eyes darted to John. "It's Hirsch."

John accepted the candlestick phone and put the earpiece to his head. "Stu, I think we may have more than one break in the Twelfth Street case. How many more reliable ex-cops do you think you and Wilker can pull together within, say, forty minutes?" His look in Mary's direction was far from elated. "Well, do the best you can. You know the rear access into her house. It'll be open. Make sure everyone takes it. I'll be waitin' here."

"You want me to go now?" Mary asked, as John hung up the stick phone's receiver.

"Yes, but use the alley as well and circle the block. He may not have identified you with the house and me yet, and it would be beneficial to keep it that way."

MORE THAN AN HOUR PASSED with John alternately making notes at the desk and pacing the floor back and forth in a fishhook pattern. The first to appear was Mary, returning with a half-filled shopping basket. Her report was that, according to the combined intelligence of three ever-vigilant block wives, the man had first appeared near the stoop sometime after seven that morning. He had relocated up and down the street at varying intervals but never ventured out of view of Mary's tenement.

Le Brun swung down onto one of the chairs. "Let's say for argument's sake that he knows that Pansy is inside The

Tombs. Only Lordis and I knew I was goin' to visit the place this mornin'. He was stationed here even before I arrived there anyway. So if he's lookin' for me, it isn't because he knows I've found the young woman."

"I agree," said Mary, taking the seat beside him. "Mercy's sake, it's a miracle he would think you were here at all, considering you arrived yesterday early and took off for the Upper East Side less than an hour later."

John rubbed his chin repeatedly with his forefinger and thumb, then flung up both hands. "Ah, why try to puzzle out this mystery on my bottom when I can get my answers on foot?"

Mary's reply was "I'll make tea."

Twenty minutes after that, Stu and Larry arrived. Stu had brought along a fellow ex-cop named Winston Brown, who looked not a day younger than seventy-five. Although only shocks of white hair remained on his crown and he spoke with the difficulty of one wearing poorly fitted false teeth, he seemed spry enough. Larry's recruit was a man who went by the moniker of Paddy Carew. Paddy was well padded and iron-haired. With his nose red and swollen, his cheeks heavily veined, and bags under his eyes the size of silver dollars, he looked as if he had spent much of his life straining whiskey through his liver.

The two extra men were so shopworn in their look that John despaired of getting much service out of them, but he held his tongue. *It stands to reason*, he reflected, *that Stu and Larry wouldn't recruit vigorous, recently retired policemen, who might be looking to nudge them out of a job.*

John first delivered an abbreviated summary of the case at hand for the benefit of his temporary employees. Then, one after the next, the four men were brought to the curtains and invited to memorize the features of the tiny man on watch across the street.

"There's no crime in havin' a shape like somebody who drove a motorized van," John said to the group. "And loiterin' on the street only merits a fine. If he's the right man, his best use to me is to lead us to the missin' prostitutes and maybe to his accomplices."

The four men nodded as one.

Le Brun angled into the center of the room to be sure he had everyone's attention. "Here's my plan: I let him follow me for a time. Then I give him the shake. That's where you four come in. I was told that the woman who escaped did so about six or seven weeks ago. Warden Carnaby said she works the open street day and night. That means she was smart enough to relocate herself to another part of the city the moment she got free. Otherwise, she would have been found and recaptured by those she got away from. Because she needs her Johns to rent rooms, she's put herself in the hotel district, from Forty-fifth down to Eighteenth Street. She's stayed exclusively on the east side of Broadway. Logically, it means that after the massacre she had been brought to an assignation house on the West Side."

"Those starting at Fifty-third and running up to just below the Boat Basin on Seventy-ninth," Paddy Carew jumped in. When everyone stared at him, he added, "Me old beat. Etched in me noggin." He tapped the side of his skull.

"Really, Carew?" Larry responded. "Now I know why you never saved a nickel."

"Y'all think it's time to get down to brass tacks, or should I wait 'til your tongues stop waggin'?" John asked to silence the laughter. He had learned that a firm voice, coupled with a few well-chosen Southernisms, was the best means to remind Hirsh and Wilker that the out-of-towner was in charge. "What's the cross street for Columbus Circle?"

"Fifty-ninth," Carew supplied.

"Perfect," John decided. On a previous summer day, he and Lordis had strolled west from Whispering Hope among winding, beautifully landscaped acres to view an area that almost rivaled

Times Square for entertainment value. Since its opening in 1857, Central Park had been the city's favorite sport riding venue. Columbus Circle, at its southwestern corner, proved the most cost-effective location for riding academies, stables, and businesses that sold horses and all forms of carriages. The motorcar was simply a "horseless carriage," and therefore displayed in the same buildings. "That huge Tichenor-Grand Company buildin' would be an ideal place to shake off a tail, would it not?"

"It and the businesses around it are crowded with the curious from noon until six," Paddy confirmed.

"Good!" John said. "That will leave him smack-dab in the middle of the target area. I'll give y'all a fifteen-minute head start." He continued with the details and rationale of his plan and finished with, "Gentlemen, this work is worth four dollars apiece no matter what. Eight dollars eventually if we find either the women or his accomplices." He plucked two business cards from Mary's desk and handed them to the temporary employees. Then he took two quarters from his pocket and handed one each to Hirsch and Wilker. "Change these into nickels. Before y'all make decisions, call here. Mrs. McMahon will act as the central dispatcher."

WHEN HE EXITED the tenement house into the street, Le Brun was careful not to glance in the direction of the loiterer. Only when he crossed the street to take the northbound Eighth Avenue Elevated at the Thirty-fourth Street stop did he confirm that he was being dogged. The pedestrian traffic was heavy; his stalker made no special effort to conceal himself among the sidewalk crowds.

John purchased his token, squeezed through the turnstile, and put himself at the uptown end of the platform, standing well back so that the little man could not get behind him. The sun was past its zenith, brilliantly lighting every northbound commuter. His stalker had positioned himself forty feet down the platform, which allowed Le Brun to pretend to be watching impatiently for the train's arrival and simultaneously to study him. The man wore a brown-and-white-striped seersucker suit. John knew that summer-weight seersucker suits were a mainstay among Southern gentlemen from the end of May until the beginning of September, but few men in New York wore them. The fashion choice made the man easier for John to spot. He wondered if the character was a transplant from somewhere south of Virginia.

What the denizens of New York jokingly called an Interboro Rattle Transit train arrived at the stop with a rumble and squeal. John took his time advancing, allowing virtually everyone else within his area to enter the car before he did. His maneuver compelled the little man to step to the side and wait, in case the car doors should close before his quarry got on.

The car was well packed. For the most part, women and children sat and the men held onto straps and swayed with the motions of the train. After John made sure his stalker had entered the door on the opposite end of the car, he faced forward, ignoring those behind him. At each stop, he swung around to allow riders to leave or enter, simultaneously checking that the little man was not sneaking up on him with a small weapon.

Eventually, the train left its elevated position and plunged into the schist bedrock of the island. At last, it arrived at Columbus Circle where Eighth Avenue, Fifty-ninth Street, and Broadway converged. John stepped briskly out of the car and fell in with the flowing masses. However, when he passed through the exit turnstile and came to the base of the stairs, he veered to his left, walked a couple paces beyond, knelt, and retied his right shoe. His follower was obliged to continue up the stairs in order not to become obvious. As he passed, John looked upward through the bars of the stair rail. From his low angle, he discerned the bottom of a holster peeking out from below the hem of the seersucker jacket. He guessed from its size that the weapon it carried was a snub-nosed revolver.

When Le Brun emerged into daylight, he found his follower waiting in front of a Liggett Drugstore. He noted Larry Wilker standing almost a full block to the south. Stu Hirsch had positioned himself on the opposite side of wide Eighth Avenue, near the Oriental Hotel. Paddy Carew and Winston Brown were not in sight.

John fetched his pocket watch from his vest, consulted it, then shook his head as if behind the time. He broke into a speed walk catercorner across the circle, weaving his way west among pedestrians, horse-drawn trolleys, and motorized Broadway Line streetcars in the direction of the Tichenor-Grand Company building at Sixty-first. Stu walked at a slower pace for half a minute ahead of Le Brun, then several moments abreast, then gradually farther behind him, so that he was sure to be passed by the stalker.

Le Brun's plan was to have his minions surround the little man and to do so in such a way as not to alert him. This required patience. The detective could not seem to run away or be ducking a tail. Le Brun entered the center hallway of the eight-story building and walked up to the bank of elevators. One was disgorging patrons and another filling with them. He watched from a distance as his stalker glanced in the front showrooms to the left and right of the main lobby. One elevator closed. The man turned and spotted Le Brun. John entered the second elevator. What seemed a minor eternity elapsed until the operator judged his car was full enough. He slid the accordion gate closed just as the man in the seersucker suit came into view. The operator yanked on his control handle, and the solid door closed as well. All the while, John avoided locking eyes with the man who had followed him.

Patrons and employees left the elevator on the third, fifth, sixth, and seventh floors, guaranteeing that when the frustrated follower watched the elevator's floor indicator, he had no way of being sure where John was in the enormous building. His expectation was that the man would wait at least half an hour near the lobby elevator wall. John exited at floor seven, let two minutes pass, and rode another car down to floor two. From there, he could march back and forth along the central hallway and look down on Broadway and Ninth in turn. He did this for almost twenty minutes before catching sight of the little man crossing Ninth Avenue and heading north. As soon as he also saw Winston Brown and Larry Wilker moving in the same direction, with Brown ahead of their quarry and Wilker behind, he dashed down the building's staircase and jogged south on Broadway to a cigar store he had passed that advertised a public phone. On the way, he encountered Paddy Carew.

"He's heading up Ninth with Brown ahead and Wilker behind!" John called out. "You should take Broadway to intercept! He's carrying a concealed revolver!"

"Okay, I'll fetch Hirsch!" Carew yelled back.

Le Brun called Mary and gave her an update and the number of the cigar store telephone. He exited onto the sidewalk and contented himself with observing the passing crowds for several minutes. A horse defecated at the curb directly in front of him. When the disagreeable smell wafted in John's direction, he retreated into the store. He engaged the owner in a detailed interview on the recent history of the cigar. He learned that about 19,000 people were employed in the tobacco industry in Havana, but that was fewer than the number in Manhattan and Hoboken. He also heard that many "genuine" Havana cigars were actually produced in Key West and Tampa.

Finally, the telephone rang. John answered it.

"It's Larry. He made a left at Sixty-fifth and hoofed all the way to a three-story on West End Avenue. Brown's watching the front, and Hirsch and Carew are on the side streets."

"I'll be there quick as I can," Le Brun said. The familiar tingle that came from a chase filled his chest. He paid the salesman for six Coronation cigars, stuffed them into his jacket pockets, and turned north.

"HOW DO YOU WANT us to play this?" Larry asked Le Brun.

John cracked open his revolver and made sure all chambers were loaded. "Obviously, the man knows me. You and Stu are carryin', correct?"

Larry patted his shoulder rig. "We always do."

"Then you two go to the front door and pretend to be Johns. Move inside quickly. He's bound to have an accomplice inside since he was out all mornin'. I'll take the rear."

John moved down the alleyway to the back of the brownstone building. Less than a minute later, the back door flew open, and a dandified man in his late thirties with macassared hair, a Kaiser-style moustache, a four-button suit, and a silk tie with a pearl tie-pin launched himself into the alley without bothering to take the two steps. John raised his revolver and pointed it at the man's face.

"Not another step . . . unless you crave ventilation," he threatened.

Brown and Carew hastened along the service alley that ran parallel to the row of buildings. John knew that neither carried a gun, but both had their hands shoved inside their jackets in a menacing manner.

"I'm just an innocent victim," the dandy complained, raising his hands.

"Sure you are," John returned. "You'll stay with these officers until we're done inside."

Without waiting for reply, John climbed the steps and moved into the building. He worked his way forward through two rooms, guided by the strident voices. Hirsch was calling

for everyone on the floors above to descend. Wilker warned two
men lying facedown not to move. The house guards alternately
hurled back threats and cursed their situation.

"We're protected, you stupid bastard," the man in the
seersucker suit proclaimed.

"Really?" Wilker said. "And who exactly would that be?"

"Don't say no more," the man lying beside him ordered.
He was bald with the remaining hair shaved down to his olive
skin. He had a war eagle tattooed to the right side of his neck.

John spotted the stick phone sitting on a small table just
to the side of a ceiling-to-floor ormolu mirror. He dug into
his pocket for the business card of 17th Precinct Lieutenant
Kasper Bergman. He picked up the instrument and gave the
switchboard operator the officer's phone number. When the
man identified himself, John said, "It's that friend of the
mayor, the police commissioner, and J. P. Morgan. I'm not in
your precinct right now, but I'm sure you'll want to come up to
where I am. I have the men you've been lookin' for since May."

"Give me the address," Bergman said.

Le Brun obliged.

"Can you hang on for half an hour?"

"Unless top brass from this precinct appear."

The connection was abruptly severed.

"I wasn't even in this business until May," the tiny man
protested.

"Do tell," John said, replacing the policeman's card in his
billfold. "Just in the movin' van business, were you?"

Le Brun's stalker drew in a surprised breath.

"I told you to shut the hell up!" his partner shouted.

Stu Hirsch kicked the tattooed man in the side. Even lying
facedown, one could tell he was clearly tall and strongly built.
He absorbed the blow without crying out. Stu said, "This one
is obviously in charge. He was watching the front door. When
Larry and I said we were here for a little matinee, he challenged

me as to who had recommended the place. I said, 'Mr. Smith.'
He said, 'Mr. Smith Who?'"

Larry laughed. "I pulled out my piece, shoved him backward,
and said, 'Mr. Smith and Mr. Wesson.'"

John glanced into the parlor, which was empty. "Were
there any girls in there when you entered?"

"Yeah, two. But they ran upstairs while I was collaring this
pygmy here."

"Go upstairs and bring everybody down. Be careful."

"I always am." Wilker let his Smith and Wesson New
Century with the shortened barrel in his right hand and the
stalker's S & W .38-caliber Safety in his left lead the way up
the stairs.

"A solemn warnin' for y'all," John told the whorehouse
guards. "I don't want to kill you 'cause I know you have much
to tell, but at the same time I'm convinced you both need killin'
real bad." He paused to let the information sink in. He did
nothing to disguise his Southern accent because he was sure
the smaller man had known John's Georgia roots before he
concealed himself opposite Mary McMahon's tenement. "First,
your names. Who you are will come out soon enough, so you
might as well tell the truth."

"Up yours," the big man said. "We're just employees of
a business."

"An illegal business," John countered. "And your buddy
spent the mornin' followin' me—"

"That ain't against the law," the smaller man argued.

"I'm gonna call you Mutt," John decided, "since you're about
as big as a mutt. Your pal can be Jeff." He did not know nor care
if either of the men knew of the comic drawing panels that had
been born the previous year in the *San Francisco Chronicle* and
then rapidly swept the country via the King Features Syndicate.
He was simply tired of the little stalker having no name.

Neither man responded. John looked in the direction

of the stairs with impatience. "Hey, Larry!" he called out. "Shake a leg!"

"One of these doors is barricaded. This is a big job for one guy," Wilker complained.

John jerked his revolver toward the stairs. "Lend him a shoulder, Stu."

As Hirsch stepped over Jeff, the man's left hand thrust out and grabbed his ankle, causing Stu to fall clumsily to the floor. An instant later, Mutt was on one knee and making ready to launch himself into John's midsection.

Le Brun slid his left foot backward for anchorage and swung his right up, catching Mutt under the chin. The vertebrae crackled in the man's neck from the force of the blow.

Jeff scrambled over Stu's struggling figure, his fingers spidering along the ex-cop's hand toward his gun. John did not hesitate. He pulled the trigger of his revolver and sent a bullet through the bald man's forehead. Blood and brains erupted from the rear of his skull.

"Jesus, Mary, and Joseph," Hirsch swore, twisting away from the corpse. "You made a mess of my cuffs."

"Better than him makin' a mess of your face," John said. "When you get your wits about you again, go help Larry." To the stalker, who was coughing, holding his jaw with both hands, and rolling back and forth in pain, he said, "Remember I said you both need killin'. Stay down or die."

John's two employees finally bulled through the bedroom door and herded a total of five young women downstairs. They all wore semi-opaque shifts that left little to the imagination of the flesh wares beneath. He studied each of the wide-eyed creatures as they passed him, growing more disappointed by the moment. They regarded the dead guard with mixed looks of disgust and satisfaction as they retreated into the parlor.

Le Brun ripped a curtain panel from one of the front windows and tossed it on the dead corpse. Then he faced the half-naked women in the parlor. "Where are Miss Lily, Miss Rose, and Miss Peony?" he asked, unable to recall the last name among the Twelfth Street women.

"No Lily, Rose, or Peony here," replied a darkly sensual woman who looked almost thirty—by far the oldest. She spoke with an accent similar to that of the dead Violet. Her lower lip had been split perhaps a week earlier and was nearly healed, but under her right eye, although disguised with makeup, was a fresh black and blue hematoma that had not changed to green and yellow. Unlike the face of Pansy, he could not after more than three months recall clearly the images of the other women in the Twelfth Street assignation house. None of the assembled prostitutes awakened his memory.

"Tell Brown and Carew to bring that peacock inside, won't you?" John directed Stu.

While everyone else waited, John asked, "Does anybody here speak English?"

"A little bit," another among the prostitutes replied.

"What country do you come from?"

"I am from Sarajevo in Bosnia, with my friend," the oldest-looking said, nodding to the woman standing next to her. "These are from Montenegro. I teach all on way to America my little English."

"Did you all wish to come to America?" he asked.

The woman spat toward the corpse. "Yes. But could not get papers. Quota problem. Man in Sarajevo say if we pay much dinara, he will put us on ship. He promise we get good work in factory that make blouses. We pay him. Two weeks we are in bottom of ship. When we come to America, we put in other boat and soon go at night to big building. We must hide and be quiet until we go on train. Not train for people."

"You were put in a freight car?" John asked. "A car with no windows or seats?"

"Yes, yes so. Long time in train."

John said, "More than a day?"

"Yes. Almost two day."

"That sounds like a load of—" Larry broke in.

John shushed him immediately and asked, "What happened when you stopped?"

"We are with many trains. Big truck come up to door. We go inside truck."

Stu and the two supplementary ex-cops appeared from the rear of the house, with Stu pushing the fashionably dressed patron forward. The customer's eyes fixed on the corpse and the bloodstained floor.

"My God!" he exclaimed. Color drained from his face.

Le Brun said, "It's a little late to ask for the Almighty's help. You've stepped into some quicksand."

"Beau Brummel here ain't carrying any identification," Carew said.

"Nor would I if I were habituatin' whorehouses," Le Brun said, giving the elegantly dressed but dissipated-looking man a hard stare.

"But I can't be involved!" the house's customer lamented. "You don't realize—"

"I've already questioned these ladies about you," Le Brun lied, "so it will go badly if you should give false testimony. How many months have you patronized this place?"

The dandy's tongue circled his lips as he weighed his words. "A year. No, about fourteen months."

"How many times a week?"

The man laughed. "A week? What kind of a man do you think I am? But these are clean girls, not like—"

John held up his hand and shook his head solemnly. "If I ask you for the time, don't tell me how your watch is made. How often in those fourteen months did the choice of ladies change?"

The dandy's eyes blinked rapidly as he cast his mind backward. "There was one group here until the middle of April.

Miss Zinnia, Miss Aster, Gardenia, and Iris. Then, suddenly, they vanished, and there was a Pansy, Peony, Lily, Daisy—"

"Daisy!" John interrupted, snapping his fingers. "And a gal they called Rose."

The patron nodded. He noted a bit of dust on his sleeve and whisked it with the side of his hand. "Then they disappeared only a couple months later. I suppose it was in June."

"That jibes. As does the constant use of flower names. You have any idea where they went from here?"

"None."

"You didn't see them in another house?"

"No."

Le Brun noted that the former cops were not listening to him but rather fixated by the sight of the all-but-naked young beauties. "Mr. Brown, why don't you go upstairs and collect some decent wraps for these ladies?" As Brown reluctantly moved to follow the directive, John pointed to the spokesperson for the young prostitutes. "What is your name?"

She pointed to herself. "Jasincka. I am Jasincka."

A photograph of the city of Sarajevo from a travel book Le Brun had skimmed flashed before the eyes of his memory. "I do not want to hear your real name, Jasincka. Tell me the name they gave you when you left the train and they took away your clothes."

"Oh. I am Amaryllis. They are Anemone, Calla, Tulip, and Dahlia."

A violent pounding on the front door nearly drowned out her last word.

Le Brun ignored the racket. "Are there other men who—"

This time the door boomed from what John guessed was a police battering ram. "Shoot!" he yelled. "They must have put wings on. Mr. Carew, time to exit by the rear. We'll settle up soon." He gestured to Larry Wilker to open the door as Winston Brown rattled down the stairs with no female clothing

in his hands and followed Paddy Carew through the rear of
the house.

Lieutenant Bergman was the first of four officers from the
17th Precinct to enter the foyer. He held his arms out to halt
the men behind him as he encountered the body on the floor.

"This character tried to kill us," John hastened to say.

"Jesus!" Bergman exclaimed. "That complicates things."

"You're welcome," John said, scowling at the head
policeman.

"Yeah, thanks." He gestured toward the women. "Put them
all in the van." He nodded at the small man, who was still on
the floor nursing his jaw. "Him in the car with you and you
between," he directed his patrolmen. He then pointed toward
the patron in the four-button suit. "And who's he?"

The man drew himself up to his full height. "I am—"

"He's a valued customer," John broke in. "And he can tell
you a whole bunch."

"All right," said Bergman. "He can ride up front with me."

"But I'm—" the man protested.

"Shut up, whoremonger!" the lieutenant commanded.

"I need to come with you, too," Le Brun said with emphasis.

Bergman stepped back to let his men work. "No room.
Come see me tomorrow morning."

John pointed to Mutt, who was being hauled to his feet by
two of the officers. "But this Jasper—"

"Will be in custody when you arrive."

"I can catch a taxi right now," John persisted.

The lieutenant ignored his suggestion and barked at his
underlings to hurry. It was abundantly clear to Le Brun that
the invasion of another precinct had made him very nervous.
What was also clear was that he had taken the risk nonetheless.

"What about the body?" John asked him.

"Who shot him?"

"I did. Self defense."

"Leave him. And leave the door open behind you." Bergman's directive was given as he retreated through the front door.

John looked at Stuart Hirsch and Larry Wilker, who regarded him in silence. He lifted two of the Coronation cigars from his pocket and offered them to his associates. "Well, don't that take the rag off of the bush!"

THE AFTERNOON EXODUS of workers from Manhattan to Queens, Brooklyn, the Bronx, Staten Island, and the heights of New Jersey had begun when Le Brun arrived at Mary McMahon's apartment. Mixed smells of cabbage and brussels sprouts permeated the air.

"I've been on tenterhooks," Mary declared as John entered. "What happened?"

Le Brun was eager to lay out the events of the afternoon in detail to his clear-thinking associate. He brought a chair into the efficiency kitchen, set it backward, and crossed his arms on the back rail as he talked and Mary finished cooking supper.

"Mutt is a minor piece on the chessboard," John said in conclusion.

Mary's head went slowly up and down as her cooking spoon went round and round. "That's clear enough. The boss doesn't spend his day doing stakeout."

John held up one hand and began counting off fingers. "So, we still don't know who Mutt works for—except that it isn't Herbert Moore or Dietrich Diefendorfer."

Mary tasted the mutton she had prepared. She dipped her head with modified pleasure. "But he was almost certainly driving that van on the night your Miss Violet and all those others were killed. Meaning, whoever was minding the women in the back of the van is probably the same person Mr. Mutt was working for uptown."

"There was a chain and lock on the rear doors of the van," Le Brun said, "so only one man was needed for the transport. But two surely were necessary to unload the ladies. And two must have cooperated to kill Diefendorfer soon after they did their dirty work over on Twelfth Street." John ticked off a second finger. "We also don't know how they learned I was in the city. I'm sure the little critter wasn't watchin' your place on a regular basis before that."

"True. Mrs. Murray would have marched him away by the ear weeks ago."

John raised a third finger. "We don't know what happened to Lily, Daisy, Rose, and Peony."

"And we don't know how deep Lieutenant Bergman is involved," Mary added. "He sure got uptown fast enough."

"More than fifty blocks north and almost completely across the island," John said. "I think I'll know a great deal more tomorrow. He's crazy on several counts if he don't let me question that tough critter."

The telephone rang. Mary answered it and held it out for Le Brun.

"It's Larry," the familiar voice came through the line, his tone devoid of its usual ebullience. "About twenty minutes after you left, a pair of older men went up to the door and knocked on it. The door was left unlocked if you remember."

"I do."

"Well, they ventured inside. They came charging down the front steps about ten seconds later. They talked on the sidewalk and decided to walk away slowly. Twelve minutes later, two mounted cops arrived. No sign of the big boss."

"Too bad," John said. "Okay, you and Stu are done for the day. Check in with Mary early in the mornin'."

"Right." Wilker hung up. The connection, however, did not go dead.

"This call is done, operator," John said. He set the receiver on its cradle.

"I hate when they listen in," Mary remarked. "You think they'd be too busy to stay on the line."

John crossed the apartment to the kitchen alcove. "That's the least of our worries. I was hopin' the man in charge would walk into the place. He's either too smart or too lucky."

"You can't complain about luck, Mr. Le Brun," Mary advised with her eyebrow cocked.

John grabbed the chair and returned it to its place in front of the desk. "True enough, true enough, Mrs. McMahon. Well, we shall see if his luck or ours is better tomorrow."

Mary began setting the supper table. "Thomas Jefferson wrote, 'I am a great believer in luck, and I find the harder I work, the more I have of it.' The way you're working at this, you're sure to succeed. Shall I set a place for you?"

"I thank you," John said, reaching for his straw boater, "but the missus-to-be is expectin' me tonight. I'd better be there because tomorrow may prove even busier than today. I'll call you bright and early to let you know when Mr. Johnny Luppis should meet me at The Tombs."

CHAPTER SIXTEEN

September 17, 1908

JOHNNY LUPPIS PLOWED a straight furrow, right to the end of the row, as Le Brun's father had said of dependable men. He was not only of Croatian birth, but he also spoke the language of central Croatia, known as Kajkavian. Pansy did indeed speak the idiosyncratic dialect. As Mr. Luppis explained it, the area had been so overrun for millennia as a corridor between Europe and the Middle East that the local language was a mixture of no fewer than a half-dozen tongues.

John had not needed to coax Lordis to attend the interview session. His fiancée had invested deep sympathy for the plight of the young woman behind bars. She brought her a toiletries set and held her trembling hand for the first several minutes of questioning.

Pansy's proper name was Anja Ljubanovic. She was the eighth of ten children from a poor farm family. Hard times had demanded that Anja make her way in the world at age sixteen. She had relocated to the coast but had barely arrived when she was told by another central Croatian refugee about a man who could smuggle them into America. It had cost her every coin her parents had given her, but she was overjoyed at the opportunity to go to the golden land of dreams rather than just another depressed part of her country.

Like Jasincka from the West Side assignation house, Anja had spent almost two weeks out of sight in the dark bowels of a freighter. Her ship came into a freight harbor in New Jersey's Newark Bay. She and her eighteen-year-old companion, who was later given the name Peony, were offloaded in the middle of the night, driven by buggy for more than an hour, and guided by a man onto a passenger train terminating in Jersey City. They were the new girls among the group, which included Violet, Lily, and Rose. Violet let it be known that she was the woman in charge. She could make herself understood to Pansy and Peony when she wanted but most often spoke in the more common Croatian dialect or in her version of English. Pansy had been a prisoner in the house for seven months. With quivering lips, she told Luppis that she was forced to service an average of eight men each day. Le Brun was sure that her youth, innocence, and beauty had put her in high demand.

Pansy's description of the owner of the Twelfth Street assignation house matched the autopsy report for Dietrich Diefendorfer. However, according to the girl-woman, he had not been the one who shot Violet, the two house guards nor the patron. Nor, to John's amazement, had the little man he had dubbed Mutt. The first of the murderers matched the man Le Brun had shot in the West Side house, right down to Pansy's recollection of the bald, shaved head and the war eagle tattoo. The second was a "man with a very large belly who had much red hair, a bushy beard, and wire-rim half glasses." In spite of his girth, he had moved with surprising agility when he first entered the house, firing his revolver with deadly accuracy. After the murders had been committed, however, he shuffled as if his weight were a great burden. Her final observation of the man, who had barked commands at the other men, was that he wore gaudy rings on four of his fingers.

Mutt had not entered the Twelfth Street house but was first seen by Pansy when she and the other surviving women were herded into the back of the van. Jeff had taken brutal charge once the sex slaves had been relocated to the Upper West Side. He was the one, she stated, who doled out the frequent punches and slaps to keep the women docile. Neither he nor the small man had ever spoken anything but English.

Anja Ljubanovic's escape, which had by her calculation occurred eight weeks earlier, was in Le Brun's estimation quite clever. The assignation house doors were always kept locked and the first-story rear windows nailed shut. Anja's main duty when not on her back and under a client was that of laundress for the house. After soaking, scrubbing, and rinsing the endless baskets of bedclothes and shifts, she fed them through a wringer and then carried loads up to the second story, where a clothesline ran on pulleys over the back alley to the building opposite. Anja had used the line to swing out through the window. As she had hoped, the nearer pulley soon detached, causing the rope to arc down. She almost managed to keep to her feet as she reached the alley, only suffering a scrape to one knee. Long before her escape, she had noted that virtually all the homes along the alley used such clotheslines. By standing on a garbage pail, she was able to reach a fire escape and, from there, to steal clothing from a neighboring woman who was roughly her size.

As Le Brun had surmised, Anja's first goal was to flee eastward across Central Park in her borrowed clothing and slippers. Once she reached Lexington Avenue, she turned south toward the hotel district, where she could continue her debasing trade but keep and manage her earnings. Her ultimate goal was to hide enough money to travel to Pittsburgh. One of her kinder johns had spoken her dialect and told her that "thousands of our kind" work in honest jobs there. Her final goal, however, had been constantly thwarted by policemen who recognized her day-and-night street presence and her eagerness to entice passing men. By her estimation, she had spent about a third of her time since escaping the assignation house sitting in The Tombs. Le Brun was privately pleased that the city had unintentionally protected her so well through the summer.

"So," Warden Carnaby interrupted, with an impatient look, "we now have a description of the mastermind." He turned his attention to John. "She also can identify the man you shot and the man who drove the truck, and that doesn't take a knowledge of English. Let's bring her down to the mug-shot collection."

Lordis had lifted a brush from Anja's new kit and begun running it gently through the young woman's hair. The prostitute's hangdog look had vanished. John was not surprised that she still appeared leery of the group, but he perceived a growing sense that Anja finally dared to hope for salvation.

"May we accompany her?" John asked, nodding to include Lordis and Johnny Luppis.

"Yes, certainly," Carnaby granted.

The gathering trouped down to the second floor, where front and profile daguerreotypes of criminals were pasted into large albums. The New York Police Department had been gathering mug shots from the earliest days of photography. Since 1857, an official wall gallery of criminals' images had also been displayed on the first floor for the benefit of officers and citizens alike.

As Anja pored over the many pages of recent criminal images, John took Lordis out of earshot of the others and fixed her eyes with his intense gaze.

"I believe I can get this pathetic victim released to my recognizance. Would you consider inviting her into Whisperin' Hope?" John had little expectation that Lordis would allow the suggestion. She had the safety of two children as her first priority, and she was truthfully only an employee of the mansion owner, who was Sally Topley. To his delight, his beloved took several seconds to give the request serious consideration. Then she offered him an apologetic look.

"She deserves the best care," Lordis said. "However, there is the danger that horrid men are looking for her, which might put Ben and Leslie in jeopardy. Also, I am not around every hour to watch her, and she is justifiably desperate enough to vanish with the silverware."

"True enough," John said. "She is obviously hell-bent on gettin' to Pittsburgh."

"What about Mary McMahon's tenement?" Lordis suggested. "Obviously, we can't communicate with her, but Mr. Luppis lives on the same block."

"Excellent thought, my dear." John shied a glance at the unwilling prostitute. "Naturally not without first consultin' with Mrs. McMahon."

Anja exclaimed with excitement and pointed at one of the photographs in the bulging album. She had found the face of Mutt, whose real name was Walter Krause. He was thirty-four and had been previously convicted of breaking and entering a private home, burglary, shoplifting, fencing stolen goods, and robbery of a butcher shop.

"Nothin' with a weapon," John noted to the warden. "Which would support Anja's testimony that the killin' in the Twelfth Street house was done by two others." He told Carnaby of the different caliber bullets.

A few minutes later, Anja recognized the scowling image of the large man with the shaved, bald head and the eagle neck tattoo. His aliases included Alvin Zark, Albert Zark, Allen

Zook, and Alfred Zedd. His age was estimated at forty-one, and his rap sheet detailed a life of crime, starting at ten years old. Among his many dubious accomplishments, he had killed another man in a bar fight but been acquitted for self defense. He had served time twice for crimes committed with handguns.

Although Anja reviewed both albums from 1905 to 1908 two times, she was unable to find the corpulent man with "much red hair, a bushy beard, and wire-rim half glasses."

"You said that Miss Ljubanovic's sentence ends tomorrow?" John confirmed with the warden.

"Yes, but I also said that the Immigration Service would like to deport her. Now we know her country and town of origin."

"That hardly seems fair," John thought aloud. "She has just done a great service for your city, and she certainly has suffered enough, both in getting here and being enslaved."

"It was all due to her ignorance," Carnaby shot back. "She knew she was doing something illegal. How would you feel if you had waded through the paperwork of applications and waited months or years to come here legally, only to hear that she is in America ahead of you? There is such a thing as fairness, Mr. Le Brun."

"How many entered this land without papers between 1620 and 1800? Certainly not with the permission of those already livin' here," John replied, even though he knew he was not going to soften the man's heart with barbed rhetoric.

"And what did the savages do with this island in thousands of years?" the warden replied.

John smiled. "Nothing. Left it as the good Lord had created it."

"Exactly!"

"Well, it's good to know that Miss Ljubanovic will be safely in your care until tomorrow mornin' when Detective Bergman of the 17th Precinct will undoubtedly need to take her formal testimony."

"I'll want an address for the woman before she leaves," Carnaby said.

"Absolutely," John replied, as he thought, *Whatever it takes to get her out of here before the Immigration folk descend on her. I'll give him her last permanent address: the bordello on West End Avenue.*

CHAPTER SEVENTEEN

September 18, 1908

THE TAXI HEADED to the 17th Precinct was filled. Le Brun had engaged it on Eighth Avenue and ushered Johnny Luppis and Mary McMahon inside. On the way, John informally interviewed the Croatian transplant. The man earned his living receiving shipments of fresh flowers from nurseries and hothouses in North Jersey via ferry boat and distributing them by nine in the morning to some fifty locations in the financial district so that the foyers and offices of the most powerful brokerage houses and banking firms in the city might be brightened each day. John learned that the man had accustomed himself to rise at three in the morning, return to his tenement building by ten, and sleep through the late afternoon so that he could enjoy the nightlife of New York. He underscored that, for Mary, he had made an exception to his routine two days running. John suspected that the four dollars he was earning might have influenced the perpetually smiling fellow's generous gesture.

Once Anja Ljubanovic was released from The Tombs into Le Brun's recognizance and thence crowded into the taxi, Johnny abandoned conversation with John in favor of the very pretty woman. John could not fault the man, who was fifteen years Anja's elder, for his rapt attentions; Le Brun was roughly the same number of years older than Lordis, who was his personal treasure. Johnny took special pains to speak in her dialect and then translate one or two important words of her replies into English for her to practice. Since the former prostitute demanded so little in living space and since she made clear that her sights imminently were set on Pittsburgh, Mary had had no trouble with the notion of temporarily furnishing a corner of her basement for Anja.

Warden Carnaby had not bothered to attend the release of the prisoner. Nor had anyone in The Tombs spoken of the Immigration authorities wanting to grab the Croat girl. The previous day, John had been careful not to mention Mrs. McMahon to anyone in the jail. His guess was that if Immigration was merely late in pursuing Anja, they would send men first to the West End address and then over to the East Side and Whispering Hope. He smiled as he anticipated conducting them on a thorough tour. In truth, had Anja hidden there, the whimsically built mansion offered no fewer than three secret areas that no average investigator could find.

As soon as Anja and Johnny fell into conversation, Le Brun raised his copy of the *Herald* and began reading.

"Oh, sad day," he lamented to Mary.

"What's happened?" she obliged.

"'Yesterday, during flight trials to win a contract from the U.S. Army Signal Corps,'" John read aloud, "'pilot Orville Wright and passenger Lieutenant Thomas Selfridge crashed in a Wright Flyer at Fort Myer, Virginia. Selfridge has become the first passenger in America to die in an airplane accident.'" John lowered the newspaper and faced Mary. "For five years those brothers have been tryin' to interest our government in underwritin' their amazin' invention with no success. How shortsighted! What about the swift delivery of vital mail and packages? Pshaw! With all this rapacious imperialism around the world, there's gonna be a big war or two before long. Can't the military see that airplanes would be far superior to hot air balloons for reconnaissance over battlefields?"

Mary merely shrugged, never one to comment when she was out of her depth.

John returned his attention to the newspaper. "Apparently, the Army bowed to somebody's pressure, and a set of trials began at Fort Myer. Selfridge was assigned to evaluate from inside the plane. Poor fellow was only twenty-six. But this won't be the end of it, Mary. Mark my words. It's just one more astonishin' advance of our age."

"And yet we can't control prostitution any better," she remarked bitterly.

Le Brun sighed. "The sinful appetites of mankind, I'm afraid, will never be controlled by technology. In fact, technology may provide other pleasin' shapes the devil hath power to assume."

The group arrived at the 17th Precinct. Lieutenant Kasper Bergman awaited them in the headquarters lobby. He explained that since the young prostitute had no permanent address and had ample reason to disappear, her testimony would be secured by deposition. The process began by placing her in the corridor just outside Walter Krause's holding cell. The tiny tough had coolly acknowledged that he knew the woman. However, the moment she laid eyes on him, she began to gasp for breath and tremble. She affirmed that he indeed had been one of her guards since her forcible removal from the East Twelfth Street assignation house. He had, she declared, committed intercourse with her against her will on many occasions. He especially liked to whip her buttocks with his belt before having sex.

"But I never hit her in the face!" Krause barked through the bars. "If she says so, then she's a liar! Al done that. Not me!"

John drew Bergman down the corridor. "What have you gotten out of him?"

"Precious little. All we have to pressure him is a third-party complaint for loitering and his employment at the house, which he doesn't bother to deny."

"What about the fact that he raped her multiple times?" John asked.

Bergman's right eyebrow cocked. "A prostitute?"

"An *unwillin'* prostitute."

"Nonetheless. For the time he'll get, this one could do it standing on his head." Bergman cast a wary look up and down the corridor. "Now, if you're willing to testify that he was the one driving the van away from the slaughterhouse on East Twelfth, even a simple accomplice judgment would put him away for at least an extra two years."

"Can't do that," Le Brun replied.

"Why not?"

"Because I didn't see his face. I'd be perjurin' myself."

"You know it was him."

"Nonetheless."

Bergman made an unhappy noise deep in his throat. "You must have been a very good lawman in your day, to be successful *and* totally honest."

"I suppose I was," John replied. "Cocky as Krause is, I'll bet you have your own set of rules for convincin' him to cooperate. He must know the identity of the fat man with the spectacles and the red beard. He might also have been a participant in haulin' Dietrich Diefendorfer up on that steel beam. Maybe you could *suggest* that I'm willin' to testify to havin' seen him in the van."

"I'll do what I can," Bergman said, with no inflection of promise in his voice.

When the more difficult part of her deposition was completed, Anja was led to a meeting room, where a kindly looking police detective asked prewritten questions while a stenographer recorded her translated replies. Mrs. McMahon sat beside her and held her hand for moral support. Johnny winked and smiled at her in between translations. Bergman and Le Brun stood at a distance, with their backs against a wall, alternately listening and conferring.

"Did you receive any trouble from the brass at the 31st Precinct?" John inquired, speaking of the unusual invasion of one district's police into another's.

"Nah," Bergman said in a cocky tone. "I checked in with their captain as soon as we got back here. The whorehouse was getting too much business, too high a profile in the neighborhood. They'd had several complaints."

"I understand," John said. He understood that the 31st Precinct police could not raid the house because of payoffs and so were happy to have another precinct do the dirty work. "An awkward situation was resolved."

"Exactly."

"You should ask them to divulge the identity of the fat man with the red beard," John suggested under his breath.

"I did. The captain swore he never dealt with such a person. We need to be satisfied with the damage we've done: another high-end house closed down, and two exploiters of innocent, young women removed."

For a full minute, both men listened silently to the patient interrogation occurring across the long wooden table. Then John cleared his throat.

"What's the status of the other women you picked up yesterday?"

Bergman's face remained devoid of expression. "We took

their depositions first thing this morning and let them go."

Le Brun was frankly surprised at the reply. "Go where?"

"Who knows? Who cares? To hell, eventually. The pimps kill the whores; johns kill the whores; the pimps kill each other. The garbage takes out the garbage."

John realized that he had forgotten just how callous Bergman was. He reminded himself that he might be talking with a man far more deeply involved in the business of prostitution than merely accepting bribes to turn a blind eye.

"Just like that, you let them go," John needed to accuse.

"Actually, it was more active-like. We booted them the hell out and told them to keep walking until they were out of our district. I suggested—to the one who speaks English—that there are still well-off sodbusters and cattlemen out in Colorado, Wyoming, and Montana looking for mail-order brides."

"What about the federal law on the books since '75 requirin' convicted prostitutes to be returned to their country of origin?"

"Yeah, right." A smirk curled the corner of Lieutenant Bergman's mouth. "That law was written by Congressmen who live in a world of 'should be' and not 'what is.' Nobody wants to pay what it would cost to allow Immigration and Naturalization to pursue foreign whores or ship them back across the Atlantic. And the men who live in this city and visit it sure don't want them to go back home."

"Speakin' of the city's men . . . " John said. "Who was that peacock you picked up along with the women?"

"Peter B. Buelow IV. He's a nothing, but his father is a prominent stockbroker with Peabody. The son plays at business. Still lives at home. Periodically in trouble over drinking, gambling, frequenting the opium dens. Your friend Kevin O'Leary can tell you all about him. A total embarrassment to his family."

"What was he able to tell you about the owner of the house on West End Avenue?" John asked.

"Nothing," Bergman said. "We let him go early yesterday evening."

Le Brun laughed.

"What?" Bergman asked.

"Maybe his loser veneer is a partial act. Might Peter the Fourth be the mastermind we've been lookin' for? Y'know, Czar Peter. Did you ask the women about him?"

"No."

Le Brun made a mental note to ask Anja what she knew about the feckless-looking dandy.

"Look, Mr. Le Brun," the lieutenant hastened to say, "prostitution is like ivy or peppermint. Once the roots get hold, you never get rid of it. Be content that you rescued some sex slaves and saw that several pimps came to justice. Wanting anything more is just asking for disappointment." Bergman pushed himself away from the wall. "How much longer are you intending to visit New York this time?"

"I can't rightly say," John replied.

"Well then, I need to get a deposition from you as well. Let me take it down in my office right now to save time."

In spite of the unexpected successes he had had in the past two days, Le Brun was not satisfied. The supply route from Croatia to the United States had not been severed. The mastermind behind the murder of Dietrich Diefendorfer and the owner of the West End Avenue assignation house had not been discovered. The unknown man's motives were still a mystery.

Unknown to Lieutenant Bergman was that John Le Brun kept spearmint for juleps in two pots at the edge of his deck. During a fierce storm years earlier, the pots had fallen to the ground and broken. John had cleaned up the debris, but a piece of spearmint root had worked its way into the soil. By the time John noticed the problem, the roots had spread. At first he had pulled out every leaf that appeared, along with its stem and all he could find of the root. However, when the problem persisted, he disassembled part of his porch, dug a pit two feet by two feet by eighteen inches deep, set a fire burning in it for an hour, then used fresh soil to replace what he had removed. The problem vanished.

John Le Brun was not one to be satisfied with a half-finished conclusion.

CHAPTER EIGHTEEN

September 23, 1908

BY THE FOLLOWING Wednesday, much had occurred but little concluded. Instead of spending his nights traipsing around the entertainment spots of New York City, Jan "Johnny" Luppis worked diligently with Anja "Pansy" Ljubanovic to develop her English. Because Anja needed to stay out of sight of both Immigration officials and sex exploitation criminals, their sessions took place in Mrs. McMahon's parlor. However, Johnny made each visit touchingly exciting by bringing small presents such as bonbons or a packed pint of ice cream. He was smitten.

Four days of shadowing the past-thirty wastrel, Peter Buelow, had strongly suggested that he was nothing more than the little he seemed to be. The exercise had cost the John Le Brun Agency a great deal of money for no contribution to the case.

Since costs were piling up, John wanted to make sure that the bills would be paid. He took himself down to the banking district and the offices of J. P. Morgan and Company. He was almost certain that he would have no problem, considering the understanding of Morgan's desires John received at the Players Club, the fact that Morgan steadfastly considered his word his bond, and that the few hundred dollars John's agency had expended on the case meant nothing to a man who once said, "If you have to ask the price of a yacht, you have no business owning one." An even more amazing story of Morgan's disdain for the particulars of spending money had come to John's ears in 1906. It seemed that the Harvard Medical School wanted to rebuild itself from scratch on Longwood Avenue in Boston. A school representative had, with protracted effort, finally scheduled a meeting with Morgan to consider a contribution for the construction of the new campus. It was to contain five massive, white marble buildings. The man rolled out one architectural blueprint after the other and began his presentation.

"I'm afraid I'm very busy this morning," Morgan interrupted. He pointed to two of the renderings. "I'll pay for this one and this one. Just send me the bills."

John entered the ground floor of the financial titan's headquarters and announced himself. He was asked to wait. About a quarter hour later, an impeccably dressed young man with perfectly coiffed hair strode out of a side door and walked up to Le Brun, who rose and prepared himself to march into the bowels of the building.

The young man offered his hand. "I'm Mitchell Rockwell," he said. "One of Mr. Morgan's junior partners. He wants to know if you have determined the identity of the man who misused his name to launch one of your investigations."

John was certain that Rockwell had relayed Morgan's request verbatim.

"I have rescued six women trapped into sex slavery," he reported, "and I have seen that several of their oppressors have been brought to justice. The counterfeiter of Mr. Morgan's stationery, however, I am still investigatin'."

Junior Partner Rockwell nodded crisply. "In that case, I have been instructed to tell you that Mr. Morgan wishes you to continue the investigation. He will, naturally, pay whatever expenses you incur." As if by prestidigitation, a business card appeared in Rockwell's right hand. "This is my personal telephone number and address. I will be your conduit and paymaster from this point on until the conclusion of the matter."

John smiled broadly. "I must say, you are the most dashin' conduit I have ever met, Mr. Rockwell."

Rockwell tipped his head to one side and flashed a beguiling dimple. "And I must compliment you on the high estimation Mr. Morgan has for your detective talents. He also declared his delight that you are raising awareness of the seamy business of prostitution in our city. He called it a 'blight.'"

"On many levels," John replied. He slid Rockwell's card into his billfold. "Let me not detain you further from your other duties, sir."

Out on the street, making his way north on Broadway with St. Paul's Chapel in sight, Le Brun shook his head in wonderment at the complex nature of John Pierpont Morgan. The long-married, flabby man with manic eyes and an acne-scarred cauliflower for a nose, had had at least six mistresses in his time. His treatment of women was far from gallant. And yet, as he had taken Mark Twain to task for presuming to become a businessman, Morgan had no qualms in vilifying any other man with an extramarital sexual appetite.

John bought a newspaper and caught the train north. He shook his head at the article on the passing of Richard "Dickey" Pearce, one of the first men to earn enough money to play professional baseball full time. John had followed the

Brooklyn man's life with unabated interest. Like Le Brun, he was not especially big, at five foot three and 161 pounds. John's features also resembled his sports hero, with his brown hair, handlebar moustache, and ever-alert eyes. What truly induced John to identify with the baseball player were two aspects of Pearce's career. First, he had been an innovator, inventing both the shortstop position and the bunt. Secondly, when he was too old to play, instead of walking away from the game completely, he had served as a highly competent umpire.

Although he had promised the afternoon and evening to Lordis, John stopped at Mary McMahon's tenement and let himself inside. He expected that Mary would not be home. She had been overjoyed to receive pavement-pounding work from her boss the previous Saturday. Because the apparent libertine, Peter B. Buelow IV, had seen Stuart Hirsch and Larry Wilker in the West End assignation house, they were risky to use as tails. Instead, Mary and her socialite friend, Alice Ainsworth, were teamed with the ex-policemen, as the tandem point guards following Buelow from his parents' mansion on the Upper East Side near Eighty-first Street. When the character ventured into crowded saloons or Chinatown "opium joints" on Mott or Pell Streets, Stu and Larry took over. In four days of watching the ne'er-do-well, he had betrayed no evidence of owning high-priced brothels. Moreover, being dragged into the 17th Precinct had, at least temporarily, cured him of visiting such places. John and Mary agreed that if Buelow behaved himself on the fifth day, watching him further would be futile.

John went about the chores of writing checks and returning calls of those who wanted detective services. About an hour into his visit, Mary entered the parlor. She looked tired and expelled air strongly enough to puff out her cheeks.

"Nothing today either?" John asked.

"Nothing. He left his parents' home at ten minutes to ten and went straight down to his father's place of business. I suppose he's putting in required presence time today."

"So Buelow is a dead end."

"We're ninety-nine percent sure. I checked with O'Leary, like your Lieutenant Bergman suggested. Peter B. the Fourth spends time in Chinatown at least twice a week. Frequents a Chinese laundry with a false door at the back. O'Leary says most white folk get tired of being fleeced by the Chinks and buy their opium and paraphernalia for use at home. Of course, Peter B. dares not waft the pungent smoke around his old man's mansion." Mary lowered her posterior wearily to a chair. "If you ask me, the prime suspect is Bergman himself. He realized how profitable it is to run the operations, as opposed to getting just a small cut for protecting them. Surely, through his own precinct arrests and access to police records throughout Manhattan, he could recruit experienced bastards to run the places, once he'd seen that the original owners were eliminated."

"He does have a stone for a heart," John granted.

"And you said he made it up to West End Avenue in record time," Mary added. "Wouldn't he just, in order to control the investigation?"

"But what about the fat man with the spectacles and the red hair?" John asked her.

"I say he's Bergman's number-two man. Bergman can't exactly run several houses while he's also playing police lieutenant."

John longed for one of his Havana cigars so he could relax enough to associate all the facts of the case. "If it is him, he can wait me out. He certainly makes enough in his city job to live off of it." He closed his eyes. "He said he just let the women from the West End house walk away. Maybe he had them transported to yet another of the high-priced bordellos."

"He would be almost impossible to shadow," Mary decided.

John said nothing.

"So, now what?" Mary asked.

"I return to Georgia," John decided. "I'll spend a couple more days here with Lordis and then take that long train ride back. In the meantime, I made certain that Mr. Morgan would continue to foot the bill on this case." He removed Junior Partner Mitchell Rockwell's business card from his wallet and set it on Mary's desk, explaining the billing process Morgan desired. Then he turned to face his agency manager full on. "Here's what the rest of you will do: whenever Stu or Larry are not busy with other agency business and feel like earnin' more dollars, they should watch the remainin' assignation houses we know about." He snapped his fingers. "In fact, they and Kevin O'Leary should compile a list of such houses throughout Manhattan. Frank Cobb, over at the *World*, told me there were some ninety in all the boroughs. But I'll bet since the high-earners mostly live in and visit Manhattan, at least sixty of them must be on this island. Use my name and get whatever information on them that Mr. Cobb has." A twinkle lit John's good eye. "Heck, you and Alice can do a bit of watchin' from time to time as well, if you're of a mind. It would go a long way toward closin' this case if one of you spotted a portly man with red hair, wire-rim spectacles, and fingers filled with rings comin' or goin'."

"And what if the 'dicks' on your staff need to investigate some of these houses from the inside?" Mary asked, through a smirk.

"I'll let you decide what gets underwritten there," John answered.

"And for how long do we keep this case open?" the agency manager asked.

John shrugged. "Until Morgan dies or stops payin' the bills."

CHAPTER NINETEEN

October 23, 1908

JOHN WHITE WAS the designated host of the New Century Club for the month of October. John Le Brun found the extremely wealthy insurance man to be the dullest member of the club. White had never traveled farther south than Jacksonville, west past Atlanta, or north beyond Charleston. The region's ex-sheriff suspected that the hunter's stew White presented had been hunted and cooked for him, and a simple inquiry of the ingredients proved that the pastry delights were not of his making. His sole personal interest was butterfly collecting, but since many of his desiccated insect corpses were delicate, he refused to transport the display cases across the water to the former Retreat Plantation for a club meeting. The host elected to speak on the migration of the Monarch butterfly, but his notes had blown overboard on the ferry. What he could recall took only ten minutes to recite. He apologized profusely for his failings, but Le Brun waved his words away.

"I for one now know a great deal more about the creatures," he said. "Another fascinatin' fact would have crammed my brain too full. I have a suggestion how we might extend this portion of our meetin', however. As y'all know, the ancient Greek philosophers preached 'a sound mind in a sound body.' What say we use our extra time to amble over to the lighthouse and exercise these old bodies?"

The suggestion was accepted by all, if not entirely with enthusiasm. The St. Simons Sound lighthouse thrust up above the trees in clear view of Retreat. It was the third iteration of the important structure and was some 104 feet tall. Garland DeBrahm had brought along his prized Kodak camera and a tripod and announced that he wanted to take a group photograph. John wondered if the shot would not look more dramatic in front of the lighthouse, and Garland agreed enthusiastically.

The members broke into subgroups. Le Brun led the way with only Merriweather Gooderly game enough to match his pace. The warehouseman puffed lightly after only an eighth of a mile, but he had enough wind to maintain a conversation.

"I was unaware that you had left for New York in September until three or four days after the fact," Merri said. "Even if I had known, I was too engaged to break away."

That was a mercy, John thought. Since learning by chance the man's secret scheme for buying Retreat Plantation and establishing a golf course and clubhouse, he had mistrusted him. He knew himself to be something of an open book regarding his attitudes toward others; invariably they appeared on his face. He lectured himself to behave politely.

"I left a day or two before you returned, so our paths may have crossed," Gooderly went on. "Perhaps in our nation's capital since I'm trying to secure business there as well."

"I see," John said neutrally.

"When I arrived in New York, I read in the *World* that you had been involved in the closing of another bordello." When John failed to reply, Merri asked, "Was the article correct?"

"It was."

"The *World* has also posted a reward of two hundred dollars for information leading to the arrest of some red-haired, heavyset character described by one of the prostitutes," Merri announced.

"A reward? I hadn't heard," said John.

"Yes, indeed. So, clearly you failed to solve every aspect of the case?"

"I failed indeed."

"Pity. Frank Cobb, the head editor of the *World*, is your personal friend, is he not?"

"I would call him a good acquaintance."

"I thought perhaps, failing to solve these linked cases completely yourself, you prevailed on him to offer the reward to someone who could."

"No, it must have been his idea . . . or Mr. Pulitzer's."

Gooderly grunted his mild surprise. "Your turn to play host for the club comes up again in February. I hope you'll speak on this business and how you have applied your sheriff experience and natural talents thus far. Or are you content to let full-time professionals of the law finish up?"

"I am bein' patient," John replied, speaking of both the cases and Gooderly. As he had in June, he felt a distinct tinge of false solicitude from the man, an oblique jab in the ribs, as if to imply, "I am better at my business endeavors than you ever were at yours, even if you play a slightly better game of chess than I." Provoked this second time, John determined to deliver a powerful counterpunch and to do it almost immediately.

The group reached the lighthouse station and fell into ready conversation with Harry Farsett, the keeper. In order to be able to get all eight members of the club in the photograph, Farsett was pressed into service. The precious camera was positioned on its tripod and prefocused by its banker owner. After several images were captured of the group of smiling men, John asked the keeper, "Would it be all right if we climbed to the top for a view?"

"No more than four at a time," Harry responded.

"No problem there," said Patrick Ebenezer. "I'm not that adventurous, and I'll wager a few others will keep me company down here."

Claudius Tatnall, Gilbert Reynolds, and John White shared his attitude, leaving John, Merri, Garland DeBrahm, and architect Irwin Jones to brave the 129 cast-iron circular steps.

When the more fit and adventurous men at last reached the top deck, the autumn sun hung low in the west.

"I can see the water tower and the turret of the Jekyl Island clubhouse," John said, facing south and leaning on the rail.

"Excellent view," Jones admired. "Look at those three behemoth yachts rafted up in the Jekyl River."

"I'll try to get a photograph," Garland said, "although they're pretty far away, and the light is failing."

When he had finished with the panoramic shot, the amateur photographer set about taking full-face shots of John, Irwin, and Merriweather as well as profile images of each looking out over the lofty railing or studying the giant Fresnel lamp and its housing.

John ambled clockwise to the western side. In his near view sat the decayed remains of Retreat Plantation. Farther away lay marshland, copses of trees, rushes, intermixed weeds and flowers, small ponds, and hillocks.

Le Brun said, in an offhand manner, "Y'know, there are more and more enterprisin' folk makin' millions around our country but not enough millions to break into the infamous Jekyl Island Club. The demand for private homes and resorts on St. Simons and Sea Islands will grow exponentially in the next few years. And why not accommodate that demand? Together, they're almost as big as Manhattan Island, and their natural attributes are the same as Jekyl Island."

"Unless yet another breakout of yellow fever strikes," Merriweather remarked, "or a hurricane like the one that damaged the Jekyl Island Club buildings. Or the entire country is hit with another depression."

"All mere bumps in the road," John countered, "which is becomin' paved over, thanks to all the horseless carriages. Those roads will also entice families to travel. Look at Retreat, gentlemen. Excellent view, sea breezes, and over there"—he pointed—"the perfect location for an eighteen-hole golf course. I can almost see the water hazards, the doglegs, the sand traps. Why are we merely rentin' the plantation when we could form a consortium, buy it, and reap the inevitable profits?"

"For a man with one good eye, you have amazing vision," Irwin Jones quipped.

"I could check on the owners' interest and what price they'd be willing to sell it for," Merriweather volunteered, the instant Jones finished his sentence. John noted that his eyes were fixed on those of Garland DeBrahm, the banker, in what could easily have been interpreted as a warning.

"Why don't you let me do it?" Jones asked. "My brother-in-law is the most respected real estate agent in the county." He laughed. "I'll bet Claude Tatnall would jump on John's idea. He's always saying 'Son, invest in land; they're not makin' any more of it.' And he would stand to make a tidy profit using the local lumber right here instead of payin' to ship it hither, thither, and yon." He shrugged at Gooderly. "A bit of a loss to you, Merri, but your Sure-Tite Warehouse will recoup it when more tourists arrive."

Le Brun smiled down on the broad sweep of unexploited lowland. *It appears that Irwin is not part of Gooderly's scheme. The excrement should strike the fan blades within the next week, and let's see what happens with the big warehouseman's secret machinations then. Maybe more than just I will be quittin' the New Century Club.*

On the way back to the clubhouse, John shared with Patrick and Gilbert his "sudden inspiration" concerning the purchase of Retreat Plantation. Irwin spoke about the idea with animation to Claudius Tatnall and John White. Merriweather Gooderly took up the rear, walking by himself.

CHAPTER TWENTY

October 24, 1908

AT THIRTEEN MINUTES past three in the morning, only hours after returning from the latest get-together of the New Century Club, John Le Brun awoke with a start. He had been dreaming. It was a confused jumble of images. The first was the drowned body of the never-identified young woman who had stolen the boat from John. The second was of her alive, standing in front of Merriweather Gooderly's warehouse. It was not the smaller one that held precious cargoes but rather the large one in which he gathered raw goods such as lumber and naval stores. Another of the lifelike people flashing through his mind included Violet, directing him to the cane that had murdered Herbert Moore, and Pansy being herded into the dark van by Alvin Zark, Walter Krause, and the shadowy figure of a large man who wore wire-rimmed half glasses and many rings and had a beard with bushy, red hair. Finally, he saw every New York City prostitute he had ever met, including Morning Mary, who had solicited John in 1906, standing dejectedly in front of a waterfront tavern while passing men in workmen's uniforms pawed them. He pivoted in his dream and saw half a dozen ships moored at nearby docks. A shrill horn sounded in his mind. He expected it to be from one of the ships, but no puff of white steam shot up over the East River. He realized that the sound was that of a steam locomotive. And yet there were no tracks or engines in the southeast corner of Manhattan.

John willed himself to awaken. He sat up in his bed, soaked in sweat and gasping for air. Suddenly, the many pieces of the complex puzzle seemed to have fallen into place.

John knew he would be unable to return to sleep. He found his slippers, scudded into them, and moved carefully into the dark kitchen. He turned on the single electric light that illuminated the space when the sun was down. With the assurance that comes from thousands of practices, he set about brewing a pot of coffee. While he waited for the water to boil, he returned to the bedroom and fetched the notepad and pencil he always kept ready by his night table. Then, with the cup filled, he began assembling facts.

LE BRUN WAS WELL AWARE of the hour the first ferry of the day crossed from the mainland to St. Simons Island. He waited on the dock as it made ready and was the first passenger aboard. It was necessary for him to walk to the home of Esau Butler, the teenager who kept the grounds around Retreat from lapsing into total ruin, in order not to have to wait for the first driver who wanted to make money transporting island visitors.

When Esau's mother appeared at her front door wearing an apron and an annoyed expression, John apologized and asked for her son's assistance. Esau emerged from the rough little house within three minutes. Sitting atop the family wagon beside the teenager, John engaged him in what he hoped sounded like a simple conversation meant to while away the journey.

"You of course know about the club a few of us have at the old King mansion, Esau."

"Yes, sir."

"And that we take turns makin' meals for each other."

"I know that, too."

"Well, when it was my turn, I must have left a big spoon behind because I haven't been able to locate it since then."

"Sorry to hear."

"A valuable spoon. Silver. Part of a set and impossible to replace. I need to get into the mansion's cellar. Do you have a key?"

"No, sir," the driver said through a yawn. "I keep all the stuff for tendin' the trees, trimmin' the bushes, rakin' and such in the old cold house. I got a key for the upstairs of Retreat, but I tries never to use it. And the inside door goin' down to the cellar is as shut tight as the outside one."

"I see." John expelled a theatrical breath of frustration, in spite of the lock-picking tools in his jacket. "Then how can I investigate for my spoon?"

A sly smile stole onto Esau Butler's face. "Once, when he didn't know I was around, Mr. Gooderly picked up a stone near the back door. He finds a key and goes right down."

John was pleasantly surprised at the news. "If I find my spoon, Esau, you shall have an extra quarter for your excellent help."

"Thank you, sir!"

John waggled his forefinger. "And of course you must never tell anyone you were spyin' on Mr. Gooderly. That might lose you your job."

Esau made a crisscross sign over his lips, then snapped the reins smartly.

"WHY DON'T YOU DO some yard work as long as you're here?" John suggested to the young caretaker. "That way, you'll be earnin' money three ways this mornin'."

"No wonder everybody say you so smart, sir," Esau observed as he hopped down from the wagon, grabbed the reins, and pulled his horse toward the cold house.

John found the key right where Esau said it would be. He cleaned it of soil, inserted it into the lock, turned the tongue back, and felt the door relax. As soon as he went through and down, he locked the door from the inside.

Throughout the South, cellars are rare enough. In the lowlands, where the water table is high, they are all but nonexistent. The fact of Retreat's cellar had not escaped Le Brun's attention. It had rather piqued his curiosity as soon as the possibility of Gooderly smuggling sex slaves into the country came to him. The cellar ran only half the length of the large house. As did so many of the stately mansions of the region, Retreat had a veranda, which once held wicker furniture and rocking chairs. The veranda and the house's first level stood three steps—twenty-seven inches—above the ground. The cellar had only been dug down thirty-six inches so that anyone descending into it would need to move either by crawling or bending almost double. John expected that the outdoor furniture had once been stored there, along with garden and orchard tools.

The claustrophobic space was lit only by a pair of windows that faced each other on the east and west sides. John was not surprised when no lanterns could be found. A makeshift floor of rough pine covered the back third of the area. At one corner of the floor, ten blankets were neatly stacked. They were relatively fresh, given the condition of the rest of the space. Eight pillows with quasi-clean pillowcases were piled alongside the blankets.

John examined the windows. Both had iron bars that obviously had been installed in recent years. He tested each and found it well anchored into the tabby foundation.

Except for the floor and the bed materials, the only other item was a porcelain chamber pot, rinsed but still smelling faintly of human excrement. To John, the space looked like an inhumane prison detention cell.

From his inside suit pocket, Le Brun produced a large, silver-plated spoon. Wherever the dirt did not seem hard packed, he dug down several inches. Time and again, he found nothing. He swore under his breath as he came off his knees. As he bent to brush off the dirt, his attention was caught by a bit of color between two of the floor stringers. He curled his fingers into a five-sided claw and eased them toward the item. On the second try, he captured it and duck-walked to one of the windows. It was half of the outer wrapping of a package printed in bright red, decorated on the top surface with a painting of rural mountains. Beneath the image were words not in English. John was certain that the package had come all the way from the Balkins.

Le Brun carefully pushed his prize into a trouser pocket. He exited the cellar, locked the door, and hid the key. He found Esau mowing the grass around the front of the mansion. He held his spoon up and grinned.

"This is a lucky day for us both!" he called out.

Esau left the mower right where he had stopped.

JOHN LE BRUN ENTERED the office space he had occupied for nearly two decades. An electric-powered clock replaced the weight-driven Regulator John had carted away when he retired. The window had been recently cleaned, and the many stacks of papers were neatly arranged in an open cabinet within its dividers. He suspected the touch of his niece Aurelia, Warfield

Tidewell's wife, in the sheriff's office. During his service, his steel-trap memory had not needed such order and therefore never got it. Warfield had been playing a game of solitaire when John entered, indicating a slow Saturday morning. It was the unique version that Le Brun had taught him. John picked up the draw deck, riffled through it, looked at the four build piles, and shook his head.

"You won't win this one," Le Brun counseled. "Too many vital cards buried beyond your grasp. It's how I felt about the business with those bordellos up in New York . . . until early this mornin'."

Warfield set down the cards in his hand, his attention fully diverted. "Tell me."

John sat. "My apologies to Charles Dickens, but mine is also a tale of two cities. Perhaps more than two." He pushed three pages of penciled notes in front of Sheriff Tidewell. "Let's begin on the day that you and I investigated and solved the business with the Goulds' stolen paintin's."

"A masterful bit of detective work," Tidewell praised.

"Masterly, War," John corrected gently. "Masterful is behavin' like a slave owner. You and I are most definitely not slave owners. But I strongly believe Merriweather Gooderly is."

The sheriff's face telegraphed his astonishment. "You believe *he's* the one behind all the crimes in New York? That's mighty far away."

"And yet *I* run a business in New York City, from Brunswick, Georgia." Le Brun let the fact sink in. "Is our fair town not the fifth largest seaport on the Eastern seaboard?"

"It is."

"And because New York City has such a high demand for prostitutes, do you believe its harbor patrol is lax in inspectin' incomin' ships for human cargo?"

"I would think not," Tidewell answered his old mentor. "But Brunswick only gets some seasonal opportunists looking to earn easy cash. Not women lacking virtue tumbling from foreign ships."

John elected not to point out that some of the young women he was working to save undoubtedly had never engaged in sexual intercourse until forced. "I don't want to put notions into your head, War. You decide." He pointed to his notes. "You noticed right away that Gooderly is extremely conceited in terms of his intelligence. I'll grant he's quite shrewd, but not as much as he thinks. He was very vexed that someone foxed him on beatin' all the security measures he had put in place over at the Sure-Tite buildin'."

"True enough."

"And what does he do the moment he realizes my reputation for what Mr. Poe calls 'ratiocination' is not exaggerated?"

"He invites you to lunch."

"He had already begun inquirin' around town about me. At this lunch, he invited me to become a member of his New Century Club. Wasn't that interestin'?"

"Especially since you don't have half the money or the social standing of any of the other members," Warfield returned, in the unguarded fashion that Le Brun appreciated.

John rocked back on two legs of his chair. "I'm the first one to admit it . . . with no embarrassment. Do you know who first said, 'Keep your friends close and your enemies closer'?"

"Probably Machiavelli," Tidewell guessed.

"He certainly adopted the strategy, but the first known writer to record the idea was a general from about a thousand years earlier: Sun Tzu of China."

"And you believe that's exactly what Gooderly set out to do with you."

"Because I am his natural enemy. Remember that the man has two warehouses in town. The second one, fairly far from the main dockside traffic, is larger. Big enough to hide illegal immigrants comin' in from across the Atlantic. At least for a day or two."

"My God! History repeats itself," said Tidewell. "That vessel, the *Wanderer,* offloaded the last illegal cargo of black slaves over on Jekyl Island."

"A full fifty years after the law was passed that ended such importations," John said. "And you recall the Ibo slaves who drowned themselves whilst bein' offloaded onto St. Simons Island. Anyone who wants to revive the practice can't do it on Jekyl anymore. Not with the passel of club guards patrollin' that shore night and day. But St. Simons is a different matter. Especially with the plantation on the far south end all but in ruins and only used once a month."

John dug into his trouser pocket and brought into the late-morning light the paper packet with the painting of the isolated mountains. "I visited Retreat early this mornin'. Managed to get into the locked cellar. I found this. I am willin' to bet the writin' is from somewhere north of Greece." He told about the floor, the blankets, the pillows, and the bars recently installed in the cellar windowsills. "The women surely anticipated a degree of deprivation makin' their illegal trip, but I'll wager they got some niceties along the way to prevent them from suspectin' their true fate. Like liquor, blankets, and pillows."

"I follow you," Sheriff Tidewell said. "But why bring them to Retreat? Why not let them stay on the ship that brought them over the ocean, right into our port?"

"An important question. First of all, because our port inspectors are diligent in their jobs, and Gooderly—not bein' a local or even well regarded around the docks—fears failure in tryin' to bribe any of them. Second, because Gooderly has the means to offload each group out at sea. Who is the owner of the largest deep-sea fishin' concern in Glynn County?"

"Patrick Ebenezer!" Warfield avidly supplied.

"A fast crony of the warehouseman and the third New Century Club member. His fleet goes out in early mornin' and comes in well before nightfall. One of his shallow-draft trawlers could come alongside an ocean vessel and pick up a cargo of women. On the way through St. Simons Sound they could use a dinghy to drop off the women at the old dock. The women, eagerly cooperatin' in their illegal arrival, would willingly hurry into Retreat's cellar. Then, at a time most propitious— say on a moonless night or when a load of lumber or cotton is ready to ship north by rail—a trawler could be sent out to fetch them to Gooderly's larger warehouse."

"What did he name it . . . Dry Goods & Lumber. But one young woman got loose along the way," Tidewell contributed.

"The one who drowned in the bay. I would guess she considered herself a good swimmer and jumped overboard a few hundred feet from land. I'm thinkin' maybe just above the lighthouse."

The sheriff's imagination had ignited fully. He pushed aside the pages of notes and leaned toward Le Brun. "I can see it clear as noon. She's a smart one. She doesn't want to be taken all the way to New York. Probably suspects a double-cross. When she gets ashore, she has no idea she's on an island. She avoids the shoreline and moves west through the deep brush."

"Wearin' those homemade shoes with no style," John added.

Right. That's how she got so many scratches and insect bites."

"And sunburned."

"She crosses the width of St. Simons, finds it's not the mainland, and doubles back. She knows she needs something that floats, and she comes upon Iley Rutledge's catboat. Clearly, she doesn't know how to sail, but she's desperate. She's knocked out when the wind changes, falls overboard, and drowns. We can't identify her because nobody in Glynn County, nobody in America, has ever seen her."

"As good an explanation as any," John praised. "An Occam's razor theory if ever there was one."

The former student nodded at his mentor's reference. "So how do we prove it? Tramp freighters often don't have set ports of call and only rough schedules. They pick up cargo as they can. Therefore, we can't know when there would be a transfer from ship to Retreat's cellar."

"I agree," John said.

Warfield gathered up his playing cards and hid them in his top drawer. "Which means Gooderly would be stowing the women and shipping them north at unpredictable times as well. So, even if I had the manpower to watch either place, or both, somebody would get wise quickly. There's virtually no spot for hidden observation near the warehouse. And there's no reason for anyone, legal or illegal, staking out the plantation."

"Which leaves us what?" John asked.

Warfield gave out a small bray. "Why should I play this game when you no doubt already have the answer?"

"I do not," John replied coolly. "If you conduct a search of the Dry Goods & Lumber warehouse, even on a carefully constructed pretext, he's going to smell a rat."

"It takes a rat to smell a rat," Tidewell exclaimed in frustration.

"I believe it's time to investigate his background," John said. "If his family was as prominent as he claims, it shouldn't be difficult to get the low-down on him. I think I'll take my semiannual trip up to Atlanta early this year."

CHAPTER TWENTY-ONE

October 26, 1908

"I AM JOHN Le Brun."

The chief of the Atlanta Police Department straightened up so sharply that it seemed to John as if he had come to attention. He thrust out his right hand and grasped John's with vigor.

"Sheriff Le Brun! I must say that I am pleased as punch to meet you at last," Chief Renfro gushed, pumping John's hand up and down. "Sit! Please." He eased his bottom onto the edge of his desk and beamed down at his guest. "You know, even before that business with the carpenter shipping stolen paintings to Talmidge Warehouse, I knew of your exploits. We had a reporter travel down to Brunswick a few years past to interview you."

"I recall," John said, wondering how long he would have to endure the praise being heaped on him.

"He should have looked you up for the Jekyl Island murders

case—"

"He was only a teenager when that happened," John pointed out.

"Well, they should have sent somebody. But he covered your solving of those club murders in London in excellent fashion."

Painted it in purple prose with a broad brush, John thought. When he had finished reading the February 1906 article, he felt as embellished as one of the Wild West celebrities in Ned Buntline's dime novels.

"Anyway, I can now repeat, this time in person," said Renfro, "that the Atlanta Police Department is personally indebted to you for helping us solve a rash of local robberies and shutting down a national fencing cooperative."

Following the solution of the missing paintings in Gooderly's Sure-Tite Warehouse, Le Brun had telephoned Chief Renfro and made him aware of the address on carpenter Quinten Banks's crate and the route it would take to get there. The Talmidge warehouse had turned out to be an innocent conduit, but the location of the receiver of the crate was filled with both precious items stolen from upscale Atlanta homes and many other items imported from several other cities. Within days, thieves and fencers from Raleigh to Biloxi had been arrested.

"I am gratified to think that you may feel a degree of indebtedness to me," John dangled.

"Indeed. How can we help you, Sheriff Le Brun?"

John handed the chief his business card. "Now merely a private detective. I wonder if one of your officers or clerks could check back on the years 1895 to 1900 and see if a certain Merriweather Gooderly had any arrests?" He spelled the name aloud.

"Certainly. It will take several hours, naturally."

"Does that name resonate with you, sir?" John asked. "I was given to understand that the Gooderlys are a prominent

Atlanta family."

The chief shook his head ponderously. "No. Now, I'm not even remotely related to our local bluebloods, but I know all the surnames. Somebody's pullin' your hind leg."

"I'm not surprised," John rejoined. "While I'm waitin' on your help, I might get a few other chores done. Could you give me the name and address of a shop that can print up a sample letterhead right quick?"

"Certainly." Renfro scribbled the information on a scrap of paper. "You tell Charlie I said to stop everything and accommodate you." He pushed the paper across his desktop.

In turn, John shoved a printed list toward the chief. "And can you confirm that these are the major railroad warehouses in the city?"

Renfro studied the list. "Seems right. All on the west side. Oh, here's one named Gooderly's. Is that the focus of your investigation?"

"Actually a single man is," Le Brun answered. "No one to concern yourself with, sir. He's Brunswick's problem, not yours. I'll be back this afternoon concernin' the background on that person."

CHAPTER TWENTY-TWO

October 27, 1908

JOHN LE BRUN stifled the urge to sneeze in the dust of the old warehouse. It was one of the dozens erected after the scorched-earth burning of Atlanta by Confederate General John Bell Hood in the fall of 1864. After the war, the relatively small city burgeoned since it remained the convergence point of so many high roads and railroads. In the detective's judgment, forty years after too-hasty construction, the drafty warehouse had almost outlived its usefulness. John looked up from his notepad and across the dusty desk at the owner, Thomas Gilmer.

"So you bought the place from Mr. Merriweather Gooderly directly," John said.

"Not a week after he had *legally* inherited it from his brother," Gilmer replied. The grandfatherly looking man seemed to be weary to the bone, although he had handled

Le Brun's half-dozen questions with patience. John had handed the man the sheet of stationery the print-shop owner had created the previous day. The handwriting on the supposed letterhead of the Greater Charleston Assurance Company was his own. It empowered the John Le Brun Detective Agency to investigate a claim for a nonexistent $10,000 life insurance policy on Algernon Gooderly. The previous afternoon, a visit to the Atlanta Bureau of Records had revealed that Merriweather had an older brother, who died in the early winter of 1899. Having experienced evidence of the Brunswick warehouseman's nefarious nature and suspecting a great deal more, John was immersed in the methodical process of learning just how far back Merriweather's criminal activities went.

"Just as he legally inherited from his brother the other warehouse over on Marietta," John said.

"That's right. That one still has the name Gooderly's on the side, even though it was taken over by Rufus Ivins." Gilmer blinked several times in quick succession, as if having trouble staying awake.

"You emphasized the word 'legally,'" Le Brun observed. "Are you insinuatin' that there might have been some illegality to the process?"

"What do you know about the two men before they came to Atlanta?" Gilmer countered.

"I heard that the family came over from England some time before. I have no proof."

Gilmer's eyes narrowed. "Well, if a Gooderly family emigrated from England, only Algernon and Merriweather ended up in Atlanta. They must also have dropped their accents into the ocean on the way over. My guess is that they came to the South as Northern opportunists. A couple more of the scores of carpetbaggers that plagued us after the War of Northern Aggression."

"Yes, I have been unable to trace any extended Gooderly

family with sons Algernon and Merriweather in these parts," John said of his Monday searches through the Bureau of Records and the *Sunny South* newspaper morgue. Furthermore, the city police records held no file on Merriweather. As far as they were concerned, he had been a model citizen.

Gilmer said, "Which suggests that Algernon owned his two warehouses outright. How he managed the financing he never volunteered. We were friendly rivals but rarely spoke. And then his younger brother appeared in the midnineties to help him manage the building just off Marietta Street." Suddenly, he came to life and snapped his fingers. "I just had a thought. A detective is like a tailor, usin' his questions like needle and thread. If he's skillful enough, he attaches many separate pieces of cloth and buttons to make a suit."

The man's verbal apostrophe suggested to John that he was not on the defensive but rather relaxed enough to let his mind do double work. "I suppose that's an apt simile."

"It's what you're doing right now."

"And, if I'm lucky, you will be a veritable sewin' machine. I'm still curious about somethin' else you said. Sounded like a critical turn of phrase. I , , ." Finally, John could hold back his sneeze no longer. He grabbed for his handkerchief too late, compelling him to cover his mouth with the cuff of his jacket.

"Bless you," Gilmer wished.

"Thank you." John blew his large nose.

"I assumed you knew the suspicions surroundin' the death of Algernon, and that is why you're in Atlanta," Gilmer said.

John put away his handkerchief. "It does me little good to be tellin' you what I heard since it's secondhand. I'm hopin' you will volunteer a more firsthand version."

Gilmer leaned backward and began a gentle rocking motion in his squeaky-spring chair. "The older brother was a lifelong bachelor and a miser of the Ebenezer Scrooge variety. He sported the same trousers until the seat wore out and then put them on backwards, if you know what I mean. His younger brother, at the opposite pole, was a spendthrift."

"Who besides yourself might I talk with concernin' their personal habits?" John interrupted.

"Several dozen downtown proprietors of clothing and shoes, as well as cigar shops and many saloons. Merri changed his fashions each season, accordin' to what was being worn in New York or Charleston. He loved the theater. That I can affirm since I often attend theatrical performances. I did not see his public drinkin' and his frequentin' of loose women, so you will need to interview others for that. The point is that he spent a great deal of money. I am sure far more than his skinflint brother would be willing to pay him."

Le Brun had, in fact, spoken with five different persons living near the former residences of the two brothers. Gilmer's observations aligned exactly. "Had you heard of any large debts Merriweather incurred, such as to unregistered lenders or bet makers?"

"Such statements I never heard."

John's careful study of Gilmer's face told him that the man wished to cast Gooderly in a suspicious light but that he was at the same time adhering strictly to what he thought was truth.

"Algernon was only forty-seven when he died," John supplied.

"That's right. He was a skinny thing. Like a walkin' skeleton. We used to say that he was too cheap to eat. When he had stomach complaints, we—those of us in the warehouse business—figured it was natural, given his physique. Algernon suspected somebody was poisonin' him. This he even confided to me."

"Did he mention his brother?"

"No. But since his social circle was nothin' to write home about, Merriweather was the first one anyone would think of. I mean, Algernon was not a church member. He did not belong to any club that I knew of. Other than his brother and his employees, he rarely dealt with anyone but salespersons, his accountant, and restaurant waiters.

"He had medical examinations," Gilmer added. "His blood studied. They tested for poisons and found nothing. He seemed to get better for a few months. I figured his problems were mostly in his head."

"Psychosomatic," John said.

"Say what?"

"In his head."

Gilmer scowled. "That's what I said. But after a season, he started having greater stomach pains, along with headaches and diarrhea. Spells would come and go. He changed the places he ate at, wouldn't let anyone into his apartment—including his brother. Made his own tea. Then one day he complained of feeling dizzy at his business, fell into a coma, and died after a day in the hospital. An autopsy found stomach cancer."

"His brother inherited the warehouses," John supplied.

"Algernon died without a will. That kind don't give a damn what happens after they croak. And they don't make wills because they never want to admit they'll die. So Merriweather had to prove that he was the nearest relative. That's what I meant about 'legality.' The process took some time, but once he got the legal documents, he sold out quick as he could and disappeared. So, now you tell me he's down in Brunswick."

"In the warehouse business there," John said.

Gilmer waggled his forefinger. "I'm seeing the light now. Merriweather wasn't the actual legal heir. He destroyed a will, didn't he?"

"I'm not at liberty to say," Le Brun recited in measured tones. "The symptoms Algernon showed toward his end are remarkably like those of someone poisoned by arsenic. Did you know that arsenic can also cause or worsen stomach cancer?"

The warehouseman's eyes brightened. "Do tell! So maybe

he accidentally gave his brother the idea to use arsenic *after* his blood was tested and found to be negative. And Merri simply hurried the stomach cancer along. I read that arsenic can be detected in fingernails and hair after a person's death. Your company should have Algernon dug up."

John nodded at the suggestion, even though he knew he had assembled not nearly enough compelling facts for a disinterested citizen of Brunswick to petition the legal authorities of Atlanta. He also knew that arsenic was present in trace levels in most drinking water and that, unless a massive amount were found, no sure declaration could be made as to the effect on the body's health.

John read the signs via body motions and vocal tensions that the warehouseman he was interrogating had endured about all he would from a supposed insurance fraud agent. He flipped his notebook closed to indicate that the interview was over.

"I thank you kindly for the time you've given me, Mr. Gilmer." He made as if to rise and then paused dramatically halfway up from his seat. "Unless you would happen to know— secondhand, of course—any information on how Atlanta's prostitutes find their way to your city."

Gilmer did not seem particularly offended by the question, but he answered in a firm tone: "I am a God-fearin', Baptist family man who never engages in drinkin', gamblin', or illicit sex, sir. That sort of information you will have to secure elsewhere."

John smiled. "I apologize for any offense. You have been quite helpful." If Gilmer had been willing to speak further, John was prepared to take him to lunch. He knew that possibility had been lost. He looked down at the list of warehouse owners he had assembled. Three names remained unchecked.

"How far is Rufus Ivins' place?"

Gilmer pointed to his right. "Go out this door. Follow the tracks. Pretty soon, you'll see the faded name Gooderly on the side of the warehouse."

"Much obliged," John said. The houses of ill repute and the saloons near them could be investigated that evening or even later. On the morrow, if nothing more damning came to surface, John would visit the city bookshops. Then it was back to Brunswick. He looked forward with perverse pleasure to learning what his suggestion to members of the New Century Club to purchase the Retreat property had wrought.

CHAPTER TWENTY-THREE

October 29, 1908

NOT UNTIL HE had stepped off the train at Brunswick Station did Le Brun learn of the death of his friend Nicodemus Mason. Nicodemus had served at the Oglethorpe Hotel since its opening in 1888. His main duty had been to act as greeter and porter, escorting guests and carrying their luggage the short distance from and to the city's train station. During the high season, he served as part of the kitchen staff. Like John Le Brun, Nicodemus was a man of promise born into an ungenerous era. He was born a slave in 1844, four years before John entered the world. He had married and quickly had two daughters. Later came a son he named Ezekiel, a child who showed much intellectual promise. Year after year, Nicodemus had scrimped to be able to send Ezekiel to the Augusta Institute, a post-bellum Atlanta college for preparing black men in education and theology. However, his wife Phillis became sick with and later died of uterine cancer. Her care ate up every penny Nicodemus had saved. Le Brun's family had focused on sending John to William and Mary until the War of Northern Aggression had broken out and ultimately left teenage John wounded and his family economy ruined. The commonality of poor luck and shattered dreams formed a groundwork for the long relationship between the two men.

During his tenure as sheriff, John had found ample opportunities to visit the Oglethorpe during Nicodemus's work breaks. They mostly spoke of national and world news and of the future of Brunswick, agreeing on most issues. Nicodemus had been such a fast friend that he even tried to pick up the game of chess when John was without competition during one summer season. He found he had little aptitude for it but occasionally gave John spirited challenge matches at dominoes.

While John was in Atlanta, Nicodemus had piloted a shay to take a hotel guest shopping. To the considerable consternation of the vacationing lady, he suffered a massive stroke and tumbled off his seat onto Newcastle Street. He died immediately.

Le Brun had known that the lifelong Brunswick native was well liked, but he had no idea to what extent until he paid a visit to the home of his son Ezekiel, who served as the printer's devil for the town's newspaper. John learned that the reason Nicodemus had sold his home several years earlier was to divide the proceeds among his children, helping solve various financial crises. Ezekiel's home was not big, consisting of four rooms and set on a piece of land at the edge of Brunswick where many black families resided.

Close by the front of the little house, four oil torches burned to brighten the early-arriving night. They struggled against fine but insistent raindrops that hissed when they met the flames. Smudges of wafting black smoke created in John's mind an image of the funeral of an ancient Greek warrior.

The road that fronted the house was of well-compressed clay, and a deep-shaded tract of woodland stood opposite. Saddled horses, carriages, and two motorcars crowded the road. The line of town residents who had come to pay their respects stretched along the stepping-stone walk from the house's front porch and onto the road, making a turn in the direction of Brunswick. Unfurled umbrellas bumped against one another. John counted twenty-two persons in view ahead of him with more coming up behind.

"Seems like it always rains when somebody good dies," observed Elvia Stevens to her daughter, Araneta.

"That's the heavens weepin'," Araneta replied.

John said nothing, even though the identical notion had crossed his mind more than once. He was tapped on the shoulder by Cornelius Harris, the headwaiter of the Oglethorpe.

"Ev'nin', Sheriff Le Brun," Harris said. "Good to see more than the people from Nick's church and the hotel."

John knew that Cornelius spoke of the salting of white people in the line.

"He was well liked," John returned.

"And for good—"

Harris's thought was cut off midsentence by the buzz of a piece of lead flying between the two men. An instant later, the air echoed with the crack of a rifle report.

Le Brun shoved the headwaiter to the ground, then hastened around one of the carriages for protection. A second crack echoed from the woods, and a shrub quivered with the passing of the slug.

A thoughtful person had twisted circlets of iron into the damp ground every twenty feet or so to provide hitching points for the many sets of reins. More than half were yanked loose by the panicking horses, and the road quickly became a confusion of buggies and animals. John followed the carriage he had hidden behind as it moved, drawing as he went the revolver from the holster at the back of his belt.

The throng of well-dressed mourners filled the evening air with screams and angry exclamations. Most of those in the line dispersed at a full run in the direction of the house. John countered their wild movements, running parallel with the road until he reached the single automobile parked there. There was no third explosive report. He popped up above the hood for a moment to encourage a response from the woods. When he got none, he aimed into the gauzy panorama of trees and squeezed off three shots from his revolver in a fan pattern. Still, he received no response. His guess was that the shooter had fled, but he remained behind the car.

One of the younger men jumped on his horse, turned it toward the direction of Brunswick's police headquarters, and sped away at full gallop.

Another shot cracked from John's side of the road and then a third. One revolver was in the hand of a white man, the other a middle-aged black man. For once, John was grateful to witness the flaunting of Brunswick's ordinance against anyone other than a lawman carrying a gun within the town limits.

"I don't believe those bullets were meant for me," Harris said loudly to the crowd. "Somebody was shootin' at Sheriff Le Brun!"

"Ex-sheriff," John said under his breath, even as he wondered if the shooter was settling a debt from the years when Le Brun executed the will of the law.

Half a dozen men rushed across the road.

"Don't go into those trees!" John shouted. The group halted instantly. Everyone grew silent in the tense moment.

"I can hear him crashin' through brush down there," a young man in the group reported. He pointed into the woods.

"Stay here," John ordered, in a voice less shrill. "It's too dangerous to chase him in the dark."

John uprooted one of the torches. Carrying it in his left hand while keeping his revolver in his right, he walked slowly across the road and through the weedy undergrowth that edged it. With his head down, he angled toward the place where he believed the shots had emanated. The leafy canopy of the trees prevented undergrowth a few paces in, allowing John to study the soft earth. After some dozen steps, he stopped and squatted. Two shell casings lay on the ground.

John grunted with pleasure. The casings told him a great deal. They were .30-30 caliber and of a type that had not appeared on shelves until 1895 when the first smokeless propellants became available to the general public. The most common rifle using the round was the Winchester lever-action, Model 1894. It was a costly weapon and, therefore, relatively rare in the Brunswick region.

Pressed into the ground were several prints. Le Brun judged that they were made by a man of normal size. He rose, stepped back, and looked at the impressions his own shoes had made in the same soil. Those of the shooter were deeper, indicating a man of more weight.

"You okay, Sheriff?" Cornelius Harris called into the trees.

"I am. May I ask a favor of you?"

"Certainly."

"Come here and see that no one walks through this area while I pay my respects," John said. "I want to be back here by the time Sheriff Tidewell arrives."

CHAPTER TWENTY-FOUR

October 29, 1908

AT LE BRUN'S SUGGESTION, Warfield Tidewell drove directly back to the center of Brunswick with his old friend. His officers remained behind to interview the witnesses to the attempted murder, take photographs and measurements of the footprints, and collect the shell casings. As they motored toward the second-floor apartment of Merriweather Gooderly, John spotted Marcus Tillman, a sailor who grew up in Brunswick but since his maturity spent most of his time on the open ocean as a boiler engineer.

"Pull over!" John directed Warfield.

Tillman slowed to watch the erratic veer of the automobile and then smiled as he recognized John.

"Hey, Sheriff Le Brun!" he called out. "Don't arrest me. I'm just visitin'."

John jerked his thumb in War's direction. "He's sheriff now, Marcus." Some pleasant words and inquiries were exchanged, but Le Brun got to his goal directly. He reached into his pocket and drew out a five-dollar bill. "Do me a favor for that time I did forget to arrest you . . . even though you deserved it: Take this around to London Street, to that three-story with the tea shop just east of Union. A fellow named Gooderly lives in the apartment on the second floor. First, see if his place is lit. Even if it isn't, go on up and bang on his door. Tell him a man just gave you this money for him and said he would know who owed it to him."

"Sounds like fun," the athletic young man said.

"Whatever happens, meet us back here once you're done."

Tillman took off at a trot. John stepped out of the automobile.

"And where are you going?" Warfield asked.

"Gooderly recently got a Ford Model K."

"I've seen it putting around town," said Warfield.

John stepped onto the sidewalk. "He probably keeps it in that stable in back of his buildin'. Let's see."

The stable held two horses and two carriages, but the last space was empty. By the glow of Warfield's flashlight, he and John discerned the muddy prints of rubber automobile tires. They retraced their steps to the street.

Marcus Tillman appeared, holding the money in his hand and puffing lightly. "No lights on. I pounded on his door enough to at least get a 'Go away!' Nothing."

John reclaimed the bill. "Say hey to your momma for me and tell her I believe the high seas have made a man of you."

Before the seaman was out of view, John said to Warfield, "Let's hurry over to his warehouses."

THE SHERIFF AND EX-SHERIFF found the Sure-Tite Warehouse well lit on the outside but no interior glow from the skylights.

"Should we bang on the door?" Warfield asked.

John pivoted and started back toward Tidewell's prized Buick, which was parked at a good distance. "For what purpose? We have no warrant. Anyway, he's probably in his automobile, gettin' rid of his rifle and shoes."

"But what's to stop him from coming after you in the early hours?"

"I welcome that."

Warfield cranked the flywheel and started the car. "If I were you, I'd be spitting tacks."

"When have you ever known me to fly off the handle?"

Warfield paused with the crank in his hand. "Right. Sorry. You don't get mad; you get justice."

"Correct."

"Well, you sure got *him* angry."

"Angry is nothin'. I am steadily turnin' his world upside down. I already engineered it so one of the other members of the New Century Club would expose his dirty dealin's over Retreat. Then I spoke with sixteen individuals up in Atlanta. The chance that he still communicates with at least one of them is good. I'd be shocked if he doesn't know I'm diggin' into his past with a steam shovel."

"And is his past as dirty as his present?" asked Tidewell.

"Decidedly. However, just how filthy is hard to tell. The man is a sly gazabo. Thinks he's Br'er Rabbit to my Br'er Fox. From the moment he let on that he had checked up on me, I never trusted the man fully. That's why I let him win a couple of chess matches against me."

"Did he win any fair and square?" John's former student asked.

"Two he did," John admitted.

"So, he underestimates you. But don't you underestimate him."

"No indeed."

Tidewell worked the clutch and wrestled the shift into first gear. "As the sheriff, I feel like I should be doing a great deal more. But I don't have the manpower or the sightlines to watch his warehouses secretly. You doubt we can get him for shooting at you. Then what *can* we do?"

"Spend a few dollars of J. P. Morgan's money and extend the caretaker's hours at Retreat. Any white man hoverin' around there would draw Gooderly's suspicion. But a black teenager who already works on the property is little cause for alarm."

CHAPTER TWENTY-FIVE

October 30, 1908

THE KNOCK ON John Le Brun's door was unexpected. The first ten feet into his home was open with a small sitting area on one side and a study/library on the other. Each side had a front-facing window with sheer curtains. He rose from his desk, where he was writing checks, and angled into the dark front corner, taking into his hand the revolver that had sat on the desk.

Irwin Jones stood on the front porch, his hands folded formally in front of him. John grinned in expectation of their conversation.

John opened the wooden door and pushed the screen door aside. "Irwin! This is a pleasant surprise."

"But not a pleasant occasion," Jones replied. The architect took in the front area with a practiced eye.

John figured that the man saw what he had expected from

an aged shotgun-style house, as he showed no emotion. John gestured to one of the stuffed chairs positioned across from his undersized couch.

"You are talkin' of the shots taken at me last night?"

Jones removed his hat and set it on the coffee table. "No . . . but that was a terrible thing. Do you have an idea of who did it?"

John sat on the couch. "The list is short. I believe I have few enemies."

Irwin smirked, as if he had his own idea of the culprit.

"Can I offer you somethin' to drink?" John offered. "I could heat up the coffee pot."

Jones shook his head. "I'm fine. The reason I say that this is not a pleasant occasion is because the task has fallen on me to bring you up-to-date on several facts that touch upon the New Century Club. Facts that my brother-in-law exposed while you were up in Atlanta."

"Do tell. Your brother-in-law the real estate agent."

"Exactly. Lamont Breckinridge. It turns out that Retreat Plantation is not being leased to our club . . . or even to Merriweather Gooderly. Gooderly has, in fact, obtained a mortgage for the whole thing."

"What?" John exclaimed, putting his theatrical experiences into practice, feigning surprise mixed with indignity, but careful not to over-emote.

The architect gave out a soft, bitter laugh. "Apparently, your excellent notion for the property came to Gooderly quite a few months ago. Perhaps even years. What we thought was our dues for rental went to almost half the payment on the mortgage."

"From what bank?" John asked.

"Garland DeBrahm's," Jones answered with venom. "You know he was the second member of the club. We believe there was collusion."

"And who is 'we'?" John asked.

"Myself, White, Reynolds, Tatnall, and Ebenezer."

John had expected the first three names. He suspected that fishing fleet mogul Patrick Ebenezer was also part of Gooderly's inner sanctum, feigning outrage or annoyance and waiting to see how events played out. Claude Tatnall, the lumberman, he was less sure about.

"You're obviously a shrewd gentleman," Jones went on. "And you have plenty of experience with criminal dealings. I hope you're thinking as the five of us are."

A cool breeze pushed the curtains inward, suggesting the approach of winter. John released a sigh. "Well, the club fees are not badly out of line. And Gooderly *is* the founder and current president. I suppose his guilt comes from misrepresentation."

"Of course it does. He flat out said we were renting the estate."

"Have any of you confronted him?"

Jones laughed again, harder and longer. "I did. He was cool as could be, naturally. He'd heard that I was going to check on the property when we were up in the lighthouse, so he had lots of time to prepare his story."

"What was it?"

"That he realized the potential but harbored the fears he expressed up on the lighthouse deck. You know, a big storm or another economic depression could delay development for a decade. He said he thought it best to lock up control of the property until other tourist ventures had started on St. Simons and the demand for a course was guaranteed. Now, however, since interest seemed to be shown by all the club members, he was willing to accept shares of the clubhouse and golf course from us, crediting one third of what we had already paid in club dues."

John scratched his ear and paused for a moment to be sure Irwin Jones had finished. Then he said, "There's no doubt he was pullin' a fast one. But because I inadvertently exposed him, we can now get into his deal on the ground floor. That might not be so bad."

Jones shot John an annoyed look. "Fool me once, shame on him . . . I think we should let him try to pay that mortgage and develop the plantation on his own. So do White and Reynolds. I haven't visited just you about this; I've spoken to a dozen of my friends and clients, warning them about him. So have Gilbert and John. We've learned that the attitudes in Brunswick toward Gooderly fall into three categories: many don't know him; more than a few think he's full of himself and a poseur; several actively don't like him. I know that DeBrahm's main banking competitor in town won't finance anything Gooderly advances."

"You're makin' him what I call persona au gratin," John joked.

Jones laughed yet again, but this time with a happy sound. "Of course, what would really put a snuffer over his candle is for you to come out against him publicly."

"I will offer my opinion if asked," John allowed.

Irwin waggled his forefinger. "I'd be more proactive if I were you. I'm betting that he was the one who took the potshots at you. You've really unblocked his hat. To be frank, I personally question if you did it inadvertently. And I'm sure he wonders as well." Jones stood. "You have a daunting reputation for maneuvering people and things for your purpose."

John also rose. He dipped his head. "In the pursuit of justice."

Jones reached into his inside jacket pocket and produced a sheet of quality linen paper. At the top was an embossed figure of an elegant house with the architect's contact information below. "This is a simple letter of resignation from the New Century Club, effective as of November first. As you can see, the signatures of John White and Gilbert Reynolds are below mine. The others are suggesting wresting the club from Gooderly, but I hope you'll sign with us right now."

Without speaking a word, Le Brun took the paper to his desk, uncapped his fountain pen, and added his signature.

JOHN HAD A QUARTER HOUR earlier tired of pacing around the Brunswick train station platforms. Once again, he raised his binoculars and surveyed the area between the station and the Brunswick River. In the distance, the Sure-Tite Warehouse was open and receiving shipments, but there was no sign of Gooderly's Ford.

At last, Sheriff Tidewell's Buick pulled up to the station.

"My Lord!" John exclaimed, throwing up his hands.

Warfield shut off the engine, reached to the other seat, and picked up an envelope. "It's not like the old days." His words referred to the years when Iley Tidewell, Warfield's father, was the judge for Glynn County. With War as his deputy, Le Brun rarely had any trouble obtaining search warrants. However, when John retired in 1906 and Warfield moved into his position, Judge Iley thought it best that he also retire so that no accusations of special favors between those who pursued and those who dispensed justice could be leveled. Nathaniel Pinkett was now the county judge, and he was known for his plodding, overcautious personality.

"Though the millstone of justice grinds slowly, it grinds fine," Warfield added.

"I believe the quotation is 'The wheels of justice turn slowly but grind exceedingly fine,'" John returned as he stepped over the first of the tracks on his way to the warehouse. "Then again, I don't have the law degree that you do."

"Ease up on me, John. I don't spend my life reading Horace and Cicero and Socrates," Warfield carped. "I like my version better anyway."

The office door to the Sure-Tite Warehouse was unlocked. John entered first. Sitting in Merriweather Gooderly's place

was another man, one who was not a Brunswick resident but
with whom John had recently spoken.

"Mr. Ivins! What an unexpected surprise," Le Brun
exclaimed.

Ivins looked at him with no surprise at all and offered no
reply.

"Sheriff Warfield Tidewell, this is Mr. Rufus Ivins of
Atlanta," John introduced. "He owns a thrivin' warehouse
business up there."

"Mr. Ivins," Warfield said, denying his hand but rather
crossing both arms over his broad, athletic chest. "Where's
Merriweather Gooderly?"

"I have no idea," Ivins replied.

"How is that possible?"

Ivins, whose watery eyes blinked often, shrugged his boney
shoulders. "He's quit the warehousing business . . . at least in
Brunswick." The man pushed himself out of the swivel office
chair, which John noted now had a thick pillow atop the seat.
"When you visited me, what was it, three days ago, I realized
how long it had been since I had communicated with Merri."
He tried a yellow-toothed smile without much success, then
rubbed the tip of his nose. "It was before I had a telephone, I
think." Ivins's fingers drifted down from his nose to partially
cover his mouth. "Anyhow, I got ahold of him here and asked
him how he was. He said he was in the midst of a major change
in his life and did I want to consider buying his two warehouses
in Brunswick. I have more and more importing commerce from
Europe and the Middle East through this port, so it made good
sense. I hopped the next train."

"I assume I came up in the conversation quite early," John
said.

"Well, yes. I mentioned that you were asking about him and
his brother. For an insurance company."

"And what was his reaction to that?"

"He didn't seem shocked. Said it was a ridiculous complaint by a distant relative." His head bobbed up and down twice.

Although neither the sideways drifting of eyes nor sweating was evidence, Ivins's movements spoke loudly to Le Brun. John assumed from his initial interview with the character that he was a practiced liar. He was sure that Ivins was prepared for the visit of himself and the sheriff.

"You are telling us that you now own both of Gooderly's warehouses?" Tidewell asked.

"Yes, sir."

"And how was this transaction accomplished?"

Ivins held firm in his place. "I arrived with a number of bank drafts."

"And you were able to inspect the warehouses, study the books, determine the assets and liabilities all in one afternoon," John said.

"That's right. I am highly experienced in my business, and Merriweather made everything readily available."

Tidewell pulled the search warrant from its envelope and snapped it open in front of the Atlanta man's eyes. "Such speed in doing major business is highly irregular. I want to see the transfers of ownership."

"I have them."

John could tell that the man had plenty of experience toughing out shady situations. He was no innocent. If he could be sufficiently squeezed, Le Brun had no doubt he would trade information about Gooderly.

Warfield stepped forward. "We're gonna have a look-see now, and I expect you to come along with us."

"Absolutely," Rufus Ivins replied. "I always cooperate with the law . . . and even private investigators." His lips curled into a smile, but he gave Le Brun the fixed look of a venomous snake about to strike.

For almost half an hour, Warfield moved among the many

crates, barrels, and stacks of boxes, checking to see if any label was addressed to Merriweather Gooderly. When none was found, he demanded that several of the crates that had appeared on the master manifest the afternoon before be opened. As the exploration took place, John isolated the three floor workers one by one. He questioned each about Gooderly's activities in the past three days and how they had learned about the transfer of ownership. Clearly, John Callahan, Steve Moritz, and Jimmy Galligan had all been kept in the dark and were not happy.

When Tidewell was finished, he announced that he wished to inspect the other warehouse. He, John, and Rufus Ivins walked the quarter-mile with the new owner asking about the warrant. Le Brun realized that Gooderly had told Ivins a good story, but that it was clearly not the whole truth.

"What about his property over on St. Simons?" John asked out of the blue. "Did you buy the Retreat Plantation as well?"

"I have no idea what you're talking about," Ivins replied.

Warfield said, "I didn't think you would. Those spoils are for Banker DeBrahm. I'll also bet you have no idea of what you've gotten yourself into."

For the first time, the Atlanta businessman looked nervous.

To the sheriff, John said, "I got over here early so I thought I'd walk around the place. By my pace, the conjoined structures are 52 steps wide and 104 long. I also noticed at the closed-in end there are no windows or doors. But there are two staggered lines of holes on the north and south ends, about ten and twelve feet up. Twenty holes in each line."

"Round holes?" Tidewell asked.

John nodded. "Looks like they were made by a large bore bit. The edges are raw, indicatin' that they were created after the most recent outside paintin' of the place. Also looks like wire mesh on the inside of each."

The side conversation further rattled Ivins. He asked, "What do you think that indicates?"

"Remains to be seen. How well do you know Mr. Cate, Gooderly's second-in-command?"

"Barely. Just that he's been with Merri for more than four years."

The trio came to the major entrance of the Brunswick Dry Goods & Lumber warehouse. The front two-thirds of the open-air complex was enclosed by heavy mesh wire, creating a ten-foot-tall fence. A peaked roof vaulted the area, intended to shelter the stored materials from harsh sun and driving rains. A single railroad track ran through large gates so that flat- and closed cars could be backed in and loaded. Both sides of the track could accommodate thousands of yards of soft and hard lumber, including resinous, long-leaf yellow pine, short-leaf pine, loblolly, cypress, and oak. A few weeks of the year, part of the space was filled with baled sea cotton. Hoists ran above the area to aid in loading.

The back end of the warehouse was enclosed in wood and held the kiln-dried lumber intended for finer carpentry such as porch rails, spindles and moldings, as well as for furniture making.

The sheriff confronted the first worker he encountered and was directed to where Elmer Cate stood, counting stacks of eight-foot-long oak planks. Le Brun hung back with the warehouse's new owner, intent on watching his long-time protégé in action.

Warfield snapped open the search warrant and held it up. He identified himself as he neared the manager. "Elmer Cate . . . this is a warrant issued on probable cause for the harboring of illegal aliens on this property."

"The hell you say!" Ivins cried out. Unlike Ivins, Cate showed nervousness immediately. "I'm *not* the owner," he said with emphasis.

"You don't need to be," Tidewell replied, using the deep end of his voice. "Come with us!"

The inside of the warehouse was explored. The back wall

presented a solid face of wood without windows or door. The sheriff walked its width, stopping and peering closely at various joints. He came to his full height and turned to John.

"Mr. Le Brun, you stated that the entire length of this warehouse is 104 of your paces."

Satisfaction animated Le Brun's eyes as he appreciated how well Warfield had picked up on his cue.

"That is correct."

"Would you be so kind as to return to the front gate and walk in a straight line to this wall?"

John obliged. He passed the warehouse employees, who had stopped working. As he neared the far wall of the warehouse, he counted aloud. "Ninety-eight, ninety-nine, one hundred."

"One hundred paces," Warfield echoed. "Which leaves nine or ten feet unaccounted for. You also mentioned two series of round holes."

"Twenty on each side, forty in all," John supplied, along with his nod.

Warfield raised his pointer finger and began counting aloud. He stopped at twelve.

"Twelve plus twelve. Only twenty-four. Another discrepancy."

John noted that the manager was awash in perspiration, his eyes wide in fear in spite of the day's coolness.

Warfield went up to the back wall. Without smiling, he said, "Gentlemen, have you ever heard the joke about the sailor on leave who had trouble reading and spent the night in a warehouse? This one section has a strange pattern of knotholes. If I stick my fingers into them . . ." He finished his sentence by fitting the first joints of his fingers into the holes and drawing backward.

Part of the wall swung outward, exposing an inner wall and a stout door with a lock.

"Open it!" Warfield commanded Cate. The manager hesitated for a moment, his tongue circling his lips. "We know about the women being smuggled in from Eastern Europe and forced to serve as whores," the sheriff told him. "Therefore, at the very least, you are an accessory to these crimes. The more unwilling you are to cooperate, the worse your punishment will be."

"This is beyond belief!" Rufus Ivins remonstrated.

Cate was a man in his early forties, of average build, with much of his crown hair gone and wearing wire-rim glasses. He looked to Le Brun more victim than criminal. John reflected that such a nonthreatening character would be perfect for reassuring illegal immigrant women that no harm would come to them. Cate reinforced his harmless, woebegone image by saying, "I've had a bad year. First, my momma died. Then I had two abscessed teeth pulled. Now this."

Warfield said, "That's not as bad as drowning," and John heard his own voice in his replacement's cadence and word choice.

Cate pulled a ring of keys from his pocket, fitted one into the lock, and pulled the door back. The space beyond ran the width of the warehouse. Its uniform length from the back wall was a little less than eight feet. At cither extreme were three levels of canvas cots, attached to the sidewalls by chains. Also in the narrow space were two ladders, piles of blankets, a few pillows, a hole for the elimination of human waste, and the wrappings for various types of food.

"This is bad," Warfield pronounced, looking first at Cate and then at Ivins.

"I just purchased the damned place," the new owner protested. "How could I be involved?"

Warfield gently but steadily pushed Ivins backward until his bottom collided with a banded pile of lumber. "Have a seat." He swung around to focus on Cate. "But *you* certainly were involved. Somebody had to be around when Mr. Gooderly made his visits North. Why don't you make an initial statement to show your willingness to cooperate? Mr. Le Brun will take notes."

Cate spoke as if his life depended on the speed of his tongue. His first words positioned him as an employee threatened with the loss of a well-paying job if he did not participate in a crime that he had no part in planning. He had been confronted with the scheme five weeks into his employment and had no idea if it had been in operation before that time. He suspected that its inception was not too much longer than four years, based on the newness of the hiding areas. He assumed that the previous manager had quit rather than become involved. Cate corroborated Le Brun's assumption that the illegal women were indeed offloaded from tramp steamers several miles out from St. Simons Island. If they arrived the night before an outbound freight train was to leave Brunswick for Atlanta, Chicago, St. Louis, Washington, D.C., or New York City, they were brought directly to an isolated Brunswick dock in the darkness. If no immediate train was scheduled to leave, they stayed for a time in the cramped cellar of the Retreat Plantation mansion.

The deliveries of women occurred at approximately three-month intervals, although the periods varied from as little as three weeks to as much as five months. Two tramp steamers that together visited Mobile, New Orleans, Veracruz, Puerto Cortez, Belize City, Colón, Port-au-Prince, and San Juan were involved.

The number of delivered women varied widely, from three to as many as ten. All were so desperate to improve their lives that they cooperated fully and rarely complained. Except for one. She had jumped from the side of one of Patrick Ebenezer's deepwater fishing vessels when the St. Simon lighthouse loomed ahead and quickly disappeared in the black ocean. Cate and two of Ebenezer's deck hands had been sent over to St. Simons Island early the next morning to search for the young woman, but she had eluded them. Cate admitted his profound relief when he learned that she had drowned.

Of the New York City brothel operations, Cate swore he knew nothing. He also had no idea if Gooderly had assignation houses in other major cities as well. His reasonable surmise was that since Gooderly only traveled personally to New York, the women were sold to other purveyors of sex, as the unfortunates of Africa had been traded in slave markets throughout the Deep South one hundred years earlier.

Proud and satisfied as he was with Warfield's handling of the interrogation, John could not help but jump in. "So, Merriweather Gooderly vanished without so much as a 'fare you well,' leavin' you high and dry," he said to Cate.

"Yes, sir, he surely did."

John turned to Warfield, simultaneously sliding his right hand under the back of his suit jacket. "Clearly, Mr. Cate will have to pay for his part in this cruel endeavor, Sheriff. But I assume he might plea himself a reduced sentence based on how much valuable information he is willin' to supply."

"Absolutely," Tidewell confirmed. He glared down at the thoroughly cowed manager. "For example, you know the destinations of the freight cars that received the women."

Cate shook his head ruefully. "I guess Washington, Atlanta, Chicago, and St. Louis were final destinations. Maybe just way stations. I tell you again: I was merely an overseer in this business."

"I refuse to believe you didn't know the name of the warehouse in each city where the women arrived," Tidewell persisted.

Cate shifted his eyes toward Ivins, who shook his head ever so slightly. Cate sighed. "In Atlanta, it was to Mr. Ivins's—"

In spite of his age, the thin Rufus Ivins hopped off the lumber stack and dashed toward the open end of the warehouse.

Le Brun yanked his revolver from its holster, released the safety, cocked and aimed it, and sent a bullet clanging into a steel stanchion just ahead of the fleeing man.

"Last warnin'!" John yelled.

Ivins slowed and then stopped. He bent and placed his hands on his knees. His lungs heaved for air.

"I could have winged him . . . even with only one good eye," Le Brun said, lowering his weapon.

"Easy, John," Warfield admonished. "I'm the law here. Gooderly didn't sell just the warehouse businesses. He must have told Ivins about the smuggling. He needs to stay in one piece . . . for now."

"I'll give you the other warehouses when I hear what kind of deal I get," Elmer Cate said to Sheriff Tidewell.

NONE OF THE FURNITURE in Merriweather Gooderly's apartment had apparently been taken when the man fled Brunswick. It was all of the finest quality. Likewise, most of the contents of the kitchen and linen closet remained. But more had been removed than John had expected.

"Every stitch of clothin', books, wall hangin's, all but two Victrola records. So he must have taken one of those machines as well. All those fancy tie tacks, cufflinks, and watches he was so proud of paradin'. Even his expensive cigars. How much can one automobile hold?" he asked Warfield, speaking of the Model K Ford.

"I'm having my deputies open every shipment in the Sure-Tite Warehouse going to any of those cities Cate listed," Warfield said. "Wouldn't it be fantastic if he put his forwarding address right where we could find it?"

"Don't count on it," John replied, as he opened Gooderly's armoire. "No shoes to compare with those mud prints. No weapon. No bullets."

"Try his desk," Warfield said.

John opened the side drawers from bottom to top. They were all empty. In the narrow center drawer, however, he found a pair of unused, carmine-colored, two-cent George Washington postage stamps. What lay beside them caused John's heart to leap. It was a claret-dyed leather appointment notebook. Le Brun grabbed the notebook and thumbed quickly through its pages.

"Shoot!" he exclaimed. "It's empty. I've seen Gooderly pull the twin of this book from his pocket on many occasions. I was hopin' he left it behind, filled with incriminatin' names, dates, and numbers."

"Maybe he got two for the price of one. Or he simply bought a second for use when he filled the one he's using," Warfield speculated.

John waved the little appointment book forcefully in front of Warfield's face. "A good find anyway! This might could be almost as valuable empty as it is filled."

"How could that be?" Tidewell asked. John told him, and he laughed. "John Le Brun, I never want to be on your wrong side."

"MR. DEBRAHM IS TOO BUSY today to see you," the bank clerk reported to Le Brun.

John feigned alarm. "Just me? Or too busy to see anyone?" He turned to the other three citizens in the bank lobby, one behind him and two at the bank's other teller window. In a much louder voice, he said, "Is there a run on the bank?"

Between the unregulated practice of free banking and no federal reserve, the nation had spent almost half of the previous eighteen years in states of either financial panic or recession. *Bankrupt* had a narrower meaning than it would in the future. The heads of the three bank customers jerked around in John's direction, taut with fear.

"Please, sir!" the clerk implored.

"Have you run out of cash?" John persisted. "Is the bank in trouble?"

The door behind the teller area burst open, and Garland DeBrahm hastened forward, his beaming expression at bizarre variance with his wildly darting eyes.

"There is no problem with the bank, people," DeBrahm declared, raising his hands, palms up. "This man isn't even a depositor."

"Thank the Lord!" John said, under his breath but loud enough for everyone to hear.

The bank owner's hands dropped to his sides. He drew in a deep breath as he cocked one eyebrow at Le Brun. "Please come around to the side door, John."

John took his time, sauntering toward the door that barred the way to DeBrahm's office and the bank's safes. When he heard the deadbolt turn, he opened the door and passed inside. He found that Garland had rushed to put himself behind his large walnut desk.

"You're here about the New Century Club, no doubt," the banker said.

"Insofar as it involves various dealin's between you and Merriweather Gooderly," John answered. Then he added, "You had better invite me to sit. This is not a simple conversation."

DeBrahm's head jerked toward a chair on the opposite side of the desk. "What would you like to know?"

John sat. "Oh, I think I already know a great deal." In rapid order, he spoke of DeBrahm being the second member of the club and of his granting of a loan for the purchase of the Retreat Plantation.

"If you think to threaten me with public disclosure of this information," the banker replied, "I will assure my depositors that the bank holds the mortgage by legal charge."

"On a rundown mansion and a plantation gone fallow," John countered, "with no immediate likelihood of development or resale."

DeBrahm began to look annoyed. "Mr. Gooderly is

sufficiently sound financially to pay the arranged principal and interest without the contribution of other club members."

"If he were still around . . . which he is not," John said, with space between each word. He watched with pleasure as the banker absorbed the news.

"What? Where is he?" DeBrahm demanded.

John shrugged nonchalantly. "Anybody's guess right now. He sold his warehouses, emptied his apartment, and vanished in his fancy horseless carriage."

"Over the dealings of a small club over on St. Simons?"

"No. Somethin' far more serious." John produced a sheet of paper with the letterhead of the Brunswick Police Department and pushed it across the desk toward the banker. "Before we continue, I must remind you that I was for many years the sheriff of this town and have now been deputized and authorized to represent Brunswick in investigatin' a heinous crime. You've lived in Glynn County most of your life; you know its history. I'm talkin' *Wanderer* and Ibo serious, except pertainin' to far paler complexions. Like the color of your face."

The banker's jaw literally dropped as the muscles went slack.

"How rude not to tell his closest pal," John taunted. "He not only forfeited a jumbo-sized white elephant to your bank but also linked himself to you."

"I am completely innocent of what you are insinuating!" Garland almost barked, struggling to reclaim his dignity.

Unfazed, John tapped one forefinger against the other. "First, you make poor use of piles of your customers' hard-earned cash." He tapped again. "Second, you do it with a man accused of tradin' in sex slaves. I doubt that there will need to be a financial crisis before your righteous depositors create a run on your bank. I believe your only possible path toward salvation is to provide information that will lead to the capture and conviction of Merriweather Gooderly."

Within the space of ninety seconds, the banker's demeanor

had changed from an image of health to that of one dying of
yellow fever. "What information?"

"For example, I would guess that Mr. Gooderly recently
removed most of his money from his checking and savings
accounts, both personal and commercial."

DeBrahm stared down at the words on the sheet of paper
and the sheriff's signature. "He removed a bit over three
thousand dollars of it. It was almost all we were holding at the
time. I told him he was foolish if he thought we were awash in
coin and paper, that he should have given the bank forty-eight
hours' warning if he wanted to liquidate accounts."

"What did he say to that?"

"He told me his sudden demands couldn't be helped. That
he had an excellent opportunity to purchase a piece of real
estate and required ready cash. He left us with less than three
hundred dollars to last the day. That's why I reacted so violently
to you when you started yelling about the bank being in trouble.
We most certainly are not, but we still lack the normal supply
of ready currency."

"Where did he say the real estate is?"

"New York City. Next to that new Pennsylvania Railroad Station."

"Let me get some of this down on paper." Le Brun reached
into his pocket for his notebook, making sure that he did not
expose Gooderly's claret-colored version. "Naturally, after what
I've told you, you will immediately freeze the balances in all Mr.
Gooderly's accounts. Sheriff Tidewell will deliver the official
version of what I've shared with you, as well as the paperwork
that formally freezes those accounts."

"Why did Sheriff Tidewell not visit me instead?" DeBrahm
asked.

"He thought you might be more comfortable talkin' with
a member of our club first," John replied. "And he had to be
somewhere else: at the front door of your house. By now he's

served your wife with a search warrant to your premises. He's particularly interested in the photographs you took at the top of the St. Simons lighthouse. You know, the ones with the front and side close-ups of Merri."

CHAPTER TWENTY-SIX

December 26, 1908

THE PRIVATE SCHOOLS of Ben and Leslie Topley closed on Tuesday afternoon, December 22. The next morning, the children and Lordis Goode boarded a southbound train. Christmas vacation promised to be a time never to be forgotten—the first of two wedding ceremonies. John had pushed Lordis gently but tirelessly, in person and by letter, to accept the date, since she was firm in her desire to delay the New York ceremony until after Sally had been released from prison. Well aware of his depression over not being able to solve the case of who killed Herbert Moore and the five persons inside the assignation house, Lordis had relented regarding the Brunswick formal expression of their commitment to each other.

The day after Christmas Day, which fell on a Friday, large masses of Northerners would board trains bound for Brunswick.

The first of the Jekyl Island Club elite would arrive on Sunday or Monday, creating circuslike crowds of common citizen gawkers. The town's population would double with vacationers, and local services would be strained to accommodate their demands. As a longtime resident, John knew this well and had argued that the only day in the festive season when their wedding would receive adequate attention was Saturday, the twenty-sixth. Lordis agreed.

As the scion of a family of lesser French nobility, John had been raised Roman Catholic. He had lapsed in regular church attendance when his wife and baby died many years earlier. Lordis was Episcopalian. Whenever she visited Brunswick, she attended St. Athanasius' Church, so that the priest was pleased to officiate at the ceremony. In attendance were a number of John's relatives, including his niece Aurelia with her husband Warfield Tidewell, three other members of the sheriff's department, and about a dozen of John's neighbors and other friends. Leslie, wearing her new white velvet dress with scarlet ribbons, served as flower girl. Ben was the ring bearer. To John's amazement, nineteen townsfolk uninvited to the reception also showed up, some bearing presents. He was so touched that, directly after the ceremony, he invited them all to join those already expected at the Oglethorpe Hotel.

The sanctuary was decorated in white with gauzy bunting, a profusion of glowing candles, and star magnolia blossoms, cleverly made from silk and paper. Lordis's dress was cream-white silk with a flowing train cut in the more free-flowing, figure-defining fashion of the new century. The luxurious material lay halfway off her shoulders, exposing her elegantly long neck to advantage. French lace decorated the sleeves and waist, and a panel of color-matched cotton formed her bodice piece and underdress. Her full veil was tulle. The bridal bouquet was calla lilies arranged in the nosegay holder she had purchased in Brunswick on her previous visit.

John wore tails. His wedding ring was newly fashioned. Lordis's ring had belonged to John's mother. Liberated woman that she was, she had selected her own engagement ring, a Mikimoto cultured pearl mounted on a gold band.

The ceremony followed the rite in the Book of Common Prayer. Warfield read a passage from Genesis, and John's sister read from 1 Corinthians. The hymn chosen by John was "The Church's One Foundation," and Lordis selected for their recessional Beethoven's "Ode to Joy."

A group photograph was taken outside the church on the cool, cloudy afternoon. John noted that Warfield and the other Brunswick policemen stood at the edges of the group, looking around the bordering streets rather than at the camera. He had also registered that all four men entered the church only after the processional music had begun. The explanation was simple: Merriweather Gooderly was still at large.

Warfield was the closest of the policemen to John. Le Brun leaned in his direction and softly said, "Isn't the fellow standin' next to the photographer the reporter from the *Call*?"

"He is indeed."

"Why is he coverin' a weddin'?"

"Because you're the groom. They're using your wedding to sell newspapers to the vacationers pouring into town. You know: 'Internationally Celebrated Detective Weds.' And then this eager ink slinger will trundle out your exploits."

John wanted to scratch his ear but feared ruining the photograph. "Heavens to Betsy! What will Lordis think?"

"She may grumble about you overshadowing her on 'her day,' but secretly she'll be proud." And then Sheriff Tidewell laughed.

"What?" John wanted to know.

"If I were you, I'd be madder at their last edition. Surely you saw the headline: 'Goode-Le Brun Nuptials Held.' If anybody tried to hold my nuptials, I'd thump him upside his head."

The photographer called for attention. He counted to three, and his flash powder went off in blinding light and muted explosion. The man immediately cautioned the group to remain in place while he reversed the exposure plate.

"Now, if I was gonna shoot me from a distance, that would have been an ideal moment," John remarked. "Do you really think Gooderly can move around Brunswick without bein' seen?"

Still looking at the tripod-mounted bellows camera, Warfield said, "He's at large, and he's already proven himself to be a vindictive son-of-a—"

"Ladies present," John interrupted.

Merriweather Gooderly had executed a successful flight from Brunswick almost two months earlier. In retrospect, John wondered if visiting the warehouses in Atlanta had been a smart idea. He marveled at how quickly the man, once warned, had divested himself of his property, cleaned out his apartment, halfway cleaned out his bank accounts, and yet still had time to try to kill his nemesis at Nicodemus Mason's viewing.

Because so few automobiles had been sold in the Deep South, Gooderly's Ford was eventually found. Warfield Tidewell had alerted police cooperatives along the coast from Georgia through North Carolina. He even alerted city and town police in northeastern Florida, in case the clever criminal decided to head in an unlikely direction, sell his car, and hop on a train. Tidewell had been right in his thinking except that Gooderly had driven west through Waycross, Albany, Columbus, and Montgomery before selling the machine in Birmingham. There, he also used excellent timing, brassy bluff, and a glib tongue to convert a pair of the banknotes from Rufus Ivins into cash. From that hub, a train had been the most likely means of transport through Chattanooga and Knoxville to Lexington, Kentucky. The third and fourth banknotes were converted there. Then the trail went cold. With so much ready cash to live on, he could become virtually nameless.

At Le Brun's counseling, Tidewell stopped pestering the police departments of major cities with the Wanted poster he had created from Garland DeBrahm's photographs of Gooderly. "You know the expression 'Give a man enough rope to hang himself,'" John had told his friend. "There ought to be another: 'Give a man enough time to hang himself.' I'll bet Gooderly was in a lather when he fled Brunswick. But once he got away, his natural sense of superiority must have kicked in. I wonder how many times he congratulated himself on the smoothness of his escape. Once two or three months have passed, I figure he'll let down his guard and return to his old ways. The best means to speed the process is to call off the hounds and let the fox think he's safe enough to come out of his hole."

With John's guidance, Sheriff Tidewell had been working steadily to solidify the case against Gooderly. Patrick Ebenezer had been given only ninety days in jail and a stiff fine for his part in transporting the women from the ocean to the land. Many of those who might have served as jurors had little pity for women who had paid to enter the country illegally. Moreover, Ebenezer had a skillful lawyer; he was friendly with Judge Pinkett, who refused to recuse himself; and many local fishermen in his employ and local packers would have suffered if his fleet stopped functioning. In exchange for a guilty plea and sentencing without a jury trial, Ebenezer painted the sex slave importer in the darkest shades. Gooderly was convicted in absentia, the sentence made harsher by the fact of his flight.

While he awaited a court date in Atlanta for receiving prostitutes, Rufus Ivins received his judgment in Brunswick. Like Ebenezer, he was also given a lenient sentence after he signed a two-page statement attesting that Gooderly had passed a remark suggestive of guilt as he signed his brother's warehouse over to the man. The words were "Life is ironic. The spoonful of honey he put in his tea three times a day is what killed him."

Because Merriweather Gooderly had been the founder of the New Century Club and Patrick Ebenezer its third member, the stigma on the little group was too great for it to survive. Like the St. Clair Club before it, the St. Simons Island club vanished without a whimper.

A week before the wedding, Warfield admitted to John that he had visited the *Brunswick Call* and made an inquiry. His reasoning was that Gooderly might have arranged for the newspaper to be sent in the mail to a false addressee so that he could keep track of local events. Warfield had worried that the announcement of the wedding might draw the criminal back to Brunswick, endangering Lordis and her young charges as well as John. It turned out that only five such remote subscriptions existed, all made long before Gooderly fled and none sent farther than Charleston.

When Warfield made his confession, John replied, "I am flattered by the value you place on my hide, but even if he did know about the weddin', he wouldn't be willin' to return and play the black side on my chessboard. I believe he's had enough of me."

At the reception, Lordis and John sat in the center of the decorated dining room at a table that would only accommodate two. Leslie and Ben sat happily with the Owlsleys and their children, Regina and Philip. The other tables encircled them in a large ring with space between for dancing. More than a dozen regional dishes were set out, buffet style, on tables against one wall. Against the opposite wall, filled bottles of wine, bourbon, rye, and Scotch whisky became empty. The collective spirit was effervescent.

John and Lordis danced to the music of "The Merry Widow Waltz," then invited their guests to the floor while the string quartet played "Will You Love Me in December." As the music played on, the couple took the opportunity to visit those still seated at the tables. While Lordis made a special effort to ingratiate herself further with the women, John took Warfield aside.

"You recall a week ago how I said I believed Gooderly has had enough of me?"

"Of course," Tidewell replied.

"That don't mean I've had enough of him. Yesterday, I received a call from my agency administrator, Mrs. McMahon."

"Is Gooderly in New York?"

"I would not be surprised. She was finally able to learn the name of the front company that purchased the two untouched brothels in the 17th Precinct."

"The ones near Union Square," Warfield recalled.

"Precisely. That company's name is Algernon Holdings." For once, Le Brun failed to drop his g.

"My God!" Warfield exhaled. "The same name as Merri's brother."

John nodded slowly. "An ironic tribute, no doubt, to the source of Merri's wealth. I was regrettin' visitin' Atlanta for a spell, but if I hadn't, we couldn't have made the connection."

"This means that Gooderly isn't merely the provider of foreign women to those houses—he's running them."

"It may mean far worse than that," John said.

"Are the two houses still in operation?"

"Doin' a roarin' business. And why not? His two competitors were eliminated within days of each other."

Le Brun watched the gears turning behind Tidewell's eyes. His head nodded twice slowly. "So, you have probably solved your most difficult case. We had a monster living among us." Sheriff Tidewell pivoted to find his wife. Aurelia gestured peevishly for him to stop talking obvious shop. He held up a forefinger that would only buy him a few seconds. "Now what do you do?"

"I bide my time and let the fox think the hunt is gettin' colder still. I was already set to accompany Lordis and the children back to New York right after New Year's. Now I have an added incentive."

CHAPTER TWENTY-SEVEN

January 4, 1909

"GONE?" JOHN LE BRUN exclaimed.

Mary McMahon threw up her open hands as if she were a magician. "Poof! Vanished into t'in air. Thin air," she corrected herself.

John sat among the members of his agency in Mary's living room. Mary, Stuart Hirsch, and Larry Wilker sat as well, occupying every chair in sight. The unofficial member of the group, Kevin O'Leary, was content to lean against a wall.

John scratched his ear and smiled. "I can't say as I'm all that surprised. He was head over heels for her the minute he saw her. And who else could she converse with in her native tongue? But we all know where they are, don't we?"

"Pittsburgh," Mary said. Everyone in the room had long since been clued into the relationship between Anja Ljubanovic, the unwilling prostitute, and her ardent translator, Johnny Luppis.

"Why should anybody search?" Larry broke in. "She'll make a good citizen. We all say, 'Good luck.' But the disappearance of Merriweather Gooderly is another matter."

John lifted one of Sheriff Tidewell's Wanted posters and held it up for all to reacquaint themselves. "You should all have a copy of this from my mailin' four weeks back. Not one sightin'?"

Each shook his or her head in glum silence.

John said, "Be aware that he might have changed his look and dress. When I saved the ingrate's bacon over those stolen Gould paintin's, he repaid the favor by cozyin' up to me. That's why I was invited to join his secret club and why he contrived to travel to and from New York with me on the train." John shook the poster. "This polecat thinks he is way smarter than he actually is. He was pumpin' me, little by little, to learn my strengths and weaknesses. I believe he was especially taken by the several uses of disguise in the Edmund and Miniver Pinckney affair. I am convinced now of his course of actions in eliminatin' his assignation house competition in the 17th Precinct.

"While Gooderly and I were en route in April, he had Alvin Zark come up behind Herbert Moore—the first victim— and stab him with—"

"Hold on a moment," Kevin O'Leary interrupted. "You were talkin' about disguises, and then you jumped onto another track."

"Sorry. But I'm comin' to it," Le Brun said. "Zark stabbed him with the blade of that sword cane. When Zark tripped Stuart inside that West Side house, he reached out with his left hand. The autopsy report on Moore said that the wound entered between his shoulder blades a little on the left side and then went through toward the right. The theory was that the tip of the blade had glanced off one of the vertebrae. It's more likely that the murderer was left-handed.

"Some time before Gooderly and I traveled here together, I had told him of this detective agency. We have all advertised it, made it as easy as possible to learn where we are headquartered. A phony letterhead was fashioned for J. P. Morgan. The fact of Moore's murder and the instructions were typed with no signature so that if I remembered Morgan's handwritin', I couldn't immediately prove it wasn't from him."

"But why would he pay so much money up front to hire you?" Larry asked.

"First, because he's an inveterate and cutthroat game player. After losing to me too often at chess, he developed an obsession to beat me at what I do best. Second, because everyone—him included—was payin' off Lieutenant Bergman and his boys to keep their houses as secret as could be. But in the case of Gooderly's competition, he wanted the sort of high profile detective work the police would never willingly provide."

"To scare all future competition away from that area," Mary understood.

"Gooderly knew from hearin' so many of my exploits that I involve myself intimately. This would mean that I was almost certain to visit the brothel across the street after the first killin'. I myself told him I was busy workin' on the case that evenin'."

The thespian in John caused him to lean forward in his chair, inviting everyone to move a bit closer. "I think he set the gears in motion durin' a March visit to Manhattan, shortly after meetin' me. As himself, he visited the competition houses several times. After meetin' all the women, he realized that the one who was called Violet was the most clever and aggressive. She longed to become a madam and run a house. He told her what she wanted to hear, and she swallowed it, hook, line, and sinker. That determined that the owner to be killed in the street was, by default, Herbert Moore. Somebody learned his

evenin' habits, makin' it easy to come up behind him right in
front of his least legitimate business. One supposed robbery
can be written off easily enough, especially if the police in
the neighborhood want to close the investigation as soon as
possible."

"And especially since Moore's wife is just as happy that he's
dead," Mary added.

John smiled and gave an admiring point of his finger
in her direction. "A second pedestrian death on the street,
however, was not what Gooderly was looking for. He wanted
somethin' spectacular that would frighten other brothel
entrepreneurs away. Since Bergman wouldn't cooperate, he
hired me to guarantee a newspaper splash. I had told him
of my relationship with Joseph Pulitzer and his chief editor,
Frank Cobb. I had also made known at the New Century Club
my revulsion over the practice of slavery . . . and especially
sexual servitude.

"So in I went and met Miss Violet—whose name should
have been Primrose since she led me so convincingly down the
path. The truth was that she picked *me* out instead of the normal
process. No doubt, Gooderly had given her my description. She
made a subtle gesture that, even so, caught my eye. I'm sure
that the day after Moore was murdered the sword cane was
brought into the house by one of Gooderly's men in the guise of
a John. Clever Miss Violet had learned how to get through not
one but two locks in Diefendorfer's study. She no doubt placed
it in the closet after Mr. D left for the day and before I showed
up. She sold me her story of witnessin' the murder across the
street and relied on my moral outrage and lock-pickin' abilities.
As soon as I left with the cane, she signaled Gooderly."

"Do you think he actually took part in the bloodletting?"
Stu asked.

"Oh, yes," John came back. "Violet might have used the
phone in Diefendorfer's study. That doesn't matter. What matters

is how swiftly Gooderly responded. He needed Violet to unlock
the back door in order to attack the two guards simultaneously.
She managed it, and her repayment was a bullet between the
eyes. She'd done her job of framing Diefendorfer for Moore's
murder, of gulling me, and of unlocking the door. She knew
too much to live."

"Bastards!" O'Leary interjected.

John ignored the outburst and continued, "Now, here's
where the disguise comes in. Gooderly is a bit tall and
overweight. That's why the prints in the woods across from
Nicodemus Mason's were larger but not too large, deep but
not exceedingly deep. For this slaughter inside the assignation
house, he needed to be there, but he also wanted to be sure
none of the survivin' prostitutes could identify him. What was
their description of him?"

Mary was the quickest to speak. "A fat man with a red
beard and moustache and wearing eyeglasses."

"Wire-rim half glasses," John refined. "And with several
rings on his left hand. All of it, includin' added weight, can be
put on easily. He can't make himself skinny so he goes in the
other direction."

"But you often made this Gooderly sound like a dandy," Stu
doubted. "Could such a character shoot someone point blank?"

"Lizzie Borden didn't look dangerous," Le Brun replied.
"Nor did Theo Durant, that San Francisco Sunday school
teacher who raped and strangled two women in his own church.
Chances are good he poisoned his brother. And if he wasn't the
one who shot at me, may I be hornswoggled. Who knows what
other physical mayhem he's committed?

"He enters the house from the front pretendin' to be a
patron. Zark is let into the back by Violet. They kill the two men
on guard. If Gooderly came in the front, then he killed Violet
because of the caliber of bullet that went through her head.
Not one but two people shot point blank. The little one I call

Mutt waited by the closed truck. Witnesses were shot. The remainin' women were hustled out the back door and taken up to the West Side assignation house. Somehow, Diefendorfer opens the door of his loft apartment to these men a few hours later. They overpower and hang him. I'll wager they also took important accounts concernin' Diefendorfer's sex business. Or businesses. Only Bergman and his minions know the truth there." John brushed his palms against each other several times. "Between the murders and my efforts through the press, that's the end of high-class competition in the 17th Precinct."

Larry said, "There is no place on Stuyvescent Avenue for us to watch that house unobserved. The one on Park, just above Union Square, offers a couple of spots that we've been using."

"And Christ but both places are doing business like Macy's in December," Stu interrupted.

Larry continued, "But even with Stu, me, Mary, and Alice taking shifts, there are blocks of time when Gooderly could enter and exit. He can't change his height much or make himself thinner than he is, but johns his age, height, and weight are at least a third of those who frequent such houses."

Le Brun said, "And, if he visits either of those two houses at all, he could easily have dyed his hair black or gray, grown a scruffy beard, and worn overalls. For all we know, he arrives regularly dressed as the trash hauler. The truth is, Gooderly may be an absentee landlord. He could just as easily be clean across the country as we sit here."

After a few moments of contemplative group silence, NYPD Detective O'Leary pushed off from the wall and exclaimed in a loud voice. "Ya can't run whorehouses from a distance. At the least, you'd be robbed blind by the managers; more likely, you'd lose the place to them. These ain't angels we're talkin' about. John hurt him bad by shuttin' down the man's swanky West Side operation an' by eliminatin' two of his bully boys. I say he's within five miles of where ya sit, and he'll come after you, John, as soon as he gets wind you're back in the city."

"So the first order of business is learnin' where he is," Le Brun said. "Then, if he's in New York City, we need to get the upper hand. And we need to do it quickly."

JOHN STEPPED OUT of the shadows of the 17th Precinct stable moments after a groomsman handed the reins of the cabriolet to Kasper Bergman. He timed his movements up and into the two-person carriage just as the lieutenant snapped his light whip.

"Your pals told me downstairs that you hadn't been in all mornin'," John said, without any preamble. "Obviously, they were lyin' on your behalf. A typical day at the office."

"I have a doctor's appointment at half past two, Mr. Le Brun," Bergman snapped, after recovering his surprise. "And I do not conduct police business in my—"

"It isn't police business I want to discuss with you," John interrupted. "It should be, but you've done your utmost to see that it isn't. Keep drivin', Lieutenant. I am here to do you a tremendous favor, if you're smart enough to accept it."

Bergman kept his eyes on the street as the cabriolet moved. "Really?"

"If you recall, I became involved in the murders on East Twelfth Street because of a note purportin' to come from my acquaintance, J. Pierpont Morgan. It turns out that, in spite of the large sum of cash that came with it, Morgan had nothin' to do with hirin' me. The actual person was Merriweather Gooderly."

John knew that Bergman would be too skilled to let his face betray his thoughts. John instead focused on the man's hands, which suddenly tightened on the reins, turning the top knuckles of his hands from pink to white.

"This is the same Merriweather Gooderly who lived in my

hometown of Brunswick and who is right now in this city."
Bergman gave no sign that John's words were wrong. Le Brun
pulled from his pocket one of the Wanted posters Warfield
Tidewell had had printed. He unfolded it and held it up so that
Bergman could glance at it. "This man is not just the owner of
assignation houses on the edge of your district but is also the
illegal importer of desperate foreign women. His actions caused
the drowning of one of those women in Brunswick Bay. He is
poison to anyone who cooperates with him in breakin' the law.
I would venture to say that if such a person were a lawman, the
poison could be lethal." John pointed to an open space at the
avenue's curb. "Why don't you pull in over there, Lieutenant,
so you can give me your undivided attention."

Bergman obliged.

"You're accusing me of complicity?" Bergman asked when
the carriage was at a full stop.

"You've accused yourself, sir. By failin' to shut down the
various houses of prostitution in your precinct . . . includin'
those owned by Gooderly. By tryin' to bar the entrance of me
and Editor Frank Cobb into a crime scene for which I had vital
information. By spiritin' away five prostitutes I found on the
West Side without proper due process."

"I merely let them go," Bergman protested.

"No," Le Brun stated flatly. "If that were true, at least one
of them would have been picked up in the weeks followin' since
their only means of survival was to turn to street prostitution.
But I have checked with the precincts that surround yours and
the registry at The Tombs. I found no booking photograph of
any of them."

"I'll thank you to step out of my cab," Bergman said. "Right
now."

In reply, John again reached into his inside jacket pocket.
When his hand emerged, it held a claret-colored appointment
book. "I trust you'll recognize this. It's what Merri Gooderly

uses to keep all his appointments and day-to-day transactions. Considerin' that he fled Brunswick at a mad dash, he did a respectable job of cleanin' out his belongin's. But he left this behind, stuck to the back of his desk's center drawer."

John used his thumb to riffle through the pages. "Upon reflection, I am mighty glad you refused to see me inside your precinct today. No doubt, you would have felt secure enough to confiscate this. But I assure you I have proof of its existence and of what you see scribbled on its pages. I have had the cover and each set of pages photographed for my protection. I have also shown this to all my employees at the John Le Brun Detective Agency. I also have my right hand on my revolver as we speak. Please recall that I had no hesitation in killin' Albert or Alvin Zark or Zook or Zed in that West Side house. I will not hesitate to put a bullet into your shoulder if you make a move on me."

Bergman's eyes were fixed on the wine-colored notebook.

"LFB," John said. "Not a very tough code to crack. From the dates, this is clearly the appointment book just precedin' the one he is usin' now." John used his thumb and forefinger to display the first page. "Do you recognize his handwritin', or haven't you paid that much attention? You don't figure much in it, but the dates and the indication of payoffs are oh so damnin'."

Without warning, John snapped the book shut. As he tucked it back into his pocket, he said, "Let me emphasize, Lieutenant, that I am not after you. I would reckon that if you should be punished for graft, then scores of others in the NYPD merit at least equal treatment. I am well aware that policemen are underpaid, overworked, and receive uneven internal discipline for lapses in duty. Further, I know that much good is done by your city's force. It would be terrible to demoralize the population with the information I possess. You alone know how much or how little support from above you can expect if I bring the truth to light. But I assure you that J. P. Morgan was not happy about his name bein' pulled into this business. So much so that he has been payin' for my investigation to continue. I also remind you that the pump of righteous indignation was primed in the late spring and early summer concernin' prostitution in this city. Most likely, if what I know came to light, you would be handed over as a scapegoat and swiftly put where you could not embarrass the many others who take their cut of the wages of vice. You would not survive a week in a New York prison."

Bergman considered Le Brun's words for long seconds. "As you say, this is not an easy problem to dispose of. What do you suggest?"

CHAPTER TWENTY-EIGHT

January 4, 1909

WINTER CLOUDS HAD been hanging so low all day that their bottoms touched the pinnacles of New York's tallest buildings, earning the structures the title of skyscrapers. As John rode north on Fifth Avenue in a Hansom cab, snow began to fall lightly. It blew into his face, causing John to squint every few seconds. The clip-clop of the horse's iron shoes were muted by the shiny asphalt beneath them. John wondered just how few years ahead a horse would be an uncommon sight in Manhattan. He checked his pocket watch and encouraged the driver to pick up the pace. He wanted to arrive at Whispering Hope just before the children arrived from their first day back to school. The conversation he had completed with Lieutenant Bergman half an hour before repeated in his ears.

The mansion stood on the southern corner of Fifth Avenue

and Sixty-second Street. It looked even less hospitable than usual to John, its brownstone walls darkening as the snow touched them and melted. He stepped out of the cab and reached up to pay the driver, then walked into the partial shelter of the front door portico. He rapped on one of the enormous door knockers and waited. He rapped again.

"John!" Ben called out.

Larry Wilker and Stuart Hirsch appeared on the street from the Park Avenue direction with the Topley children walking beside them. Ben clutched in one hand the locomotive of his Christmas-present train, which he had brought to school to make the other boys envious. He waved with the other hand, and John returned the greeting. John pivoted around, expecting the door to open at any second.

"Where's Lordis?" Leslie asked, as she approached the stoop.

"I don't know," John replied.

"She said she'd be here to greet us," Ben pouted.

"I have the key," said Leslie. She captured a sturdy chain around her neck and pulled from under her dress the massive front door key.

John turned back to survey the street. "She did indeed promise to be standin' here."

Stu and Larry were already on the alert, Stu with his hand inside his coat seeking the revolver in his shoulder holster.

Leslie pushed one of the large front doors inward and rushed into the foyer, calling Lordis's name. Ben followed. John backed up the steps and into the shelter of the house, as did the two ex-policemen.

"Children, stay with me!" John commanded, not wanting them to witness a sight that might scar them for life. "Larry, look upstairs. Stu, take the basement." He closed the front door.

Although the wedding in Brunswick had precluded the purchase of a Christmas tree for the mansion, it was nonetheless decorated with holly and mistletoe and dozens of painted glass ornaments imported from Italy. The festive mood seemed mocking to John. The only sounds were the heavy tread of quick-moving shoes upon wooden floors and the calling of Lordis's name.

One of the front door knockers sounded. John pulled his revolver from its belt holster and yanked the door open. Merriweather Gooderly stood on the second step, smiling like the St. Nicholas in a Thomas Nast drawing.

"Happy New Year!" he wished in a joyful tone.

"Where's Lordis?" John demanded.

"Safe and sound and being treated like a lady," Gooderly replied. He reached into his trouser pocket and pulled out her wedding band and the engagement ring with the pearl. They were joined by a light-blue ribbon tied in a knot. "So, she is now Mrs. John Le Brun! I had no idea until I saw her hand. She told me you two were just married in Brunswick. But how could I have known that? I am a refugee. I get no news from there. My closest friends won't even answer my telephone calls. One of my former warehousemen was kind enough not to hang up. He told me that Rufus Ivins and Elmer Cate are on ice. Ergo, my supply of willing whores from Europe has been effectively severed."

John revealed the revolver and trained it on Gooderly. From behind him echoed the voice of Wilker.

"Nobody upstairs," he reported. "Who are you—"

"Fetch Stuart," Le Brun ordered quietly. He listened to Larry dash away. To Gooderly, he said, "A bit harder to bushwhack me in the middle of this city."

"Especially when you're not out in the open unless surrounded by your henchmen." The ex-warehouseman's smile dropped. "Except when you have them walk the children home. With that steel-trap mind of yours, you obviously remembered that Lordis told me which schools Ben and Leslie attend. But nobody volunteered where the three of them live. Nevertheless, here I am, and gone she is." He waggled his forefinger at John. "I want you to remember that I left the children alone. The only one who should suffer for the mistreatment you've visited upon me is you."

"Mistreatment assumes innocence," John countered.

"Bring your protection with you, by all means," Gooderly said, looking past John at Larry.

"Where are we goin'?"

"Just across the street into Central Park."

John turned and addressed his employees. "This is Mr. Gooderly standin' before you."

"Yes, this is what I look like when not in disguise," he admitted. "Actually, I've almost met both of you before. You and the two women in the John Le Brun Detective Agency have spent a great deal of time watching my place at Union Square. Late this morning, we were able to corner Mrs. Alice Ainsworth and scare the bejesus out of her. I'm so glad *she* knew where Lordis lives. Imagine! The quarry stalking the prey." Gooderly blinked as a snowflake tumbled onto his eyelashes.

John stepped outside, re-holstering his revolver. Over his shoulder he said, "Stu, stay here with the children. Make sure the doors and back windows are locked."

"Yes, you do that, Stu," Gooderly said with mock sincerity. Not waiting for a reply, he turned smartly and headed briskly in the direction of Central Park, which lay just across Fifth Avenue.

John caught up with him in several strides. "What exactly do you want?"

Gooderly kept moving, although he had already begun to pant slightly. "Right now, I want to sit in the park. Indulge me."

They passed through the Children's Gate and walked down a gentle decline toward the stone benches that had the chessboards cut and polished into their surfaces.

"You really don't need your friend following us," Gooderly said. "You're in no danger. Neither is Mrs. Le Brun."

"I believe you. You need us both to be alive," John said, holding up his hand so that Wilker would maintain his distance.

"Absolutely." Merriweather swiped at the snow accumulated on the bench and the table with his glove, then walked around to the opposite side, cleaned the bench, and sat. "I discovered these chess tables while waiting for you. Have you ever played on them?"

"Yes. Lordis and I have."

"Is she any good?"

"Better than you."

Gooderly laughed. "Of course she is. Sit!"

John sat opposite his foe and looked at the arrangement of light and dark squares. "You took the white side."

"Shouldn't I? The advantage is, after all, mine."

"We have no pieces," John pointed out.

"We don't need them. Just play the game with your mind. Here are the rules: not only do I make the first move, but your queen is captured even before that. Even given that you are a slightly better player than I, how long would you last?"

"To mid-game."

"Not more than twelve white moves before defeat is obvious." Gooderly folded his arms across his chest. "Now, stop thinking game, and start thinking real life."

"I'm sure of one thing you're after. You want me to contact Sheriff Tidewell and have him unfreeze the bank accounts in DeBrahm's bank," John said. "Four thousand one hundred and twenty-one dollars and nineteen cents, plus accrued interest since you skipped town."

"It *is* my money," Gooderly said.

"Much of it was earned from helpless sex slaves," John riposted.

Merri's face screwed into a smirk. "Would-be illegals, half

of them already whores—or eventual whores in their own countries. Females brought into this world who obviously couldn't be cared for. Surplus humanity . . . the byproducts of peasants rutting in rude shacks, obeying the same sexual imperative that rats and cockroaches do." His face suddenly softened. "Look, I'm here to make you a deal. You forced me into selling my warehouses at a loss of $2,700."

"I would have expected a worse loss," John said frankly.

Merri nodded affably. "It would have been so, if Ivins had known that you had figured out my smuggling operation. I let him think I had to flee because you learned I poisoned my brother. He actually thought he could continue where I left off."

"*Did* you poison your brother?"

"Obliquely. A few months after he got his bill of health, he and I went to the opening of a farm cooperative market near the warehouses. The various orchards, farms, dairies, and so forth had giveaway drawings to attract future clients. One apiary offered a basket of four jars of honey. Algernon won the drawing. I had a packet of arsenic in my pocket—ready for any opportunity. I bought two bottles from the same stall, adulterated them with the arsenic, and found an opportunity to switch my bottles with two in Algernon's basket. He did the rest, over a period of three months. There's no way anyone can prove what I just said. Ivins should have realized that. But he was greedy for my businesses."

"And you want that $2,700 loss out of my hide as well."

Gooderly shrugged. "Not all of it. Because I underestimated you, that part of my losses is my fault. Therefore, you only owe me half—$1,350 from your own assets. Secondly, you worked hard to improve this city because you love New York. Your rich buddies are here, you're a member of two classy clubs, it has all the swank and fun that Brunswick couldn't possibly produce. You feel proprietary about it. I understand completely. I insist that virtue should *not* be, as the saying goes, its own reward. Which shows I'm not a heartless monster."

John longed to respond but realized that any remark might set off the amoral megalomaniac.

The assignation house master plowed on. "You and the other pious moralists here are making a dishonest living harder and harder to earn. So I'm resolved to relocate. I'm in the process of clearing out of your beloved city. But that requires considerable money and that can't happen overnight."

Gooderly shivered. He rose from the bench and took two steps backward. "If you want your wife returned unharmed, you hand me the money you owe me in gold. You must also arrange for me to get every last penny out of my accounts in DeBrahm's bank. Then, you must sit like a lamb and mind those kids. You'll get your beautiful wife back with not one of her gorgeous shafts of hair harmed. You're a worthy opponent, but you must not forget that I have the upper hand. If you don't follow my demands to the letter or if you capture or kill me, I guarantee that she will be whisked across the Hudson and tossed into a common whorehouse far away. She'll be chained, wrists and ankles, to a four-poster, and she'll earn someone a small fortune. She's still a handsome, sensual woman, whom an unending line of men forty or older would love to ravish. She will service nonstop, day and night, because the rate for her will be set at two dollars. If she maintains the daunting high spirits she's shown since we took her, she'll simply be turned into an opium fiend."

Le Brun had expected a detailing of lurid images, but an acid-like fury spread throughout him nonetheless.

"Now," Gooderly went on, "how long must I wait until I get my money from you and from DeBrahm's bank?"

John said, "I can't promise any sooner than two days. Before bank closin' hours on Wednesday."

Gooderly stood and brushed off the seat of his trousers.

"That's what I expected. When you get it, I want yours in those new $20 gold coins, plus the last fifty in silver dollars. The bank money should be in $10 silver certificates, fifty to a paper band, nonconsecutive. Plus $130 in silver dollars. In a physician's bag. Understood?"

"Perfectly. But I don't hand over anythin' except to you. And that don't happen until I see Mrs. Le Brun."

"I won't carry a weapon. I expect the same of you."

"I understand," John replied.

"Wonderful. Stay well until we meet again."

"Where will that be?"

Gooderly pulled a slip of paper from his trouser pocket and handed it to Le Brun. "Here's the location. Four o'clock on Thursday. Bring no police or detective employees with you. Otherwise we'll need to reset your delivery date. And Mrs. Le Brun will be hobbling on crutches the rest of her life." He made a small bow and began walking toward the center of the park. After half a dozen steps he paused and turned. "Oh, I almost forgot. You also owe me the five hundred dollars I advanced your agency to solve Moore's murder. That whore Violet solved the crime, not you. Eighteen hundred and fifty dollars from you, John Le Brun."

CHAPTER TWENTY-NINE

January 7, 1909

"I DON'T LIKE this one damned bit," Mary McMahon fumed. "I don't care that he proclaimed himself less than a monster. He's going to murder you and drag Lordis away to wherever he's relocated."

Her husband, Martin, had taken Thursday off, in case one more man unfamiliar to Gooderly and his cronies should be needed. He stood in his living room among Larry Wilker, Stuart Hirsch, and Kevin O'Leary and nodded in tacit agreement with his wife.

John smoked one of the Perfecto cigars he had bought the previous day. He exhaled and, in a casual tone of voice, declared, "You know what I learned yesterday? Never smoke a cigar aged less than three years. Otherwise, there's too much ammonia in them."

"You can't downplay this," O'Leary said sternly. "With such a clever enemy, there is no such t'ing as bein' a hundred percent sure of the outcome."

"How's that girlfriend of yours?" John inquired.

"She's livin' with me now," Kevin replied.

"Aren't you afraid you're makin' the same mistake over again?"

Kevin sighed peevishly. "I ain't marryin' this one."

John consulted his pocket watch. "And is the ex Mrs. O'Leary still with the trombone salesman?"

"I suppose. She hasn't come crawlin' back to me. Are you sure Gooderly won't make the exchange in that Rexall Drugstore on Union Square?"

"Correct."

"But the real location will be somewhere in the 17th Precinct," Stu broke in.

"Correct."

"Even though Gooderly shut down both his brothels Tuesday night," said Larry to Le Brun. "Just as you predicted he would."

As men unknown to Gooderly, retired policemen Paddy Carew and Winston Brown had been engaged to watch the two assignation houses near Union Square. Paddy had sharply noticed that, even though evening lights glowed within his assigned house, potential clients knocking on the front door of his assignment were not admitted. From a dark vantage point in the house's back alley, he had watched as eight limp sacks the size of average women were carried by a pair of burly men into a closed motor van. Winston had also noted that the house he watched was lit but not accepting patrons. Both had telephoned the John Le Brun Detective Agency, and John had immediately sent Stuart Hirsch to the Erie Railroad Terminal in Hoboken, New Jersey. Moments later, he dispatched Larry Wilker to the freight yard of the Lehigh Valley Railroad in adjacent Jersey City. Within two hours, two large crates had been moved off a Hudson River ferry and been delivered to the Erie freight yard. Both crates were loaded into an empty boxcar toward the front of a thirty-car consist. The car's position strongly suggested it would not be uncoupled from the train for a long distance into the run. Two of the four large men who had managed the two crates climbed into the car carrying suitcases. The other two had sealed the door and walked back to the Erie's passenger terminal. Stuart had noted the number board on the locomotive and checked with the freight master. The freight train was bound for Chicago with stops at Binghamton, Corning, Meadville, Leavittsburg, Marion, Lima, Decatur, and Rochester.

John's crew decided that the prostitutes in Gooderly's two midtown assignation houses had been drugged and boxed into the crates. It would be unlikely that Gooderly would set up shop in a small city like Corning or Decatur. Further, the journey to Chicago would be long enough to risk their lives; he might kill some of his precious cargo if he took more time forwarding them to another large Midwest city. Booming, venal Chicago was to be the site of Gooderly's new operation. The mixed freight consist with no ice cars for perishables was scheduled to leave Hoboken at 2:42 A.M. and take a non-express twenty-two hours to reach Chicago. Because John did not trust the Chicago police force any more than he did the NYPD, he arranged for the Pinkerton Agency to have several detectives watch for the train's arrival and discreetly follow the two crates wherever they might go. Even to Pinkerton officials, he had not disclosed the contents of the crates.

"I don't know how you can be so sure where Gooderly will take you," Larry persisted.

"For one thing," John said, "because I have played more than a dozen games of chess with the man."

"And for a second thing?" Stu asked.

"You'll see. Just be where the carriage stops. At 4:20 P.M. and not a moment sooner. Two revolvers each, fully loaded."

"Are we sure the Topley children are safe?" Mary asked. "He could deliver Lordis and, at the same time, have someone drag them off the street on their way home from their schools."

"I've taken care of that," John assured. "They spent last night with members of Lordis's Leper's Club. Nobody knows the members unless they are already part of the club. If anyone has been watchin' Whisperin' Hope today, he would conclude that both young-uns never left the house."

"So that's it?" Martin McMahon wondered. "You can't use the leverage of J. P. Morgan or Joseph Pulitzer or a dozen other influential men at the Players Club or the Manhattan Club? Surely, they can assemble a squad of honest patrolmen in plainclothes to blanket the area and swoop in when John gets to Gooderly and his wife?"

"Are you kidding?" Stuart Hirsh exclaimed. "It's been not even ten years since Tammany Hall appointed Bill Devery Chief of Police. Devery's the one who said, 'If there's any grafting to be done, I'll do it.' Sure, a couple dozen honest cops could be assembled, but by the time you'd done it, another hundred would have gotten word to Gooderly for a ten-dollar payoff!"

"I'll live or I'll die with the plan I've put together," John affirmed. He rose from his chair and nodded at Mary McMahon. "Time to go."

THE EARLY JANUARY AFTERNOON was balmy, inviting shoppers, shoeshine boys, street corner hawkers, travelers, and loiterers to Union Square. John noted with relief that not a uniformed patrolman was in sight. He looked at the buildings that surrounded the tree-filled square. Every structure was commercial except for four houses that were all younger than fifty years, and every commercial structure was four to sixteen stories high, uniformly rectilinear and filled with lines of gleaming windows. One block above the more northern of Gooderly's assignation houses, the newest of the steel building skeletons awaited its curtain walls.

Le Brun waited for a streetcar to pass before continuing across the wide street. A distant church bell had begun to sound out the hour of four o'clock. John reached the curb in front of the Rexall Drugstore just as the last clang echoed down the Broadway canyon. He entered the store.

A thin, average-sized young man in his early twenties awaited Le Brun. He wore his pea jacket open so that John could see his plaid shirt and vest. Together with the poor-boy cap, gloves without fingers, three-day-old beard, and hard-set jaw, he was the cliché image of a street tough. He squinted myopically. While John returned the stare, he privately wondered exactly how many young men were willing to do such dirty work rather than learn a trade in a city that snapped up diligent laborers.

John decided to think of the tough as Squint. He did not fit the description Stu had given of either man who returned from the Erie freight yard. It meant that at least three henchmen rather than the expected two remained in the city to serve Gooderly. *The best-laid plans of mice and men,* John thought, taking a deep, fortifying breath.

His face fixed resolutely straight ahead, the young thug swaggered toward Le Brun. As they were shoulder to shoulder, he said in a half voice, "Follow me." John pivoted and fell in behind him.

The drugstore was large. Squint continued to the back aisle away from the eyes of the pharmacist, the counter clerk, and the customers. As Squint slowed, John dropped his physician's bag. Its muted noise was enough to cause the tough to spin around. John caught him in midspin and shoved him hard against an open space of wall.

"What the hell?" Squint exploded.

"Quiet down, Sonny. Just checkin' you for weapons," John said, expertly patting him down. He laughed softly as he fished from the pea jacket's right pocket a glasses case containing oval lenses inside brass frames. He handed the case and spectacles to their owner. "Put these on, and stop worryin' about whether or not you look mean enough."

"Now I gotta frisk *you*, ya bold bastard!" Gooderly's minion complained, as he replaced the case and glasses in his coat pocket.

"I'm prepared." Le Brun stripped off his suit jacket so that the ruffian could clearly see he had no gun in a belt or shoulder holster. He raised his arms so that they appeared over the lines of shelves in the center of the store. The man imitated John's patting actions but in a slower, more methodical fashion, starting from the detective's sleeve cuffs and moving down to the cuffs of his trousers. He nodded his satisfaction as he straightened up.

"You're clean. Now the bag," he said, nodding at the case. "Open it up!"

Le Brun turned the latch and spread the leather bag's mouth wide.

"Okay, I see the gold and silver coins," Squint said. "But I've got to make sure the bills are real and their serial numbers are not in order."

John looked up suddenly and focused just past the tough's shoulder. An instant later, the same shoulder was touched by a small hand inside a white, calfskin glove.

"Young man . . ." the owner of the hand said crisply.

Squint yelped and spun around, facing a little woman wearing a long coat and carrying a large purse. Under her broad-brimmed hat, her hair was gray and her complexion pale. She wore pince-nez spectacles with a light-blue tint.

"Oh!" the woman said, taking a step backward. "I'm so sorry. I've frightened you."

"No you didn't," Squint countered. "Just surprised me is all."

"I'm glad to hear it!" the little lady said brightly even before Squint finished his sentence. "I wonder if you would do me a favor." She twisted around and pointed to the top shelf of the display unit set against the store's back wall. "Would you fetch me that package of mustard plaster up there?"

Squint shot a look at Le Brun, then returned his attention to the woman. "Yeah, sure." He reached up and hauled down the package. "Here."

"Thank you so much." The gray-haired lady cocked her head to one side and looked past him at the physician's bag. Then her partially shielded eyes darted upward. "Doctor, is this the best treatment for a sore back?"

"It's better for healin' wounds than helpin' soreness," John told her. "You should immerse yourself in a bath as cold as is comfortable when you feel back soreness. And take two Bayer's aspirin every six hours to relieve the inflammation and pain."

"Oh, thank you, Doctor!" the woman gushed. Without warning, she thrust the mustard plaster material back into the tough's hands. "I won't be needing this. Please return it." Having made her declaration, she executed a stiff about-face and moved with mincing, slightly bowed steps in the direction of the pharmacist.

Squint turned an exasperated look at Le Brun, who smiled and shrugged. He shoved the package of mustard plaster onto the nearest shelf.

John once more held the doctor's bag wide open. Squint picked out a banded pack of bills and methodically thumbed through them. He stirred around the paper and coins to be sure nothing else lay in the bag. Then he picked up a second packet.

"You're gonna get us robbed," John warned. "Two fellas are walkin' this way."

Squint took John by the shoulder and pushed him toward

an emergency door in the back of the store. In a mocking tone, he said, "I thought you were a famous detective. That old biddy didn't know you. This way, Doctor! Close your bag!"

As soon as the pair appeared in the afternoon light, a Brougham carriage moved toward them from the curb at the north end of the block. It stopped directly in front of John. He looked up at the driver and recognized Stu Hirsch's description of one of the men who returned from the Erie Terminal. John expected that when he climbed into the enclosed carriage, Squint would follow. Instead, the young man slammed the door shut, and the light coach jolted away from the curb at a reckless pace.

Le Brun could do nothing except hold onto a strap with one hand and the doctor's bag with the other as the carriage executed several wheel-rocking turns. He struggled to note the names of the streets and avenues that the driver took. A maze-like progress was being created by his maneuvers. Eventually, the coach slowed. John looked out the back window. One by one, all the tailing motorcars, trucks, and horse-drawn transports within a block disappeared. At that point, the driver reversed the carriage's general southward route and took Broadway north. At East Fourteenth Street he turned right, made a left onto Irving Place, continued north for three blocks to Seventeenth, and finished with a sharp turn into a shadowy alley. John realized that, for all the thirty-odd blocks they had traveled, he was within a thousand feet of where he had been picked up. He was not in the slightest surprised.

The Brougham stopped. In the narrow alley, the sounds of the city could be heard only faintly.

"Some ride. Do you drive in Sunday's Carriage Parade in Central Park?" John goaded.

"Get out," the driver answered, half reply and half command. He possessed the deepest bass voice John had ever heard.

John alit from the Brougham holding the black satchel.

"Wait there!" the driver directed.

John listened to the man gee and haw and watched him work the reins to guide the horse into one of the mossy-roofed stalls on the east side of the alley. In spite of the horse's labored breathing and flanks glistening with sweat, he gave it no care but headed directly toward John after he leapt down. He secured the reins only lightly, indicating that he expected the carriage would get more use almost immediately.

As Stu Hirsch had described, the man was large and intimidating. He stood almost a full head above the detective. His motions were crude and awkward, as if an excess of muscle took the grace from his stride. Compensating for his large proportions and unrefined gait, he dressed in a conservative suit of muted gray and wore a derby hat. He did not pause as he passed John but maintained his stride, heading to the rear of the nearby structure and up its back steps. John knew it had to be the more southern of Gooderly's two Union Square assignation houses.

As soon as John entered the house, walking into a storage room, he saw that it was lit by neither gas nor electricity but rather by a pair of candles in brass holders.

"Had the power turned off, eh?" John said. "Definitely moving out."

The man said nothing. He led the way up four steps, past a narrow staircase, and along a hall to a large room that John supposed had been designed for formal dining. It was lit by six candles, most of them burned halfway down. Le Brun recognized from the total absence of city sounds that the room lay in the center of the well-insulated house. Two other door frames split the walls to his left and right. The doors were closed. The far wall was mostly hidden by a marble-fronted fireplace and walnut cabinets on either side. The fireplace was cold. A table built to accommodate twelve occupied the center of the room, but only four chairs were pushed up against it.

"Put it there." The curt driver pointed first to the satchel and then to the table and, without looking back, walked to the door toward the rear of the house. John countered, hastening to place himself with his back to the fireplace where no one could surprise him from behind. He set the leather case between two candles on the long table.

The driver returned, passing through the east side door. He continued on, moving to block the door through which John had entered the room. Then Lordis appeared. She looked disheveled and angry. When she tried to rush to her husband, a hand thrust out from behind and grabbed the nape of her collar.

"Not yet, Lady," her captor warned. The second man from the Erie freight yard pushed her gently toward the west side door.

Lordis attempted a brave smile for John. He smiled back. He saw that her hands had been tied.

The last through the doorway was Merriweather Gooderly. Over his suit, he wore an expensive light-gray topcoat with black velvet lapels. All vestiges of facial hair, including his usual sideburns, had vanished.

"So, you fulfilled your part of the bargain," Gooderly said to Le Brun. "No police or fellow detectives following you. No weapons."

John casually gripped the back of his left hand with the fingers of his right. "As you said in the park, you have the winning position."

"Just so." Merri nodded in Lordis's direction. "As you see, I've kept my part. Not one hair on your wife's beautiful head has been harmed." He flicked his fingers to signal John to take a step backward as he moved toward the doctor's bag. John complied.

Gooderly slid the satchel toward the middle of the table, then turned the latch. His eyes widened in direct proportion to the opening of the satchel's mouth. "Look at all those gold coins! And the silver dollars. But is every bill in these packs random? Let's see." He lifted the first band of twenties and began to flip through them, noting the serial numbers.

John changed his attention to Lordis. "We always seem to end up in dinin' rooms when things get dangerous," he commented, reminding her of how they had ducked under another massive table, that one inside Whispering Hope.

Lordis nodded. "True."

"Why don't you two cut the gab until I'm finished?" Gooderly commanded. "I'm trying to concentrate."

A half minute passed in silence. The sex slaver's musclemen fixed their stares on John, who tapped his right forefinger repeatedly against his wrist. One of the men shot him an annoyed look. John hunched his shoulders as if in apology and tucked the finger under his shirt cuff.

"All here. All genuine," Gooderly announced. "Which means we no longer need you alive, Detective Le—"

The words had apparently been an arranged signal to the guards. With nearly identical motions, they lifted their hands toward their chests.

Le Brun moved much more quickly. When he withdrew the fingers of his right hand from his left shirt cuff, they held a derringer. In one smooth motion, John cocked it and aimed at the man directly opposite him. He pulled the first trigger. Trapped in the enclosed room, the explosion was all the more raucous. The man's head snapped back so swiftly that the derby tumbled down his chest and onto the floor.

Lordis, who had stood to the left of her guard, her collar still locked in the left-handed grip of her captor, swung around as his right hand dug into his jacket. Her tied hands delivered a blow upward into his nose, breaking cartilage. As he reacted blindly to protect himself, she slipped from his grasp and dove under the table. A second later, Le Brun sent a second slug of lead crashing through the man's temple into his brain.

The men fell almost in tandem, the first maintaining his vertical position for a moment purely by muscle memory. They hit the wooden floor with heavy thumps. The first man's left leg kicked out, caught a chair leg, and sent it toppling backward onto his corpse.

John threw the derringer at Gooderly and rushed toward him.

"Goddamnit!" Gooderly screamed. He had jumped back involuntarily from the sight of the derringer and then the blasts of the two shots. The derringer flew harmlessly past him. He took another two steps backward as he registered John's rush, clawing desperately into his topcoat and suit jacket to reach his revolver. He found it and swung it wildly toward John when his assailant was still six feet away, cocking it with his opposite hand.

"Stop!" Gooderly shouted.

John pulled up abruptly and raised his hands. He expected Lordis would quickly be able to kick the chair in front of Gooderly hard enough to crash into him, giving John a moment to finish covering the distance and dive under the barrel of the gun. His hopes were dashed, however, when Gooderly continued to retreat until his back met the corner where the east wall met the south one.

"Bergman!" Gooderly shouted. "Get your ass in here! Bergman!"

Several seconds passed before the police lieutenant appeared in the east doorway. He wore plain clothes and had his police revolver drawn. He paused to take in the condition of the room. He went into a squat.

"Get out from under the table, ma'am," he ordered Lordis.

"She's no ma'am," Gooderly said hotly. "She's a pain-in-the-ass harridan." He tilted his torso to the side and glowered at Lordis. "Get up, whore!" To Bergman, he said, "She might as well get used to the title since that's what she's about to become. Now I'll harm *every* hair on her head. I'll have her shaven bald and offer her as a curiosity."

Lordis crawled out from the side where she had stood, rose with dignity, and brushed herself off.

John shook his head. "I never once saw a leopard change its spots . . . and you weren't goin' to be the first, Gooderly."

"Checkmate in Persian means 'the king is dead,'" Gooderly said loudly, mopping the copious lines of sweat from his forehead with the back of his free hand. "You knew the game had to end this way if I was ever to be rid of you," he told Le Brun. His weapon wavered from his extreme agitation. "I don't know how you managed to conceal that derringer, but it was an effort worthy of you."

"I didn't anticipate you'd be cowardly enough to need two men with you. I thought one of your goons would be left behind in the drugstore and that two bullets would be enough."

"I'm too smart to underestimate you, Le Brun. Care to tell me where the derringer came from?"

"You stole the notion of disguises from my stories," John said. "My agency manager became a little old lady with a sore back in the drugstore to distract your less-than-brilliant young tough after he had patted me down." He had placed the derringer under the stacks of bills and piles of coins in the doctor's bag before leaving Mary McMahon's. When he raised his hands to allow himself to be examined, Mary had responded to the signal and timed her approach as the old woman. Her polite assault allowed John time to remove the little gun from the satchel and shove it nose first under a rubber band that encircled his left wrist.

"Thanks for telling me," said Gooderly with acid in his voice, as he glanced at the pair of dead thugs. "So kind of you not to take the mystery to your grave."

"We should have left the children at home and taken this beast to see himself in 'Dr. Jekyll and Mr. Hyde,'" Lordis declared coolly to John, speaking of the occasion when Gooderly accompanied them to the moving pictures.

Gooderly laughed. "What strange final words to send your husband to eternity with." He gave Lieutenant Bergman a quick glance. "Shoot him!"

Bergman sniffled and then was silent again, causing Merriweather to look at him once more.

"You want him dead, you shoot him," Bergman said quietly.

"Goddamnit!" Gooderly ranted. "What the hell have I paid you all that—"

Swiftly, Bergman raised his revolver and sent a bullet crashing through the bridge of Gooderly's nose. The heavyset man fell like a steer in a meatpacking house. Both John and Lordis shrank back from the sudden sight.

Bergman looked down at the latest corpse. Addressing it in the same quiet voice he had when Gooderly was alive moments before, he said, "You were done paying me, jackass. Anybody who quits the city and still expects to be protected ain't half as smart as he thinks he is." Bergman lowered the revolver.

"The plan was to take him alive," John said.

Bergman shook his head vigorously. "That was *your* plan. In spite of the scenario you laid out to protect me and my men, we would have suffered too much scrutiny your way." He stuck his head out of the doorway and called out to an unseen colleague, "Go upstairs and make sure all the candles are snuffed." While John untied Lordis's hands and Bergman dug into Gooderly's left jacket pocket and fetched out a small, dark-red notebook, the lieutenant explained, "It's the two boys I brought with me to Diefendorfer's brothel back in April. Where is the previous notebook you promised me?"

"Not on me. I'll send it to you in due time," John said, after kissing Lordis on the cheek. "I figured you might let him kill me and Lordis before you finished him."

"And I figured you could take care of yourself," Bergman

said, elevating his chin in a defiant manner.

John pulled out one of the chairs and gently guided Lordis down onto it.

"One way or the other, he needed killin' . . . as my husband sometimes says," Lordis pronounced. "Who knows how many women beyond the drowning victim died because of him. He probably killed his own brother . . ."

"He admitted he did," John supplied, neatening her hair with the gentle stroke of his hand.

"He bushwhacked my husband and almost killed him. He shot a guard and a prostitute in his competition's house. He hanged—"

"You don't have to convince me, Mrs. Le Brun," Bergman interrupted. He holstered his revolver.

"I will give you somethin' beyond what I promised you," John told him. "I know the location of the house he recently opened in Chicago. All the women from these two Union Square houses were shipped there."

"As were the ones whom you rescued from that West Side house," the lieutenant admitted. He dipped his head in apology. "Sorry I lied to you about releasing them onto the streets. He didn't tell me where he was sending them."

"You can be a hero to them and to the editors of the Chicago newspapers. Maybe a promotion will result," John dangled.

The worldly wise lieutenant shrugged. "Maybe."

"Are you all right?" John asked Lordis.

"Right as rain," she replied.

John offered his elbow for his wife to rise. To Bergman, he said, "I wish you better days. You know, there are crooked men, and then there's swamp scum." To Lordis, he said, "Let us go, my love. There's a right smart Brougham awaitin' us in the alley. Its owner has no more need of it." With his free hand he closed the latch of the satchel and grabbed the handles. "My money is in here," he told Bergman.

"More than your money is in there," Bergman said, "but I'll trade it for that red notebook."

"We both earned that money," Lordis declared with attitude, taking the physician's bag from John. She looked down at Gooderly's corpse, licked her thumb and middle finger, and extinguished one of the candles. Then she led her husband out of the room.

CHAPTER THIRTY

January 8, 1909

JOHN'S MIDAFTERNOON LUNCHEON with J. P. Morgan took place in the Ladies Restaurant annex of the Metropolitan Club so that Lordis could join them. Morgan had insisted on meeting Le Brun's new wife, and the club proper would allow no women to enter. John's note to the Morgan junior partner, Mitchell Rockwell, sent early that morning had asked when Le Brun might travel down to Wall Street to inform his benefactor of the successful results of the investigation. He was, therefore, frankly astonished when a telegram deliverer knocked on one of Whispering Hope's doors less than an hour later, asking if he and Lordis would instead dine with Morgan at the exclusive capitalist club that stood only three blocks south of the mansion.

Immediately after John introduced Lordis to the Titan of

Wall Street, Morgan took her hand, brushed it with his lips, smiled, and said, "I caught a glimpse of you two years ago, standing on a dock."

"Yes," Lordis confirmed. "Alongside your very wonderful yacht."

Morgan's smile widened at the compliment. "You looked exquisite at a distance, but not half so beguiling as you do at this table." He snapped his fingers for the nearest server's attention and ordered a bottle of Moët et Chandon Brut Impérial to accompany a plate of seasonal fruits and finger sandwiches. Without waiting for any response from the waiter, he swung his attention back to Le Brun.

"So, my investment was well spent," Morgan said, glowing.

"Well spent indeed," John replied. From one of his jacket pockets he produced the phony letter that began his involvement in the Twelfth Street murders case. "A souvenir for you."

Morgan glanced at the sheet, then crumpled it up and dropped it on the table. "Trash," he proclaimed.

John said, "Just how you wish the results to be manipulated are partially up to you. If you'll allow me, I shall attempt to recapture the events for you so that you may make a fully informed decision."

Morgan spread his arms in invitation.

John knew the financial pirate to be one of the quickest minds he had ever met, perpetually with or ahead of any conversation. Further, the man's motile facial expressions clearly betrayed whether he was captivated or bored. John spoke rapidly and raced through the earliest happenings of the case, but as he saw that Morgan was enraptured, he dared to add details. He praised the robber baron for underwriting the investigation after it had seemingly come to a dead end, which redoubled the old man's interest in experiencing the case vicariously. He knew that Morgan's habit was to pontificate on any subject on which he had knowledge. But of the solving of criminal schemes, the financier was beyond his depth and had been in awe of Le Brun since the former sheriff's solution of the Jekyl Island Club murders.

Concerning the events of the past week, John went into the greatest detail. He confided how he had fooled Lieutenant Bergman into accepting the contents of the claret-colored notebook as Gooderly's incriminating notations. He explained how consultations with his ex-policemen employees and Kevin O'Leary had led him to trust that Bergman would not double-cross him at the last minute. He revealed that, in spite of the risk he was willing to take alone, he had allowed Stuart Hirsch and Lawrence Wilker to watch Gooderly's two abandoned assignation houses, join at the one where the Brougham stopped, and ready themselves to slaughter Gooderly and his henchmen in a hail of lead if Lordis and John had not emerged safe and sound. As the food was set down before the diners, Le Brun concluded.

"I realized no one was followin' us on the way out of the house. Now, I had gained some knowledge from openin' the locked closet in the pantry of 223 East Twelfth Street. So I decided to open several of the cabinets in Gooderly's storage room. *Mirabile visu!* In an orange crate sat not only papers detailing Gooderly's past pimpin' but also his arrangements for his grandiose Chicago assignation house. In another crate, I found the papers he and his men had taken from Dietrich Diefendorfer's loft after they hanged him." He bent slightly toward Morgan.

"Now, here's where I need your counsel, Mr. Morgan. How do you think Lieutenant Bergman should be handled, both in print and by the city government?"

Morgan folded his hands over his large belly. "I believe your assessment is correct. Ten years ago, the business of policing was a mess. Separate divisions all over this island. Since then, with Progressives like that egomaniacal Teddy Roosevelt taking charge, it's gaining public respect. There's no advantage in depressing the average citizen over Bergman's antics. Since before Babylonia, bribes, graft, and kickbacks have been part of the spoils of those in power. By all means, make him a hero in print and let's see if he begins to live the lie."

Le Brun nodded. "Based on your assessment, I shall forge the entries to that red notebook and send it to Bergmann. He won't spend more than a minute or so pagin' through it before he burns it or drops it in the East River. Now, what about those in power in Chicago if Bergmann fails to inform the various newspaper editors? To whom should that pertinent information be given?"

"It won't make a bit of difference there," Morgan came back immediately. He blinked several times as his encyclopedic mind collected his thoughts. "The corruption in that town makes New York look like the garden of Eden before the apple tree bore fruit. Nevertheless, I'd send the information to the head editors of the *Chicago Daily News, Tribune, Broad Ax, Defender,* and even that new one . . . the *Examiner*. Also to the mayor's office and the chief of the Chicago Police. If a hundred husbands are shamed into foreswearing the use of brothels, it will be worth it."

"Here in New York I've promised to provide the information first to the *World*."

Morgan looked at Lordis. "You don't read the *World*, do you Mrs. Le Brun?"

"Rarely," Lordis replied, truthfully. "I prefer the *Wall Street Journal*, where I learned about you saving the entire nation's economy two years back and also the wonderful acquisitions you've made for the Metropolitan Museum of Art."

John winced inwardly. Although Morgan adored praise and was a willing captive to beautiful women, his passions could not make him blind enough not to register such blatant blandishments. At the same time, Le Brun knew that the man was victim to deep depressions during the dark days of winter and desperately sought out means in that season to raise his own spirits. In spite of her excessive flattery, he suspected the afternoon luncheon with Lordis was a perfect tonic.

"Good to hear," John Pierpont responded. "No genteel woman should read such a rag. The last thing I want to do is make that scandal-monger Pulitzer richer."

"I'm returnin' several favors from Frank Cobb," John explained. "Will you let him put in his editorial that you underwrote the investigation?"

Morgan's chest elevated. "I suppose." Then he rolled his eyes. "I understand Cobb offered $200 for the arrest of the person behind the Twelfth Street murders. Don't you dare allow him to name me as the recipient. You two take it for your honeymoon, wherever it might be."

"One of the Windward Islands," Lordis supplied quickly. She showed the table's host the sailboat charm that John had recently given her for her bracelet, as a promise for the trip. "We can't take that vacation, however, until Sarah Topley is released from prison and readjusted. I'm caring for her children."

Morgan nodded, indicating that he clearly remembered the details of the trial that he had subtly engineered as a favor to the former sheriff from Brunswick, Georgia.

"Before that, when she is again free, then we shall have a second wedding here in New York," Lordis announced. "You, kind sir, will be among the first invited." Having accomplished her goal for the afternoon, she flashed her beautifully even teeth at Morgan and touched the back of his left hand.

"Thank you very much," Morgan responded. He rearranged the table flowers with his free hand so that he would not have to meet her gaze and betray that only a present would arrive on that festive day. He retrained his piercing eyes on John. "And now that this frustrating case is solved at long last, what can possibly challenge you, Mr. Le Brun?"

John finished a sip of champagne. "Well, I came into a tidy sum of money just yesterday. I'm thinkin' of investin' in the development of a spectacular golf course and clubhouse over on St. Simons Island. Myself and a few well-heeled friends. Perhaps you'd like to make some money along with me."

Morgan's black eyebrows shot up at his former adversary's brassy suggestion.

Lordis laughed.

ABOUT THE AUTHOR

BRENT MONAHAN was born in Fukuoka, Kyushu, Japan, in 1948, as a World War II occupation baby. He received his Bachelor of Arts degree from Rutgers University in music. He received his Doctor of Musical Arts degree from Indiana University, Bloomington. He has performed, stage directed, and taught music and writing professionally. He has written thirteen published novels and a number of short stories. Two of his novels have been made into motion pictures. *The St. Simons Island Club* is the fourth in a series of John Le Brun novels. The series started with *The Jekyl Island Club*, which was first published in hardback in 2000 and is still in print. Brent lives in Yardley, Pennsylvania, with his wife, Bonnie.

Experience Brent Monahan's
John Le Brun series again or for the first time.

  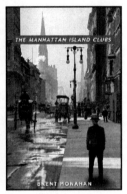

| Book One | Book Two | Book Three |
| Available Now | Available March 2016 | Available March 2016 |

Fall 2016

John Le Brun will return once again in
The St. Lucia Island Club

CPSIA information can be obtained at www.ICGtesting.com
Printed in the USA
BVOW02s0453171215

430468BV00012B/265/P